P9-CJT-114
2/17

ROYAL INSTITUTE OF MAGIC

The Last Guardian

VICTOR KLOSS

An Original Publication From Victor Kloss

Royal Institute of Magic – The Last Guardian
Written and published by Victor Kloss
Cover by Andrew Gaia
Formatted by Frostbite Publishing
Copyright © 2016 by Victor Kloss
All rights reserved.

***

This novel is a work of fiction. Names, characters, and locations are either a product of the author's imagination or used in a fictitious setting. Any resemblance to actual events, locations, organizations, or people, living or dead, is strictly coincidental. No part of this book may be used or reproduced without written consent from the author. Thank you for respecting the hard work of this author.

***

www.RoyalInstituteofMagic.com

— CHAPTER ONE —

Unlikely Allies

Date: *3rd January 1603*

Michael Greenwood glanced up at the extravagant house, and knew there was going to be trouble. Rumour had it that this was the most expensive residence in London – a rumour, no doubt spread by its owner, Lord Samuel, Guardian of Elizabeth's Shield.

Michael gave a firm rap of the iron-wrought handle, and waited. He wasn't armed, as he knew Samuel would never let him inside with a sword or spellshooter. He shouldn't have any need for weapons, but with Lord Samuel, you never knew.

Michael heard the sound of footsteps from within and composed himself. Lord Samuel had requested the meeting, and though he hadn't said what it was about, Michael had a good idea.

Queen Elizabeth's Armour.

The specifics of the conversation were a little harder to guess, as the queen's instructions had been very clear. Those entrusted as Guardians were to safeguard their designated piece of armour until the dark elf king, Suktar, returned.

Michael was still pondering the matter when the door swung open. Samuel's butler was dressed in an immaculate, tailored black suit, which was probably more expensive than anything Michael owned.

"Mr. Greenwood," the butler said with a slight bow. "Do come in. Lord Samuel has been waiting."

Michael stepped inside to a grand hall that was almost as big as his entire house. A lavish staircase ran up the middle, and split two ways to an open gallery. There were large portraits lining the walls, most of them of Samuel, though a few were of his family.

"This way, please, Mr. Greenwood," the butler said, directing him with a pristine, white-gloved hand.

Michael followed the butler through several drawing rooms, each lavishly decorated by Lady Samuel, until they reached a set of double doors, which the butler pushed open and walked through, Michael following just behind.

As magnificent as the previous rooms were, this one rivalled the queen's palace. Perhaps that was the idea, Michael thought.

A huge, glistening chandelier hung from the ceiling, casting a soft light on thick carpet and lavish furniture. The room was so large, it was divided into sections. There was a reading area and a section for music, complete with a grand piano. Small tables, decorated with flowers, vases and antiques, were dotted everywhere.

"Greenwood. You decided to turn up, I see," a deep, overbearing voice said.

Lord Samuel sat, legs crossed, on a black leather couch, holding a drink. It had been only a week since they had last met, but Samuel seemed to have managed to gain a few pounds, mainly around the chin. His hair, too, somehow seemed thinner, but he compensated that with a thick, perfectly groomed moustache.

He didn't get up, nor did he offer Michael a drink. The couch Samuel sat on was large, but the big man somehow seemed to consume most of it, so Michael chose a small chair nearby. He noted the spellshooter strapped to Samuel's waist, but was careful not to show any concern.

"I shan't waste both our time with social pleasantries," Lord Samuel said. Michael had to resist the urge to put a finger in his ear to partially mute Samuel's booming voice. "You must know why you're here."

"Not really," Michael said with a shrug. "I'm assuming it's something to do with Elizabeth's Armour."

"Of course it is," Samuel said, tapping his glass impatiently. "But more than that, it's about the mistake our queen made, most likely due to her poor health."

"What mistake is that?" Michael asked.

"You know very well," Samuel said. His face looked a little red, but Michael couldn't tell if it was from the drink or his simmering anger. "I'm referring to the fact that she put you in charge. She made *you* the Head Guardian."

Michael couldn't help noticing the contemptuous way in which Lord Samuel said "you".

"It was her choice," Michael said, keeping his voice light.

"Impossible," Lord Samuel said. His moustache twitched as he shook his head. "Her decision was clearly clouded by her ill health. Have you seen her recently? She won't last much longer."

Michael couldn't argue that point. The queen was now confined to bed and, with a heavy heart, he knew it wouldn't be long before they had a new commander at the Institute.

"I saw her recently and was sorry to see that she was so poorly," Michael said with a nod.

Samuel seemed to relax a little at this. "Then you agree that her decision was not made with a clear mind?"

"No," Michael said firmly. "I remember well when she summoned us and told us about her armour. She was as lucid as you or me."

"Absolute nonsense!" Lord Samuel said, slapping a great big

thigh. He gave Michael a sneer, his perfectly groomed moustache rising up to his nose. "Do you really think she would choose you, a baker's boy, over me on such an important mission? It defies all logic and reason."

Michael could always tell when Samuel was getting worked up by his large nostrils, which would start flaring. They were doing so now, reminding Michael of a pig sniffing for food.

"I believe she had a reason for her choice," Michael said, keeping his voice calm. "I think we should trust her."

Lord Samuel hauled himself up with surprising ease, and starting trooping round the couch.

"I don't believe it," Lord Samuel said. "I can't believe it. Do you realise what sort of responsibility she has entrusted you with? Suktar will return one day, and your bloodline will be responsible for finding the Guardians and gathering Elizabeth's Armour to stand against him."

"I'm aware of that."

"I don't think you are," Lord Samuel said, shaking his head. "No, it's madness. I cannot accept it."

Michael had to quell his own frustration. "What do you suggest?"

Lord Samuel turned to him, and placed both hands on his chest. "Let me take on the burden. I have the resources. My family is large, rich, and powerful. We have the ability to track the Guardians over the centuries, if need be."

Michael saw a sincerity in Samuel's small, brown eyes that wasn't born of selfishness, but genuine concern.

"I'm sorry, Samuel," Michael said. "Queen Elizabeth chose me for a reason. I truly believe that. I will not betray her on this. Those are my final words."

Michael decided against mentioning the real reason he felt the queen chose him – it would only infuriate Samuel further.

"Stubborn boy!" Lord Samuel said, slapping a hand on his thigh. "You risk jeopardising this entire mission with your stupidity."

Michael stood up, his eyes narrowing. "We are done here, I think. Is there anything else you wanted to go over?"

Lord Samuel's hand hovered over his spellshooter, and Michael's heart lurched, but he pretended not to notice. Samuel stood very still, staring hard at Michael.

"I will not," Lord Samuel said stiffly. "I cannot allow my family to be led by the family of a baker's boy. It is demeaning, insufferable and it will not be endured."

Michael stared right into Lord Samuel's brown eyes. They looked slightly bloodshot, whether from the drink or simply from his blood boiling, Michael didn't know. What he did know was that Lord Samuel was on the verge of one of his famous outbursts. Michael could remember only too well when Samuel last lost his temper – little of the Diplomacy meeting room was left undamaged.

Eight feet, Michael estimated. Eight feet between them. Could he leap that far and reach Samuel before he drew his spellshooter? Despite his bulk, the man was no slouch, especially with a spellshooter.

Michael inched forwards, pointing his finger at Lord Samuel. "This isn't a game, Samuel. The future of our nation, of the world, is at stake," Michael said. He kept his anger in check, mostly. "I don't want your sense of self-importance getting in the way. You are responsible for the shield. Remember what the queen said? The Guardian of Elizabeth's Shield will be responsible for blocking Suktar's deadly blows, so that the Guardian of Elizabeth's Sword can strike the killer thrust. That means your family and mine are going to be working together. It might not happen in our lifetimes, it might not happen for centuries, but it *will* happen."

Lord Samuel stared at him, his hand inching closer to his spellshooter. Michael eased forwards a little more, and continued talking.

"When it does happen, your descendant had better be a little more accommodating to mine. Do I make myself clear?"

The moment he spoke, he knew he'd gone too far.

Lord Samuel drew his spellshooter so quickly that Michael barely had time to move.

"You've made yourself abundantly clear," Lord Samuel said. "Now, get out of my house."

Michael resisted the urge to duck for cover and held his ground. "Hide the shield well, Samuel."

Samuel's finger twitched on the trigger. "Get out, *now.*"

Michael knew he was in danger, but he bit his lip and remained where he was. He was the Head Guardian; he had a responsibility, no matter what Samuel thought.

"The shield," Michael said again, his voice soft. "I need to know that you have a well-thought-out plan for keeping it safe."

To Michael's surprise, Lord Samuel gave a little smirk. "The shield will be well hidden. It will make finding your sword look hopelessly simplistic."

Michael knew he wasn't going to get any more from Lord Samuel without risking getting his head blown off.

"We'll be in touch," Michael said with a little salute.

Michael left, expecting at any moment to feel the soaring heat of a spell smash into his back. To his great relief, it was only curses, not spells, that Lord Samuel let fly as he departed.

— CHAPTER TWO —

Danger in the Sky

Present Day

Can you stop that thing from spitting acid?" Charlie shouted, as he darted left to avoid a spurt of green liquid. "I happen to value my life."

"Working on it," Ben grunted. He was straddled on the wyvern's neck, and had a huge acid-resistant toothbrush with which he was attempting to brush the wyvern's teeth. "Come on, Thomas, do we have to go through this every single time?"

There was laughter coming from around the paddock. From the corner of his eye, Ben could just make out a dozen apprentices, Aaron amongst them, watching on as he, Charlie, Natalie and Abigail attempted to clean the most ill-tempered wyvern in the Institute.

Despite the fact that apprentices were supposed to rotate cleaning duty, to better understand each beast, they had landed the task of cleaning Thomas every single week for the last month. Of course, it didn't take a genius to work out why – Aaron was the one responsible for the rota.

"Got it!" Ben said triumphantly, as he cleaned the last bit of rot from the wyvern's front teeth.

"Oh, well done," Abigail said. She was standing just out of harm's way, but still inside the wyvern's paddock. In her hands was a clipboard that she was looking at intently. "Next are the ears. Are you ready, Ben?"

She bent down and produced a soapy sponge from a bucket next to her. With a throw of considerable accuracy, she launched it up to Ben, who reached out a hand and snagged it, while still holding on to the wyvern's neck. He went to work on the back of the ears, trying to ignore the smell of pus. He took a quick glance down and saw Charlie working on the wyvern's body, and Natalie the tail. They had tried several different cleaning combinations, but this one worked the best.

"Don't forget inside the ears! Remember what happened last time?" a voice said, laughing.

Ben would have liked to identify the voice, so he could clobber him round the ear when he'd finished, but he was too busy hanging on for dear life. His left hand slipped a little and he almost lost his grip on the wyvern, resulting in more laughter.

"Done with the body," Charlie said, wiping a hand over his brow. He looked up at Ben, who was slowly losing his grip. Wyverns didn't like having their ears touched, and Thomas was especially sensitive. "You almost done, Ben? I'm getting hungry."

"Getting there," Ben said, snaking his way back up the wyvern. He dropped the sponge, and Abigail immediately threw up a Q-Tip that must have been at least a foot long. Ben caught it expertly. He took a deep breath, and made sure he had a firm grip on the wyvern. This was always the worst part. Cringing slightly, he shoved the Q-Tip into the wyvern's giant ear, and turned it. There was a squelching noise that always made Ben's stomach heave. The wyvern cried out and reared its head, shooting acid skywards. Some of it fell back down on Ben, but his protective jacket stopped the acid from reaching his skin. He pulled the Q-Tip out and applied it to the other ear, receiving the same treatment from the wyvern.

"Done!" he said, leaping off the wyvern, and landing next to Abigail. He quickly threw the Q-Tip in the bucket and the four of them moved out of harm's way. The wyvern gave Ben a baleful look, before waddling away, back to the centre of the paddock.

"Twenty-seven seconds slower than last week," Aaron said, tapping his expensive-looking watch. "I'm a little disappointed. You will keep cleaning Thomas until you can get the job done in under ten minutes."

Ben checked his anger. He was too exhausted to come up with a retort, though Natalie and Charlie gave Aaron hateful stares, which Aaron seemed to enjoy and responded to with a pleasant smile. Ben couldn't help noticing that while most of the apprentices were caked with sweat and dirt, Aaron looked as though he'd just bathed and dressed. There was not a hair out of place. However, few people seemed to care that he'd done no actual work. Indeed, many of the female apprentices probably hadn't even noticed, being too busy staring at that strong jaw and dark, smouldering eyes.

"Let's get going," Aaron said. "Thanks to your less than impressive time cleaning old Thomas, you've made the rest of us late for lunch. I've half a mind to make you clean the dishes to make up for the damage."

Tiredness suddenly forgotten, Ben was about to tell him what he thought about that idea.

He never got the chance.

A high-pitched screeching noise made them all jump. As one, they turned their heads skywards, and immediately saw the perpetrator. It flew at an altitude similar to a small plane, but Ben could still make out its massive bat-like wings on its long, slender body.

"Get inside, now," Aaron said, humour forgotten.

Even as they moved towards the rooftop door, Ben saw a

couple of Spellswords burst out and run to a pair of giant eagles. Within moments they were airborne, and gaining altitude, fast. But as swift as the eagles soared, Ben knew they were unlikely to catch their target.

Ben followed the rest of the apprentices inside, and they headed down the main staircase. Stomachs were rumbling, but lunch was the last thing on their minds.

"That's the fifth ptryad this week," Charlie said. "They're getting braver to be able to scout Taecia so easily for the dark elves."

"Our Spellswords will catch them," Ben said, trying to sound convincing.

"I doubt it. As well as being the ultimate spying beast, they can also fly at a great pace. With their insanely keen eyesight, they'll spot the eagles and be halfway home before the Spellswords can get that high."

"You're full of optimism this morning," Natalie said, giving Charlie a poke in the back. She and Abigail were a step behind Charlie and Ben as they headed down.

"Sorry, I can't help it. At this rate, they'll know Taecia inside out before the end of the month."

"Does that matter, though?" Natalie asked. "They'd never dare invade Taecia."

"No, but I've read about those ptryads. They can hear a bee buzzing from a mile high. The Institute has already had to cast spells to make sure they're not eavesdropping on us."

"They might be nasty, but they look cool," Abigail said with a distant smile. "They are so graceful, the way they fly."

Charlie scratched his nose. "Yes, I think you might be missing the point here."

Ben leapt down the last steps, and headed towards lunch, his stomach rumbling. "You guys haven't forgotten about Dagmar, have you?"

"The meeting? No," Natalie said. "I wonder what she wants to talk about."

"I think I can guess," Charlie said, though he didn't elaborate with apprentices everywhere. "Did you see how serious she was? Even more so than usual. I think it's important."

"I saw," Ben said. "Come on, let's grab some lunch, and worry about that later."

— CHAPTER THREE —

The Crimson Tower

I have several announcements to make," Dagmar said.

Ben and the rest of the apprentices stood to attention, ears perked. Despite the increasing turmoil from the dark elves, Dagmar remained as unflustered as ever. He sometimes forgot that she was so small, such was her presence. She held her baton and stood so straight Ben long suspected that there might be another baton thrust down her back. Her only concession to extravagance was a pair of green shoes that would have been too big for most people double her size.

"For those of you able to cast level-four spells, we will be supplying long-range tracking spells, which you are to fire at any ptryads you see. Needless to say, if you are in the Seen Kingdoms, make sure you do it discreetly."

There weren't many apprentices who could cast level-four spells, but Ben was one of them.

"Secondly, for those who took exams at Barrington's, your results have come in."

Dagmar pointed to her desk, on which were several white envelopes. There were a few intakes of breath, though Ben barely reacted. He had taken the bare minimum of subjects and wasn't overly optimistic about his results. The exams were mandatory and were ordinarily an important part of the education system, but with Ben's plans firmly set on becoming an Institute member, he really wasn't that bothered and was glad to be done with school. Charlie, on the other hand, was shifting from foot to foot, clearly desperate to find out what his results were. He was one of the few people who would continue to study at Barrington's, taking advanced levels.

"Thirdly, the executive council has asked me to brief you on the latest situation with the dark elves."

There was an inevitable murmur of voices, which Dagmar quickly silenced with a raised hand.

"As apprentices, there is much I cannot tell you, but at the same time, your position gives you the right to know more than those outside the Institute."

She paused, scanning faces. There was an expectant, almost deathly silence. Ben was just as eager for information as the rest of them. It had been a month since they had found the Guardian

Krobeg and Elizabeth's Breastplate, and it didn't take a genius to notice that the dark elves had since made rapid, almost frightening progress in their quest to conquer the Unseen Kingdoms. To make things more frustrating, Ben, Charlie and Natalie had made little progress in searching for the final two pieces of Elizabeth's Armour, as well as the missing Guardian.

"The dark elves have now conquered seven Unseen Kingdoms, and another seventeen are in lock-down mode, only accessible if you have a special pass, issued by the Diplomacy Department. We are helping those kingdoms as best we can with resources and Spellswords, though we are stretched. However, that is not the most pressing matter at the moment."

Ben wasn't sure if she paused for dramatic effect, but it certainly worked, as he could see some of the apprentices physically craning their necks forwards, willing her to speak.

"It has probably not escaped your notice that we are beginning to fortify the south coast of England. We have established small outposts, and are working on stationing larger defensive units there."

"Why are we doing that? Surely the dark elves are focusing on the Unseen Kingdoms?" a new voice asked, clearly unused to Dagmar's policy of silence. Thankfully, she accepted the question without reprimand.

"It seems as though the dark elves' ultimate goal might end up being not the Unseen Kingdoms, but the Seen ones," Dagmar said.

Ben had strongly suspected that might be the case, but it still shocked him to hear Dagmar say it with such frankness. Several more voices piped up, but Dagmar's fleeting generous mood had disappeared.

"We do not know this for sure, but we cannot rule it out, for the consequences would be great," Dagmar said. "For now, the executive council does not wish to reveal any more information on this."

There was a groan from the apprentices, but nobody dared venture any further questions. Nevertheless, Dagmar waited for complete silence before continuing.

"I have one final announcement, and it is by no means the least important. Just because the dark elves are causing mischief, that is no reason to start slacking on your studies. There will be times where you will be expected to help the Institute, but that simply means when you are studying, I expect you to work harder. You all have deadlines to make, and several of you will soon be graduating to Institute members. Do I make myself clear?"

There was a military-like chorus of agreement, though Ben couldn't help noticing one or two disgruntled looks.

"Good. Dismissed," Dagmar said, and she promptly clomped out of the room.

Charlie and Natalie darted towards Dagmar's desk and,

amongst a multitude of arms, grabbed their exam result letters. Ben did the same, with considerably less enthusiasm. He ripped it open, his heart giving a little flutter as he took out the small slip of paper. As soon as he saw the results, his concern turned to relief.

"An A and three Bs," Ben said, smiling. "Not bad, given that I barely did anything."

"Six As!" Natalie said with a squeal of delight, flinging her arms round Ben's neck.

Charlie, however, was looking at his card with genuine confusion. "That can't be right. They've only given me an A for Geography."

"Only an A?" Ben said. "What were your other results?"

"Eleven A*s." Charlie shook his head, looking genuinely put out. "My parents aren't going to be happy. They were expecting A*s across the board."

"They'll be fine," Ben said, wrapping an arm around Charlie's shoulder. "Now, we should get going. Dagmar is expecting us, remember?"

A meeting with Dagmar was normally enough to focus them, but as they left the room and walked down the corridor, Charlie was clearly still thinking about the exam results, right up to the point when Ben rapped on Dagmar's door.

"Come in," Dagmar said.

Ben led them into the office, which was neat as always,

though lately he had noticed a sizeable number of files on her desk. Dagmar remained seated, but she stopped writing and looked up as they entered. Ben, Charlie and Natalie approached the desk with their customary deference.

Dagmar pulled out a rustic red key and placed it on her desk. "That's your key to get in."

Ben frowned. "Sorry, key to what?"

Dagmar returned to her writing for a moment, before looking up again. "You didn't think we were going to have a meeting here, did you?"

"What's wrong with here?" Charlie asked.

Dagmar finished her writing with a flourish and put her pen down with a sharp snap. "Too risky, with the dark elves."

Ben couldn't hide his surprise. "You think the dark elves have got in here? I thought the Institute was the most secure place there was."

"Yes, it's secure from a direct attack," Dagmar said. "But the dark elves are masters of infiltration, and the executive council is concerned that their reeters might have sneaked in."

"Reeters?"

"They are tiny lizards. They can get into almost anywhere, and are nearly impossible to detect as they are masters of camouflage."

"So we're being listened to?" Charlie asked, looking around furtively.

"Unlikely," Dagmar said. "The Institute has sophisticated magical defences, so even the smallest bug shouldn't be able to get in. But it's better to be safe, especially given what we will be talking about."

"Makes sense," Ben said, pocketing the key.

"Your destination is the Crimson Tower," Dagmar said.

"Ooh!" Natalie exclaimed, before she could help herself. "Sorry – I've heard a lot about the tower from my parents, and I've always wanted to go there, though they never let me."

"It is only used for very specific purposes – confidential meetings being one of them. I trust you know where to go?"

"Oh yes," Natalie said.

"Good. I will be there within the hour. I will meet you there," Dagmar said.

She picked up her pen and began writing again, signalling the end of the meeting. But as they were about to exit the door, Dagmar cleared her throat, making them turn.

"Make sure you shake off your tail," Dagmar said, looking pointedly at Ben.

"My tail?"

"Aaron's lackeys," Dagmar said. There was rarely a hint of emotion in her voice, but Ben was sure he detected a modicum of disdain when voicing Aaron's name. "He'll have a couple following you. I'll leave you to deal with them, but they absolutely cannot know we are going to the Crimson Tower."

— CHAPTER FOUR —

A Special Gathering

I see them," Charlie said the moment they left Dagmar's office.

Two apprentices – a boy and a girl, with faces that looked uncannily like a weasel's – stood chatting idly at the end of the corridor.

"Should we confront them?" Natalie asked.

"No point," Ben said, as he led them down the grand staircase. "They'll follow us anyway. They'd never disobey an order from Aaron."

"What's Aaron's problem?" Charlie said. "Why does he keep hounding you?"

Ben waved a dismissive hand. "Oh, you know. He thinks I stand in the way of him being the future Spellsword Director."

"That's ridiculous," Natalie said. "It'll be years before you'd be considered ready for that position. You're not even an Institute member yet."

"I know it's ridiculous, but Aaron's dreams of grandeur rival Napoleon's. Anyway, as long as he doesn't get in my way, I really don't care. I'm done with him."

They reached the ground floor and Ben led them outside. He threw another quick glance over his shoulder and saw their two followers exit a moment later.

"How are we going to lose them?" Charlie asked.

Ben pulled out his spellshooter in answer.

"You're not allowed to fire at a fellow apprentice," Natalie said with a reproachful frown.

"Yeah, that's unfortunate, because I had some great ideas. But I'm not casting it on them. Those idiots didn't bring their own spellshooters, so they're not going to be able to counter anything."

With that, Ben pointed his spellshooter into his chest, and casually fired. A small white pellet barely had time to absorb into his jumper before he did the same for Charlie and Natalie.

"What was that?" Charlie asked, flinching as the spell hit him.

"Camouflage spells, level one. They're going to have trouble seeing us." He gave a little wave. "Come on, let's speed up. Natalie, you know the way to this tower place, right?"

"The Crimson Tower. Yes, it's been a while, but it's not something I'd forget," Natalie said.

Natalie picked up her pace, and headed west. Ben glanced back, and saw the perplexed look on the faces of the two weasels following them, standing and looking about in confusion. Within moments, they were out of sight. Ben made a mental note. Aaron wouldn't make the same mistake twice – next time, their pursuers wouldn't be so easy to shake off.

The west side of Taecia was Ben's favourite. The buildings were well spaced out and many of the houses had small gardens, despite being in the heart of the town. The restaurants were a little nicer and Ben often caught a whiff of something that made him salivate. The shops, too, were a little bigger, a little more upmarket. They were far beyond his financial means, but that didn't stop him from window shopping here from time to time. There were magnificent antique shops selling ancient treasures, libraries with books on magic that had Charlie bug-eyed, as well as the more traditional magic, armouries and service-based shops. Ben couldn't help noticing that here, at least, the citizens didn't seem as concerned about the dark elf threat. One possible reason was the Institute's presence here. There were several buildings, big and small, with the Institute's insignia on them. Many were occupied, but some seemed to sit there without any purpose, except possibly reassurance.

Ben was so busy enjoying the walk that he didn't spot the

Crimson Tower until it was in plain sight.

"There it is," Natalie said with a smile. "Beautiful, isn't it?"

Natalie wasn't wrong. The tower was slender with an elegant steeple that towered over the other buildings in west Taecia. But it was the colour that made the tower really stand out. It was a hundred shades of red, as if someone had carefully applied a Photoshop filter. The sun seemed to gleam off it, constantly changing shades.

"That is cool," Ben admitted. "What is the tower used for?"

"Important and confidential meetings," Natalie replied. "I'm surprised Dagmar managed to get us in, to be honest."

They made their way through a few more well-to-do streets, before finally reaching the tower's base.

"Ah, I thought I'd meet you here!"

It had been only a couple of weeks since they'd seen Krobeg, Guardian of the Breastplate, but already Ben thought his stomach looked a little larger. Ben still hadn't got used to the gleaming silver beard, which had changed colour the moment Krobeg had claimed the armour. He had a friendly face, bushy eyebrows and a rather large nose, which probably proved useful for smelling the culinary delights he cooked. As if to reinforce his love for food, his jacket was stitched with the pattern of a bubbling cauldron.

"I didn't realise you were coming," Ben said with a smile and a handshake. Krobeg's hands were similar to Dagmar's feet –

large.

"Nor did I, until this morning," Krobeg said. "Got a message from Dagmar. She said it was important. It took a bit of mad scrambling, but I managed to get my friend Abbot to cover the cooking for me. When it comes to a roast lunch, I have to admit, he's almost as good as I am."

"I could use one of your roast lunches," Charlie said, patting his stomach.

"You're welcome anytime," Krobeg said.

Ben glanced about with a frown. "If you're here, shouldn't we have brought Abigail?"

"I think Dagmar will bring her," Natalie said. "She spends a lot of time with Dagmar these days, working on her mental toughness, so that she can master the helm."

Ben felt a little guilty. As Head Guardian, it was his job to make sure everybody was ready, but he was grateful for Dagmar's intervention. She was better equipped, and far more knowledgeable than he.

"Should we wait for Dagmar here?" Natalie asked.

"No," Ben said, pulling out the key. "She wouldn't have given us access if she wanted us to stand outside."

Ben inserted the key into a large keyhole and turned, noting that there didn't appear to be any door handle. There was a soft click, and the fiery red door seemed to shimmer. Ben watched in astonishment as it quickly faded away, leaving them staring into a small hallway. Ben exchanged glances with the others, and then they stepped inside.

"Oh, my word," Natalie said, squinting and instinctively throwing up her arms in a protective gesture.

A mighty fire in the centre of the atrium burned bright, sending flames towering all the way to the turret. There was no wood or foundation for the fire; it seemed to emerge directly from the floor. Just like the building outside, the flames were a multitude of reds that constantly changed, from deep crimson to faint pink.

"The Flame of Defence," Natalie said, finally putting her arms down. "It can be commanded by the top Institute members to attack any infiltrators."

"I can't feel any heat," Krobeg said, raising a hand towards the mighty flames.

"No, but when the fire attacks, the flames can reach a thousand degrees."

"Well, that explains why there are no guards here," Ben said. "They don't need any."

"The question is, where do we go?"

The answer became clear the moment they looked about. There was only one way they could go – up, via a spiral staircase that ran the perimeter of the tower. It wasn't long before the staircase opened to a gallery. But to Ben's surprise, there were no doors, only a short landing, and then more stairs. Ben walked to the next set of stairs, wondering at the point of a gallery. He soon saw why.

A peculiar stone archway stood at the base of the stairs. It was black and engraved with silver hieroglyphs. At the top was a large, green eye that took them all in with an eerie, knowing stare.

"Security, just like in the Dragonway," Ben said.

"It should be safe, right?" Charlie said, looking at the big eye anxiously.

"Yeah, we're supposed to be here, remember?" Ben said. He rubbed his chin. "I've always wondered what would happen if we went through when not allowed."

"There are two possibilities," Krobeg said. "If it's a minor offence, the archway won't let you through. If it deems you a serious security threat, you will pass through, but you won't come out the other end."

"Where do you go?" Charlie asked in alarm.

Krobeg shrugged his massive shoulders. "I'm sure somebody at your Institute can answer that question, but not me."

Charlie pulled out an impeccably clean handkerchief, and dabbed his glistening forehead. "Well, you've turned going through the archway from a simple matter into one of life or death. Thanks."

"Calm down, we've got clearance. We're not a threat," Ben said.

Ben walked up to the archway. He had intended to walk straight through, but couldn't help hesitating as Krobeg's words reverberated round his head. *If it deems you a serious security threat, you will pass through, but you won't come out the other end.*

Ben shook himself. He was being ridiculous. Nevertheless, it took some effort to suppress his natural life preservation instincts. He walked quickly through the archway. There was a moment's resistance, stronger than the one he experienced in the Dragonway. His heart threatened to exit his mouth, before the resistance subsided, and Ben was through.

He turned, and gave them a smile, trying to hide his relief. "See? Nothing to it."

Krobeg gave a shrug and then followed Ben through, looking fairly relaxed about it. Only Charlie cringed when passing under, as if he was hiding some sort of secret the archway might detect.

Another flight of stairs followed, which led to another gallery, and another archway. The only difference was the colour of the eye – this one was blue.

"I bet they have different roles," Natalie said, as they passed through the next archway.

Ben kept looking for a door, but they didn't find one until they reached the very top floor and had passed through three more archways. It had another lock, and Ben produced his key again. He expected it to lead to a corridor, but it opened up into a single room. Ben frowned. Could there really be only one room in the entire tower?

His frown evaporated the moment he looked around. The walls were painted in a swirling red and seemed to give off a comforting warmth. There were two distinct sections of the room. Nearest to them were a bunch of soft leather couches, each with its own coffee table. At the back was a conference table, lined with formal chairs.

"Oh, look at those," Natalie said.

She was pointing to the vases, filled with incredible bouquets of fresh flowers. There was a large one on the conference table and another on the largest coffee table. But something even more delightful overpowered the smell of flowers. Small plates of appetisers were placed all over the room – sausages, vegetables, chips, and all kinds of dips.

"I guess someone knew we were coming," Ben said. "I'm fairly certain Dagmar wouldn't have done all this herself."

"It's the pixies," Natalie said with a clap of delight. "There are three that live and serve here. You'll never see them, but they make sure the place always looks perfect when company is expected."

Charlie and Krobeg were rubbing their hands together.

"Well, I guess we should tuck in. It would be criminal to let good food go to waste," Krobeg said with Charlie nodding furiously in agreement.

"Shouldn't we prepare ourselves while we wait for Dagmar?" Natalie said. "I don't think it would create a great impression if she comes in and sees us stuffing our faces."

The door behind them gave a sudden creak just as Ben was about to reply. They turned as the door swung open.

— CHAPTER FIVE —

Revelations

Dagmar and Abigail stood in the doorway. Dagmar's stern, rigid expression was a stark contrast to Abigail's soft smile. But Ben did not focus long on expressions – his eyes went straight to the helm tucked under Abigail's arm, and then to Dagmar's feet, where he gave a gasp of surprise, one that was immediately echoed by Charlie and Natalie.

Dagmar was wearing Elizabeth's Boots.

Abigail was holding Elizabeth's Helm.

"Take a seat," Dagmar said, nodding to the conference table at the back of the room, ignoring their startled expressions.

Ben managed to drag his attention away from Elizabeth's Armour, and they all sat down. The flowers and the food trays were temporarily ignored, bar a subtle lick of the lips from

Krobeg.

Ben had forgotten how simple yet beautiful the helm was – a slender, simplistic design that ordinarily wouldn't have looked up to the rigours of battle, if not for the power within.

To Ben's surprise, Dagmar removed her boots, and placed them on the table, next to the helm. Though Ben had never seen them together, it was clear that they belonged to the same suit of armour. A sudden grunting noise made Ben turn, and he saw Krobeg removing his jacket, revealing Elizabeth's Breastplate beneath. It came off smoothly, leaving a remarkably unbashful Krobeg in his undershirt. But with three pieces of Elizabeth's Armour sitting on the table, Krobeg could have stripped naked and nobody would have noticed. The breastplate dwarfed the other two pieces, but its craftsmanship was every bit their equal.

There was a brief, almost reverential silence, as they took in the three pieces of the armour, sitting in front of their respective Guardians. Ben had never seen all the pieces in one place, as they were normally hidden by each Guardian, and he felt a flash of unease seeing them all together, even if it was in the safety of the Crimson Tower.

"Now I see why you wanted to hold the meeting here," Ben said, his throat feeling a little dry.

Dagmar gave a quick nod. "Security is paramount. Not just because of the armour, but the topics we will speak of."

"Why did you bring them here?" Charlie asked, his eyes

locked on the helm.

"I will get to that in due course," Dagmar said. "First on the agenda, I need to give you a briefing on what is happening with the dark elves."

"I thought you already briefed during muster?" Charlie asked with a furrowed brow.

"I'm talking about a proper briefing, not the bare minimum waffle I give the apprentices," Dagmar said with a perfectly straight face.

Dagmar took each of them in, her keen, stolid stare appraising them with a thoroughness only Wren could match.

"The dark elves are coming, and they are coming soon," she said. "The executive council thinks the attack will occur within three months. I told the apprentices that an attack on the Seen Kingdoms was a possibility, but the fact is it's a certainty. The dark elves are planning to invade the United Kingdom."

Ben felt his mouth go dry, and his question came out as a croak. "Are we sure about that?"

Dagmar nodded. "We have suspected for a while. Between the Institute's extensive spy network and the strategic Unseen Kingdoms Suktar's taken, it has become fairly obvious."

Ben struggled to come to terms with Dagmar's declaration, and he wasn't the only one. Charlie was massaging his cheeks, a look of utter disbelief on his face.

"So the dark elves are going to invade us? What, like a full-scale invasion? An army?"

"An army, with the dark elves' full range of military units behind them. Aerial and combat beasts, mighty spells, war ships, and thousands of skilled warriors."

"Blimey," Ben muttered. "Has the Institute told the British government about this?"

"It is a delicate matter," Dagmar said, forming her fingers into a steeple. "Communicating it in a way that will be believable and asking them to gather their army is not a small thing. We have several prominent people in the government and, more significantly, within the royal family who know about the Institute, and we are working on it."

Charlie seemed to recover a little, though that didn't stop him pulling out his handkerchief again. "Okay, let's say the dark elves do invade and the United Kingdom is caught unawares, surely our military will wipe the floor with them? We have tanks, planes, guns and bombs."

"Do not underestimate the dark elves," Dagmar said, giving Charlie a stern look. "They will be well prepared. Guns will be useless. Stronger fire power may penetrate their magic, but it will bring many casualties, as the dark elves will arrive and launch straight into hand-to-hand combat. Any fire power the British use risks harming their own. It will be carnage unlike anything the British have seen since World War II."

Ben felt like all the air had been sucked out of him. He

wanted to come up with some sort of reason why this scenario was impossible, but he couldn't get his brain or his vocal cords working. Charlie and Abigail, the only other British residents, looked equally stunned. Natalie's face had turned pale, while Krobeg looked grim.

"They are moving quickly," Krobeg said, finding his voice first. "Three months for a full-scale invasion. When we found the breastplate, a little over a month ago, I don't recall the situation being so urgent."

Dagmar nodded. "You are right. The Institute cannot understand the dark elves' sudden haste, especially as they are normally so methodical and thorough. I have had words with Wren and even the prince, and they are also confused. However, we in this room should know why they are moving with such haste."

Ben knew the answer even before Dagmar continued.

"We have forced Suktar's hand. We now have three pieces of Elizabeth's Armour and all but one Guardian. I wouldn't say he is scared, because I don't believe Suktar knows of that emotion, but he is deeply concerned, and he wants to move before we get the rest."

Ben put a hand on his forehead, struggling to comprehend the words that were coming out of Dagmar's mouth. "So you're saying we're the reason for the war that's about to happen? We're the reason thousands of dark elves are about to invade the

United Kingdom?"

"We're the reason it's happening so quickly," Dagmar said.

Ben let out a deep breath. "That's mad."

"And the Institute doesn't know the reason behind the dark elves' haste," Natalie said. Her eyes had a distant, haunted look.

"That doesn't matter," Dagmar said with a rap of her hand on the table. "What matters now is that we find the two remaining pieces of armour, and the single remaining Guardian. That is why I requested the armour be here today, to remind you of its significance in ending Suktar's reign."

At this, she turned her laser-like stare to Ben, who met it with a feeling of discomfort.

"We're working on it," Ben said. "The problem is, we don't have any leads."

"I find that difficult to believe," Dagmar said. Her voice wasn't accusatory, just matter-of-fact. "Your parents were responsible for the sword. Surely they left a clue or a trail? After all, it is you, not they, who is the Guardian."

Ben gave a rueful smile. "If they left a clue, then it's a really subtle one. I've been through our old house several times. I've been through all the stuff that got sent to Grandma's, but I haven't found anything. Remember, they kept the whole Royal Institute of Magic thing from me. I think they were planning to tell me, eventually, but they were forced to go on the run."

Dagmar gave the merest narrowing of her eyes, before

nodding. "Very well."

"But you're right," Ben said, clenching his fist and pressing on. "I'm certain that if I keep looking, I'll uncover a clue somewhere. I must not be looking in the right place."

"What about the shield?" Krobeg asked. "Do we really have nothing for that either?"

"Nope," Charlie said, idly tapping his fingers on the table. "And the shield is worse. At least with the sword, we have the Guardian and so have some idea where the sword might be. With the shield we have nothing."

"Well, we need to find something, and quick," Dagmar said. "I will get you access to every nook and cranny within the Institute, so you can expand your research."

Charlie brightened considerably. "That might help."

"I hope so, because we are running out of time. Remember, once you have found the sword, Ben, you will need time to harness its power if you are going to use it to confront Suktar. Don't expect to simply pick up the sword and immediately be able to use it."

"I hadn't thought of that," Ben admitted.

Dagmar placed her hands on Elizabeth's Boots. "I have spent many hours with the boots, and I'm confident I can utilise their magic. My role will be to navigate us to Suktar, wherever he may be." She turned to Abigail. "How are you feeling with the helm?"

"I'm doing well, thanks to you," Abigail said. "It was scary at first, flying without my body and reading dark elf minds, but I'm getting the hang of it."

"Wow, that's intense," Ben said, looking impressed. "I can't believe how well you've done. So, what is your role to be?"

"I will need to be able to read thoughts, to determine what the dark elves are going to do and learn their secrets." She gave a little gulp and continued. "Eventually, I may have to enter Suktar's mind."

"We don't know that yet," Dagmar said, coming as close to sympathy as Ben had ever seen. "But you are making rapid progress, and I am happy. And what about you, Krobeg?"

"Nothing so subtle," Krobeg said, giving a grin and tapping his breastplate with a hairy hand. "I'm a one-man fighting machine. The breastplate gives me strength, increases my reaction time, and provides incredible regeneration. I guess I'm the bodyguard. I have been practising every evening and I'm improving each day."

"Good," Dagmar said. "That just leaves the sword and the shield."

Ben, who was feeling a little useless, leaned forwards and piped up. "Well, we know the sword is supposed to deliver the killer blow, and the shield is responsible for protecting me from Suktar's strikes."

"Providing we get them in time so you learn how to use it,"

Dagmar said with a subtly raised eyebrow.

"We'll find them," Ben said, grinding his teeth. "I've already got some ideas."

Ben couldn't tell by Dagmar's response if she knew he was exaggerating a little, but he didn't care. He was the Head Guardian and he still hadn't found his own piece of armour. That had to change, and it had to change now.

"Good," Dagmar said. "Remember, if you need anything sensible from me, do not dally. We cannot afford to waste time."

Dagmar looked as though she was about to rise, signifying the end of the meeting, but, to Ben's surprise, she turned her attention to Charlie and Natalie.

"There is one more thing I need to mention. When the time comes and the Guardians assemble to find and destroy Suktar, it can only be the Guardians who go."

It took Charlie and Natalie a second to realise what she was implying. Natalie, who was normally so deferential when addressing senior Institute members, looked at Dagmar with shock. Charlie was only marginally less put out.

"Are you suggesting that Charlie and I shouldn't go?" Natalie asked, the outrage in her expression mirrored by her voice.

"That's exactly what I'm saying," Dagmar said. "You would jeopardise the mission."

"No," Natalie said, shaking her head so vigorously her hair

spun around her shoulders. "You can't stop us going. I won't let you. We've been with Ben from the start. He might need us."

Natalie turned to Charlie for support. He looked troubled, and Ben knew why. Would he side with reason? Or would he let the heart rule for once?

"It wouldn't be right to exclude us at the very end," Charlie said eventually. "We have got this far together and had success. We should finish the job together."

"Irrelevant," Dagmar said with typical lack of emotion. "The final journey will be like nothing you've ever encountered. Your mere presence could hinder us."

Charlie and Natalie both raised their voices in protest. Dagmar sat there, unflinching, but Ben was sure her tolerance would last only so long. It was time to act.

"Okay, that's enough," Ben said, slapping his hand on the table. Natalie and Charlie reluctantly quietened down. Ben turned to Dagmar. "As the Head Guardian, whether they come or not is not your decision to make. It's mine."

Ben spoke firmly, trying to replicate Dagmar's understated authority. She gave him a hard stare, and then, to Ben's surprise, he saw a subtle upturn of her lips – or had he imagined it?

"You are right," she said, after a moment's tense silence. "That is a decision I will leave to you."

And with that, she reached out, grabbed a cucumber sandwich, and left.

"Well, that was intense," Krobeg said. His hands snaked out and within moments he was sampling five different appetisers, smacking his lips and licking his fingers.

Ben expected Charlie to follow suit, but found that he and Natalie were both looking at him, expectantly.

It was then Ben realised just exactly what he'd got himself into. He had to make the call as to whether Charlie and Natalie came on the final journey. Was Dagmar right? Would they jeopardise their chances? They weren't Guardians; they weren't even powerful Institute members. What role or value did they bring, other than support and friendship? Was that enough?

Ben met the gazes of Natalie and Charlie. "I need to think about it."

"What?" Natalie asked, leaning forwards. "What is there to think about?"

Ben had to think fast. "Let's just focus on finding the last two pieces of armour and the remaining Guardian. Then I'll make the decision."

Natalie gave him an angry stare, and looked ready to give him another earful.

"That sounds reasonable," Krobeg said, before Natalie could launch into another tirade. "Ben has enough on his mind already. Let's not give him something else to think about until the time comes."

To Ben's relief, Natalie sat back, partially mollified, though she didn't look happy. Charlie, Ben noted, was far less put out.

Ben gave Krobeg a grateful smile. "Alright, when everyone's done stuffing their faces, let's get out of here. We've got a lot of work to do."

— CHAPTER SIX —

A Tenuous Lead

Despite their renewed urgency fuelled by Dagmar's briefing, Ben still found their time to do any research for the last Guardian limited by the Institute's own plans.

Ben was one of a handful of apprentices given extra lessons on spellshooting and swordsmanship by a senior Spellsword, Volvek – an elf who was well known for his talents in those two particular fields. The lessons were exhausting, but Ben made progress in leaps and bounds.

"It is a contingency plan," Volvek said, when William asked the reason behind the lessons. "Apprentices talented in certain areas are being further trained, in case they are needed when the time comes. I sincerely hope you are not."

The same went for Charlie and Natalie. Natalie received

extra Diplomacy lessons and spent at least a couple of hours a day dealing with questions from citizens arriving at the Institute, both commoners and nobles. Charlie was already incredibly competent as a Scholar, and so he was used more for research regarding the dark elves – how would they most likely attack? What might their strategy be?

They each enjoyed the challenges, but along with their continuing third-grade apprenticeships, it restricted their free time significantly. Not even Dagmar had the power to change their schedule, as she couldn't give a valid reason to do so.

Nevertheless, they met regularly, sometimes with Dagmar, to discuss what they had found. To Ben's immense frustration, very little progress was made, and they left dejected but determined to do more the following week.

Two weeks passed in the blink of an eye with little progress made. To make matters worse, the planned dark elf invasion started to impinge more and more upon their Institute lives. The Institute had recalled several hundred members from the Unseen Kingdoms now that they were no longer under immediate threat. It made the place even busier than usual and finding some privacy for their research that much harder.

Ben consoled himself with the fact that this weekend, the four of them, Abigail included, were going over to his grandma's to do a real thorough search. Ben was hopeful that they might spot something he had missed.

It was with that slightly comforting thought that he left his Trade lesson, and headed down to the apprentice floor to grab a few things from his locker. He decided to take a less-known route, fed up with the constant traffic. He ended up on the far side of the apprentice floor, which had the rare phenomenon of being almost empty.

"Josh, I need a word. You've been avoiding me."

Ben paused, just as he was about to round the corner. That was Aaron's voice.

"I've got nothing to say to you," Joshua said a little tersely.

"I know that, but I believe you will change your mind after I have spoken to you."

Aaron's voice was soft, persuasive, but Joshua's grunt indicated that it didn't have the usual desired effect.

"You misjudge me," Joshua said.

"I think not," Aaron said. Ben could almost see his charming smile attempting to work its magic. "We have a mutual adversary: Ben Greenwood."

Ben's stomach jumped, and his heart started beating so loudly he was afraid it would give his position away.

"He is no adversary of mine," Joshua said. "In fact, most of the time I try to pretend he doesn't exist."

"Sounds like you're not part of the Ben Greenwood fan club," Aaron said. "He has one, you know – such arrogance. If that is your opinion of him, how can you tell me he is not an adversary of yours?"

Silence. Ben had an enhanced hearing spell, but he was afraid to cast it. Since the increase in security, any unauthorised spells could immediately get reported.

"What was it he did to you?" Aaron said, his voice suddenly soft. "Tease you? Betray you? Lie to you? He has done all three to me."

"It is none of your business," Joshua said. Ben was expecting anger or impatience, but he detected neither in Joshua's voice.

"Fair enough," Aaron said. "Well, I don't want to impose myself, but I know you two have quite a history, and you would be well placed to help me. Can I tell you my plan, at least? You can make a decision, and I won't hold it against you either way."

"No," Joshua said with a sudden forcefulness. "I don't care what petty squabbles you have with Ben. Gaining revenge will not make me feel any better."

But Aaron wasn't finished. "I can feel your anger, Joshua. Why don't you at least tell me something about your grievance with Ben? It will help, trust me."

"Even if I wanted to, I can't. It's a family secret – something that happened many years ago. I made a promise."

Ben's mind was momentarily cast back to the scene he felt sure Joshua was referring to. His dad and Joshua's uncle had had a row at Joshua's parents' house. For some reason, the argument escalated, and his dad ended up killing Joshua's uncle. Joshua, then just a child, had witnessed the whole thing.

"Very well," Aaron said. It was remarkable how his voice went from friendly and endearing to uncaring in a heartbeat. "I'll find someone else. You weren't my first choice anyway."

Ben's stomach lurched at the sudden sound of footsteps. They were coming right to him. Quick as a flash, he darted away on tiptoes, and opened the door into a nearby room. It was packed with storage boxes, but thankfully empty of people. He waited three minutes before poking his head out. Apprentices walked the corridor, but, to his relief, Joshua and Aaron had gone.

Despite being run off his feet with the apprenticeship and the extra Spellsword lessons, Ben thought the day still seemed to drag out, and it felt like an age before he met up with Charlie and Natalie. Dagmar had managed to get them access to one of the most magically secure conference rooms, located on the Diplomacy floor, which they could use as long as it was empty.

It was six o'clock, and Charlie was munching on a baguette. They often had little time for dinner and so would grab what they could before getting back to work. Now they were third-graders, and over sixteen years old, the Institute felt they could be pushed a little harder with their schedule.

They were seated around the circular table in the conference room. One quick glance at Charlie and Natalie, and Ben could tell they had no news.

He leaned forwards on the table, giving them both serious looks. "I think I might have a possible lead."

It was as if someone had crept up behind Charlie and Natalie and said "boo". They both stared at him, food momentarily forgotten.

"A real lead?" Charlie said.

Ben raised his hands. "Don't get too excited. It's tenuous at best, but it's something, and given that we have nothing else to go on, I think it's worth pursuing."

Ben had their complete and undivided attention.

"It's Joshua," Ben said.

Seeing them both frown, Ben retold the conversation between Joshua and Aaron, ensuring he got every detail right.

Their responses were, typically, quite different. Natalie clapped her hands, her pretty face flushed with hope. Charlie, however, looked thoughtful.

"I'm not saying this is nothing," Charlie said. "That whole incident with Joshua's uncle and your dad was never properly resolved – even Wren thought the whole love story thing was rubbish. But, if that is what Joshua is referring to, what more can we learn? And how would it help us?"

"We can't learn anything more with what we have," Natalie interjected, completely undeterred by Charlie's cautious manner. "But we can find out more."

"What could we hope to find?" Charlie asked.

"At worst, nothing," Ben admitted. "But my dad was involved, remember? And many strange incidents in the past have been answered by his motivation to preserve the secret behind Elizabeth's Legacy."

To Ben's surprise, Charlie nodded with agreement, rubbing his cheeks. "That is true. Perhaps something happened where he had no choice but to kill Joshua's uncle."

"I hope not," Ben said. "But the point is, we have a lead involving my dad. Maybe it could give us a clue to the location of the sword."

"Yes, that's possible," Charlie admitted.

"Possible?" Natalie asked, staring at Charlie with mock exasperation. "It's the best – well, only – lead we've had since we found Krobeg and the breastplate."

Ben felt his mood rising now that he had won Charlie's approval. "The question is, who do we ask? Joshua and I aren't exactly best buddies. He tries his best to pretend I don't exist."

"I don't think we should approach Joshua. Not yet anyway. I think we should go to his dad, Arnold."

"He's not easy to get hold of," Ben said. "He's out at some Unseen Kingdom half the time."

"No, he's back," Natalie said, her back almost leaving her chair with excitement. "Most of the Institute members have been recalled to focus on the UK. I saw Arnold the other day."

"So did I," Charlie said. "Though he was surrounded by half a dozen other Wardens. He's a powerful man, and won't be easy to catch alone."

"Don't worry," Ben said with a smile. "I have a plan."

"How is that possible? We only came up with the idea seconds ago."

"True," Ben said and shrugged. "It's not really a plan, more of a germ of a potential idea. But work with me here. I'm on a roll."

— CHAPTER SEVEN —

Arnold and the War Room

Catching Arnold alone turned out to be more difficult than Ben had anticipated. Arnold spent much of his time in the Warden Department, surrounded by an entourage and often within earshot of Draven himself. Ben soon learned that Arnold was part of a group of three Wardens who were essentially second-in-command, directly below Draven.

Ben, Charlie, Natalie, and even Abigail took turns trying to catch him alone, but with the craziness of the impending dark elf invasion, it was nigh on impossible.

"What's this plan of yours, then?" Charlie asked.

The four of them, including Abigail, sat in the common room, looking a little frustrated. It had been three days now since Ben had overheard Joshua and Aaron, and they hadn't come close to getting a moment alone with Arnold.

"I didn't think it would be this difficult," Ben admitted. He was leaning back in a soft chair, one leg on a coffee table. "Clearly what we're doing isn't working. We need to try something else."

"We could go to his house," Abigail suggested. She had a cup of tea and drank it in tiny sips.

"I don't think he goes home anymore," Natalie said. "Most of the senior Institute members work here twenty hours a day, and then sleep somewhere in Taecia, either here or at a hotel. I don't know how we'd find out where Arnold sleeps."

"We could follow him," Charlie said.

"Tried that already," Ben said. "He's staying at the Hotel Jigona. I thought I might be able to catch him on the way there, but several other Institute members were with him. Then I thought maybe I could knock on the door where he was staying. I traced him all the way to his room. I was about to knock on the door, when I spotted his wife and Joshua there. I had to bail."

"What about Dagmar?" Abigail asked in her soft voice. "She said she would help if we needed it."

Ben lifted his second leg onto the coffee table. "Tried that as well. Nobody can accuse me of not trying here. She and Arnold are not on speaking terms for some reason, and she said any request for help would be met with a great deal of suspicion, and the last thing we want is questions being asked. But she did say that if we can't find another way, come back to her."

"Well, as far as I can see, there is no other way," Charlie said. "It would probably be easier getting hold of the US president right now."

Ben removed his legs from the table and sat up. "I'll catch him today."

"What? How?"

"I'd much prefer to get him alone, for obvious reasons, but if I can't, then I'm going to approach him while he's surrounded by his people."

"That's risky," Charlie said immediately.

"I know, but we've wasted too much time on this already. I'll take the risk."

They ended the meeting on that note, and agreed to meet later that evening.

"If I'm not there, you may want to get Dagmar," Ben said with a smile as they left.

Ben knew from experience that five o'clock was a good time to try to catch Arnold. Many of the Institute members left for a quick dinner, before returning between 5:30pm and 6pm. Arnold, however, often got someone to get him his food, so he could keep working. The hardest part was staying up on the Warden floor without attracting attention, but Ben had that worked out. At 4:45pm he went upstairs. The atmosphere changed the moment he entered the Department of Wardens;

Ben could almost see sparks of electricity flying from the tension in the air. Institute members regularly ran down the corridors, and those who didn't were deep in conversation. There were apprentices too, and they always ran, zipping down the corridor, often with notes or strange small boxes that piqued Ben's curiosity.

Ben stepped behind a couple of apprentices, picked up his pace, and followed them into the War Room. Somehow, it looked even busier than his last visit. The room was also set up differently. There was one huge table surrounded by Institute members, who leant over it, talking, gesturing and generally causing a great deal of noise. Ben could just about get a glimpse of the map on the table, and he couldn't help gasping, despite his attempt at remaining inconspicuous. It was laid out in three dimensions; the colours were vibrant, and the texture and detail were incredible. It looked like it was just the south of England, allowing for greater detail because of the smaller area. Ben knew he should have been used to the incredible things they could do with magic, but it was still startling to see the small Institute garrisons in miniature 3D on the map.

Ben had to tear his eyes away, and quickly searched for Arnold. He wasn't at the large table, but at a smaller one, set up for senior members. Papers and cups of tea littered the surface.

Ben attempted a quick head count, focusing on the members and apprentices in the room. When he had a good estimation of numbers, he left, not wanting to risk getting spotted. He walked no more than twenty feet down the corridor until he reached a door that said "Unseen Activity". Ben, however, didn't enter, but stared at a large map on the wall, detailing populations, terrains, political information and economies for each region. It was a map he was supposed to learn back to front by the time he finished the third grade, and it was the perfect excuse for standing outside. If anyone questioned his presence, he would say he was studying. If he saw someone like Draven, he would simply step into the room, where he could really study, as he had several steps to do on his Warden checklist in the Unseen Activity room.

Ben positioned himself so that he could see the map, but also see the door to the War Room in his peripheral vision. He held the clipboard he had brought along in one hand, and started making notes. He had to be careful not to write complete nonsense, in case someone checked it. He had debated leaving the clipboard behind but decided its presence would lend an authentic air to his studies.

Ben had counted between fifty and sixty members in the War Room. Thankfully, he hadn't noticed Draven, but in an ideal world he would want fewer than a dozen members in there before he approached Arnold. Just as he predicted, it wasn't long before the members started filing out in twos and threes to grab some dinner. It was surprisingly difficult looking at the map and keeping track of how many members left. Ten minutes passed and Ben counted twelve. Fifteen minutes passed, and the number was up to twenty. That meant there were still at least thirty members in the War Room. Ben cursed silently. It wouldn't be that much longer before some of the members started returning. Once that happened, his chance was gone. How much longer should he wait? Another five minutes passed, and several more departed. Ben started getting impatient – was twenty in the War Room too many? If the members were spread around the table, then there might not be too many people near Arnold. Five more minutes, he said to himself, then he would move. To his delight, those five minutes yielded another ten people leaving. There were now just ten members left inside. Ben had the sudden urge to give it five more minutes – at this rate everyone bar Arnold would be gone.

Two Institute members rounded the corner, and promptly re-entered the War Room.

Ben clenched his fist in frustration. He had waited too long. Served him right for dallying.

He left the map and headed for the War Room. It occurred to him that he hadn't given much thought to what he was going to say when he approached Arnold. He wasn't one for thinking too far ahead, but, nevertheless, his mouth suddenly felt dry as he tried to visualise the conversation. Ben grit his teeth. He couldn't afford to back out now. He reached the War Room door, took a deep, calming breath, and entered.

He took the room in quickly. As he had predicted, there were only a dozen or so members in the room, and several of them looked ready to head for dinner. His eyes went to the small conference table, and he immediately spotted Arnold. There were two others with him; both had four red diamonds floating above their shoulders. With only a moment's hesitation, he headed right towards Arnold and his colleagues. Arnold had the same thick, blond hair and slightly stuck-up nose as his son. His sharp blue eyes looked tired, and the normally impeccable suit he wore had signs of wrinkles, which, for someone like Arnold, was a strange sight.

"Yes?" a rather curt voice said.

The Institute member next to Arnold had spotted him first. Arnold turned, and Ben saw surprise etched in the fine wrinkles of his face.

"Ben Greenwood," Arnold said. "Can I help you with something? We are rather busy here."

"I'm sorry, sir," Ben said, pleased that Arnold remembered his name. "I wouldn't bother you unless it was extremely important. It's about that incident with your brother and my father. I really need a few questions answered."

Ben cursed himself most vigorously the moment he had finished talking. What sort of pitch was that? It was horrible. Why should Arnold care? Quick as a flash, he started trying to re-word the question in a slightly more sensible manner.

But to Ben's immense surprise, Arnold didn't laugh or tell him to leave. Instead, he gave Ben a serious look, those blue eyes seeming to grow distant. After what seemed like an eternity, Arnold gave a nod, and turned to the two members by his side.

"I will be back presently," he said.

They watched in surprise as Arnold stood up.

"Let us find somewhere private to talk," Arnold said.

Ben couldn't believe his luck. He followed Arnold to the door, trying to conceal his exaltation. Finally! This was his chance to speak to Arnold in private.

The gruff voice from the other side of the door sliced a knife through his good mood. Ben looked up just as Draven came thundering through the door, alongside Wren.

"Greenwood? What are you doing here?" Draven asked, coming to a juddering halt in front of them.

For some reason, Draven didn't have that weary, bedraggled look evident in many of the senior Institute members working twenty hours a day. That might have simply been because he always looked scruffy, with his ragged beard, his nasty scar that ran along his chin, and his terrifying expression that was more commonly associated with an attack dog. Ben was comforted by the Spellsword Director standing next to Draven. She, too, looked untouched by fatigue, but that didn't surprise Ben one bit. She always looked agelessly perfect. Her fine silver hair was piled on her head, heightening her presence, in stark contrast to the diminutive Draven. She wore a dazzling green dress, matching the five green diamonds floating above her shoulder. >

"It's okay, Draven. He came to see me," Arnold said.

"Can't it wait? We are far too busy to deal with trivial matters, especially a troublemaker like Greenwood," Draven said, giving Ben an accusing look.

"No, actually, it can't," Arnold said calmly.

Ben had to conceal his relief. Many people would back down against the sheer aggression of Draven, but Arnold appeared unflustered.

"Really? What could possibly be more important than the imminent invasion of the dark elves?"

"It's a personal matter," Arnold said, keeping a completely neutral face that would have done Dagmar proud.

Draven gave Ben a hard look, but he knew he was off the hook with Arnold backing him up. However, it wasn't Draven who made Ben's skin tingle and his stomach give a little lurch, but Wren. She was looking at him keenly, her grey eyes seemingly seeing right into his soul.

"Is everything okay, Ben?" Wren asked.

Of course. Ben had told Wren something of Elizabeth's Legacy, using the most general terms he could muster. He had been in a tight spot, and had had no option. He didn't regret it, but he had wondered more than once if she had done anything with that knowledge. Ben had told her little more than the fact that there were several families responsible for obtaining an artefact that could defeat Suktar. But, in the present circumstances, that was huge.

"I'm fine, thank you," Ben said.

Wren smiled. "Just remember, if you need anything, please don't hesitate to ask. I am always available."

Draven gave her an incredulous look. "Are you mad? You're almost as busy as me. How can you make yourself available like that?"

"What I do or don't do is my concern, Draven," Wren said calmly. She turned back to Ben and Arnold. "We won't disturb you two any further."

Wren and a very reluctant Draven moved aside so that Arnold and a now perspiring Ben could leave the War Room.

— CHAPTER EIGHT —

Arnold's Story

Arnold led Ben up three floors to the Diplomacy Department. Ben noted that those members who weren't too busy talking or lost their own thoughts gave Arnold a respectful nod.

They went through the double doors and started walking at a brisk pace until they reached a series of doors separated by just a few feet, indicating either one big room or lots of small ones.

Arnold stopped by one of the doors. "Ignore the sign; it's one of the only secure rooms that is free right now."

Ben was thankful for the warning. The sign read "Enforced Negotiation Room #3."

There didn't appear to be any handle. Arnold extended his

forefinger to the door, touched it lightly and turned. There was a soft click, and Arnold pushed the door open.

True to the room's designated purpose, it was dark and uninviting. There were two uncomfortable-looking chairs separated by a small table.

"Please, take a seat," Arnold said, gesturing to one chair while he took the other.

The moment Ben sat down, his heart seemed to double in speed. He hadn't given a good deal of thought about what to say, preferring to let instinct take over. But he remembered with some ruefulness how that had worked out when he approached Arnold earlier. He was determined to be more careful here, and think before he spoke.

But Arnold beat him to it.

"I'm sorry I haven't spoken to you earlier," Arnold began. "As you may have seen, it's mad at the Institute right now, especially for Wardens. It's a bit of a nightmare to be honest, but we're doing as best we can."

"I totally understand," Ben said. "I was hoping you might be able to tell me a little more about the incident where my father killed your brother. I can't stop thinking about why my dad would do such a thing."

Arnold gave a sympathetic nod. "I understand. It doesn't take a genius to realise what we told everyone wasn't the truth. Wren tried on numerous occasions to get it out of me, but I held firm, though it's not easy withholding anything from Wren."

Ben felt a thrill of excitement that threatened to lift him off the seat, but he managed to remain calm.

"Do you know what really happened?"

"Bits, but not all," Arnold said. There was a flash of pain in his eyes, making him pause.

Despite Ben's feverish excitement, he was careful not to rush him.

"The reason for the fight had absolutely nothing to do with misplaced love," Arnold said. "Frankly, I'm surprised that lie managed to stick, though Greg could be very convincing when he wanted to. Barry, Joshua's uncle, and I were good friends with your parents. But exactly a week before Barry had the incident with Greg, things started to sour."

Arnold stopped, and became reflective, as if he were pondering a sad memory.

"He stopped coming out to dinner, and he stopped working on projects with us. He was pre-occupied, that much was obvious. But when I questioned him, he would say everything was fine. When I pushed further, he got angry. He even threatened me with his spellshooter once, though he immediately regretted it, saying I couldn't understand. I will always remember those words: *you couldn't understand.*"

Arnold paused again, and Ben counted an impatient ten seconds, before nudging Arnold on. "Did you ever work out what he was talking about?"

"Some of it," Arnold said. "This much I know: Barry was persuaded to change sides. I strongly suspect the dark elves were responsible – that's what Greg said, and I believe him. Why the dark elves chose him, and for what purpose, I don't know."

Ben knew exactly why – the answer screamed inside his head so loudly he feared Arnold might hear. *The dark elves were using Barry to try to get the sword.*

"That's interesting," Ben said with remarkable calm given that his heart rate was going a mile a minute. "Is there anything else you can tell me?"

Arnold nodded, and leaned forwards a fraction, so that his red diamonds were almost above Ben's head. "There is one more thing – Joshua knows more about this than I do. I am sure of it."

"He hasn't told you everything?"

Arnold paused again, his eyes once more becoming distant, and sad, Ben realised. "We are not on speaking terms right now."

This was something Arnold was clearly not willing to elaborate on, so Ben tried another angle.

"What makes you so sure that Joshua knows more than you?"

"Several reasons. Firstly, he was there. I know he was young, but I also know that he has since used sophisticated memory spells on himself to re-live the incident. He has done this several times, most recently just last week. But that's not all. He's hiding something, I'm sure of it. I tried getting it out of him, and he as good as admitted I was right, but stubbornly refused to say more. I feared the dark elves may have got to him as well, but thankfully that fear proved unfounded."

Ben's excitement waned just a fraction when he thought of Joshua. "We don't exactly get on either, especially when it comes to that incident. I was really hoping you'd be able to talk to him."

Arnold gave a sad smile. "I know you'll find this hard to believe, but you have a better chance of getting through to him than I do. Parents can be the last person their child wishes to confide in sometimes."

And sometimes it's the other way round Ben thought.

"I can give it another go. The worst he can do is to tell me to get lost."

"Good," Arnold said, nodding. "Do you know why I'm telling you all this? I'm not in the habit of revealing skeletons in the closet, especially when it's my family's closet."

"I'm not sure," Ben said. The truth was, he couldn't believe how lucky he had been with Arnold opening up so freely.

"It's because of Joshua," Arnold said. "He needs help, I know it. Something is on his mind that has changed him. It's not just you he's been acting unfriendly to. He has lost many of his friends with his antisocial, unfriendly behaviour. I would really appreciate it if you could find out what it is, for both our sakes."

Ben saw then how much Arnold was hurting. His only son wasn't talking to him – but worse than that, Arnold knew there was something very wrong with Joshua, and Arnold was powerless to help.

"I'll talk to him," Ben said with a confident nod.

Arnold gave a relieved smile, and extended his hand, which Ben shook.

Now it was just a case of working out a devious plan to get Joshua to talk. Ben suspected he would have an easier time cleaning Thomas the wyvern blindfolded with his hands tied behind his back.

— CHAPTER NINE —

Akrim's Vintage Antiques

I don't think we should approach Joshua in the Institute," Natalie said.

The three of them sat in their favourite spot in the common room. It was busy, but as they weren't talking about anything confidential for once, the common room was an easy, convenient place to meet.

"Why not?" Charlie asked.

"I just think the Institute seems to bring out the worst in him. I saw him at a coffee shop a couple of days ago and he gave me a smile, believe it or not."

"I believe it," Charlie said, looking a little put out. "He was always trying to woo you when we first met, remember? He's changed a lot since then."

"Only in the last few months has he really changed, though," Ben said. "His dad can confirm that. So what do you suggest? We go over to his house?"

"No," Natalie said immediately. "I don't even know if he's there right now. He stays at the Hotel Jigona with his parents a lot of the time. Trying to catch him there with his parents around would never work. I think we should try to catch him during his lunch hour. He nearly always eats out by himself now. I think that's our best opportunity."

"I like it," Ben said. "Let's get him tomorrow lunchtime and beat whatever secrets he's hiding out of him."

"I like the beating part," Charlie said.

With a plan set in place, and the first bit of progress made towards the other pieces of Elizabeth's Armour, Ben was able to relax and switch off that evening for the first time in weeks, enabling him to sleep better than he had in some time.

*

He was so focused on getting to lunch the following day that he didn't even mind when Aaron had them spend an hour shovelling shit in the winged chimpanzee paddock, where they tried to avoid being thrown about by the "playful" animals.

"My goodness, you do smell," Aaron said, as he and Charlie finished up. Thankfully, Natalie and Abigail had been exempt. "Make sure you shower and change clothes before you enter the lunchroom, or else you'll ruin everyone's appetite."

Ben resisted the urge to gather a piece of chimpanzee pooh and fling it at Aaron's face. Instead he and Charlie rushed to their locker room, grabbed a change of clothes, then quickly showered and got dressed.

Ben halted as they were about to head down the stairs and leave.

"What's up?" Charlie asked. "Natalie's waiting for us outside."

"So will a couple of Aaron's lackeys," Ben pointed out. "Remember how they love following me?"

Charlie cursed. "I'd forgotten about that. What do you want to do? We're supposed to be following Joshua, remember? We can't afford to waste time losing Aaron's people or else we'll lose Joshua."

In response, Ben took out his spellshooter and, making sure nobody was looking, fired a spell into Charlie's stomach.

"What was that?" Charlie asked in alarm.

"A tracking spell," Ben said. "You follow Joshua with Natalie, and I'll catch up to you using the tracking spell once I've lost Aaron's idiots."

Charlie frowned, and then looked about with a worried expression. "That was risky, firing a spell here, with the Institute so tight on security."

"I know," said Ben. "But it's only a level-one spell, so I'm hoping I'll be okay."

Charlie left Ben, and headed downstairs. Ben went to wait in the common room, figuring it was best not to hang around where he'd just fired a spell. The room was almost empty as most people had gone to lunch. He forced himself to wait at least five minutes, so that Charlie and Natalie would be safely clear, before heading downstairs.

If last time Aaron had employed a pair of weasels, then this time it was a pair of gorillas. Both wore spellshooters, and neither made any attempt to conceal their intentions.

"Where you going?" a deep, slightly slow voice said. You could tell Timothy was below average intelligence just by hearing him talk. "Your friends have left without you."

Ben stopped and stepped up to Timothy, who was a good head taller than him. "What's my destination got to do with you?"

Timothy was clearly taken aback, and there was a moment of uncomprehending shock as he tried to compute Ben's words. He clearly wasn't used to people talking to him in such a manner.

Ben grinned at him and his friend, Paul, who was only marginally smaller, but just as slow.

Without warning, Ben sprinted out the Institute door.

He must have made it thirty feet away before he even heard them respond in shock, and head after him. Ben ran through the Institute gardens and out the gate, getting a suspicious stare from the guards. He turned right and picked up the pace, so that he was flying through the streets, taking random lefts and rights.

Timothy and Paul never had a chance. Even if they had started pursuing as soon as Ben fled, they would have had difficulty keeping up, without casting some sort of self-enhancement spell. But with Ben's head start, he lost them within minutes. Ben ran for a good five minutes, mainly for the exercise, before finally slowing to a walk. He checked behind him several times, but saw no sign of his pursuers. Satisfied he was alone, Ben focused on the tracking spell he cast on Charlie and immediately took a left, and picked up the pace again to a rapid walk.

The tracking spell took him west, which was unsurprising. Some of the more upmarket restaurants were in the west district, and Ben could well see Joshua having expensive taste. The tracking spell gave him some idea of proximity to his target, so Ben was a little surprised when he got to the main eatery section and found that he was still a good few minutes away. His surprise increased when he passed all the restaurants, and kept going.

It wasn't until he arrived at a quaint, cobbled street, lined on both sides with antique shops, that the tracking spell blinked out. Ben saw Charlie and Natalie down the street and hurried to catch up with them. They were standing outside *Akrim's Vintage Antiques*, looking surreptitiously through the shop window.

"What's going on?"

Charlie didn't take his eyes away from the window, but instead beckoned Ben to join them. Ben placed his head against the window to get a proper look. For an antique shop, it was remarkably uncluttered, making good use of the space; the shop seemed to go on forever. In the distance, Ben could just about make out Joshua deep in conversation with a gnome, who Ben guessed to be the store owner. In his hand Joshua was holding what looked like a key.

"Yes, it's a key," Natalie said, confirming Ben's guess with her superior eyesight. "The shopkeeper gave it to him several minutes ago, and they've been talking ever since."

"So he came straight here?" Ben asked.

"Yeah, which I was bummed about, as I was hoping he'd choose a nice café where we could grab something. Now we're going to go the whole of lunch without eating," Charlie said.

But the disappointment in Charlie's voice didn't match his obvious interest as he stared at the key in Joshua's hand. Ben was also curious about the key, but he was more interested in talking to Joshua.

"Shall we go in?" Ben said. "The place is relatively empty – now is probably a good time."

They nodded, and Ben led them inside. The door rung a soft bell as they entered, indicating to the owner that he had new guests. However, he and Joshua were so engaged in conversation that the owner didn't seem to notice. This suited Ben perfectly as he was eager to hear what they were talking about. With a subtle nod, he directed them to spread out amongst the shelves. Ben chose the most direct route to Joshua that still gave him a little bit of cover from the right-hand shelf, which he could hug against if needed. The wooden floorboards were old but solid and made no sound as Ben crept forwards until he was within earshot of Joshua and the store owner.

"...I'm sorry, Master Wistletop, but beyond the letter, there isn't much more I can tell you. Were my great-great-grandfather still around, I'm sure he could oblige you, as the one who originally safeguarded the key for your family. I honestly thought nobody was going to reclaim it, such was the time that had passed since it was placed under our care."

"I understand," Joshua said. He felt his pocket, and Ben was fairly certain he was feeling the letter the owner must have just given him. How Ben would have liked to read it. From this distance, he could get a better look at the key, and he was impressed. It was an old-fashioned thing, cast in what looked like gold and studded with rubies. Ben had become pretty good at spotting enchanted items, and he suspected the key to be magical, in some shape or form.

"Is there anything else I can help you with, Master Wistletop?" the little gnome asked politely, but with a subtle edge that suggested it was time for him to move on.

"No, thank you," Joshua said. "You have done more than enough. Thank you for holding on to the key for so long."

The gnome gave a little bow. "No problem at all, Master Wistletop. At *Akrim's Vintage Antiques*, we are known for our trust and honesty. And I have to be honest, your great-great-grandfather paid us well for the privilege of storing it."

"It was well spent," Joshua said.

The gnome gave another bow. "Thank you, once again. Now, if you'll excuse me, I need to deal with my other customers."

Akrim turned towards Ben, who was the closest. Ben acted instinctively, swiftly but casually picking up a small eagle statue and earnestly examining it.

"Ben!" Joshua said, his voice full of surprise and not a small amount of suspicion. "What are you doing here?"

Ben turned, still holding the eagle, and gave a casual wave. "Oh, hey, Josh. It's Natalie's mum's birthday soon, so we're just looking for gifts. Nat heard good things about this place, so we thought we'd give it a try."

Ben spoke loud enough so that Charlie and Natalie would hear his story.

"Hey, Joshua," Natalie said brightly, stepping out from between the shelves, and walking up to an increasingly surprised Joshua. "I didn't know you liked this place. Do you come here often?"

The question was perfect. It put Joshua, who had been looking at them suspiciously, straight onto the defensive.

"Sometimes," Joshua said. "It's one of my mother's favourite antique shops."

"Oh, cool," Natalie said, giving Joshua one of her dazzling smiles. "Are you looking for anything in particular? I see you're still empty-handed."

Joshua had slipped the key into his pocket the moment he had spotted Ben. But, unlike Ben, he wasn't quite as adept at coming up with stories, and faltered – the gaze from Natalie probably didn't help.

"Er, no," Joshua said. "I'm still looking actually. I think I'll try upstairs. I hope you find something nice for your mum."

"Thanks," Natalie said.

Joshua ignored Ben and Charlie completely and wandered up the stairs, disappearing out of sight.

"Can I help anyone?" Akrim asked.

Ben thought fast. "Yes – Charlie, you said you wanted some advice on something, right?"

"Er, yes," Charlie said, looking flustered and trying quite clearly to indicate to Ben with rather unsubtle hand motions that he had no idea what to say.

Ben ignored his protests and turned to Natalie. "Stay with Charlie, unless you hear noises or if it sounds like Joshua is losing it; then I may need your help."

"You don't want me to come up with you?" Natalie asked.

Ben had seriously considered it. Joshua would certainly be less inclined to blow him off with Natalie there.

"No," Ben said. "This is between our families. But I may need you, if things get out of hand."

Natalie looked dubious, but she didn't protest, and went over to help a relieved Charlie, who was already struggling to deal with the store owner.

Ben turned and headed slowly up the stairs. He touched his spellshooter for reassurance. He shouldn't need it, and it would be mad to use it in an antique shop, but you never knew with Joshua.

The top floor was different to the bottom. There were no shelves; instead the room was filled with display tables, upon which were antiques, arranged in such a manner that each had plenty of room to breathe. It almost reminded Ben of how an Apple store might have looked hundreds of years ago. Instead of everything being pristine white, here the tables were made with vintage wood that fit perfectly with the antiques themselves.

Along the walls were old paintings and maps, and it was a map that Joshua was staring at, near the back of the room. He turned the moment Ben hit the top stair. Unless Joshua had suddenly become very good at hiding his emotions, Ben didn't detect any surprise upon his arrival.

"I knew you were here because of me," Joshua said quietly,

turning back to the map.

"How did you know that?" Ben asked with genuine interest.

"My father," Joshua replied. He said no more and Ben didn't push him, despite his curiosity. It was vital to stay on track, and not go off on a tangent.

"Do you know why I'm here?" Ben asked, moving forwards slowly. He wanted to be close enough to have a proper conversation without having to shout across the room. At the same time, he didn't want to scare Joshua off.

"I know." Joshua turned away from the map to face Ben.

Ben was taken aback by how tired Joshua looked. There were rings under his bloodshot eyes, and his normally stylish, blond hair looked unkempt.

"So – do you want to start talking or shall I?" Ben asked. He stopped a good ten feet from Joshua, feeling that he needed the space. As it was, Joshua made his first glance towards the stairs, before turning back to Ben.

"What did my father tell you?" Joshua asked.

Ben knew it was a stalling tactic, but this was as talkative as Ben had seen Josh in a long time and he didn't want to upset what he had. So he quickly recited the salient points in Arnold's briefing.

Joshua listened with genuine interest, though Ben was certain he already knew all of it.

"He's mostly right," Joshua said. "My uncle Barry was the

bad guy. I have re-watched the memory a dozen times. He tried to kill Greg." Joshua then showed his first sign of anger, his face seeming to darken. "But I am equally sure your dad could have avoided killing him. Greg was far better at combat than Barry, and could have simply disarmed him."

Ben had to work a little to keep his voice neutral. "Maybe, but you said yourself that Barry was the bad guy."

"He was," Joshua said in a raised voice. He took a deep breath, and continued in a slightly calmer manner. "But that doesn't mean he had to kill him. He could have taken him in."

Ben knew arguing the point would be pointless, and would probably result in Joshua's anger getting progressively worse, so he moved on.

"Do you know why Barry was there in the first place? Do you know what their original argument was about?"

Ben knew immediately he had hit onto something. Joshua seemed to physically recoil at the question. For a moment, Ben thought Joshua was going to make a move for the stairs.

"Barry wanted something from Greg," Joshua said, his voice suddenly going so soft that Ben struggled to hear.

Joshua paused and stared at some item on the table. Ben tried not to hop on either foot, so eager was he for Joshua to continue. Instead he counted inside his head – he made it to thirty before Joshua looked up again.

"He wanted something," Joshua repeated. "Something

important and powerful. Not for himself, but for the evil that had seduced him – the dark elves."

It was only by some miracle that Ben managed to stay calm, though he could feel his arms vibrating by his sides, and every nerve inside his body seemed to be tingling.

"What did he want?" Ben asked, aware that his voice was shaking slightly.

Joshua closed his eyes for a moment, and gave a subtle shake of the head. "That, I cannot tell you."

"What?" Ben said, unable to contain the sudden intensity in his voice. "You cannot or you won't?"

The question seemed to genuinely fluster Joshua. "I won't, and I'm not certain I can."

Ben had managed to keep relatively calm up till now, but for Joshua to suddenly shut down was too much to bear. He stepped forwards with obvious intent.

"Joshua, this is important."

"I know how important it is," Joshua replied, matching Ben's sudden increase in intensity.

"Then tell me," Ben said, clenching his fists.

Joshua seemed to be seriously considering the matter, but he didn't speak.

"Okay," Ben said, taking a breath. "At least tell me if you know where the thing that Barry was looking for is."

Joshua immediately shook his head. "That I definitely

cannot tell you, and it is none of your business."

Ben's eyebrows shot up even faster than his rising anger, which was quickly coming to a boil. He wanted desperately to tell Joshua how important the item they were searching for was, but he couldn't.

"Look, Joshua, I need to find this thing. It's far more important than you realise, trust me," Ben said. It wasn't difficult thrusting all his conviction and belief into his words, as they were perfectly true.

But Joshua was unmoved. "This is something I need to do myself." He took a step back and, all of a sudden, drew his spellshooter.

"What the hell are you doing?" Ben said, loudly this time.

Ben heard someone come flying up the stairs. "Joshua – don't be silly! You can't fire that in here."

Joshua gave Natalie the merest of glances, then turned back to Ben.

"It's just not possible," Joshua said, his voice suddenly soft. "It cannot be. It's not meant to be."

And with that, Joshua lifted his spellshooter, and fired a spell into his chest.

He disappeared in a flash.

— CHAPTER TEN —

A Nasty Surprise

"Damn it!"

"I make that the tenth time you've said that, and we only left the shop five minutes ago," Charlie said.

Ben held up a clenched fist. "I was so close to finding where the sword is."

"You don't know that for sure," Natalie said.

"No, but at the very least, we might have got another lead," Ben said, his voice still bubbling with anger. He set a quick pace, on the off-chance that Joshua had teleported back to the Institute.

"I wish I'd heard the conversation myself," Charlie said in a thinly veiled accusation aimed at Ben. "I'd have a much better understanding of the whole thing. Instead, I had to keep Akrim entertained, pretending that I was considering paying nine hundred pounds for some incredibly boring rock."

"I don't understand why Joshua thinks he has to do this himself," Natalie said. "Frankly, I'm not even sure what it is he's trying to do. And I really don't understand his last statement, about how 'it cannot be' and 'it's not meant to be'."

"Gibberish," Ben said. "There's no other explanation."

He missed the dubious expression exchanged between Charlie and Natalie, but neither felt the urge to correct him, especially as they hadn't been there for the full exchange.

To nobody's surprise, Joshua wasn't anywhere to be found at the Institute. Ben was half-tempted to go to his house to see if by some chance he had gone home.

"He'd never be at home," Charlie said. "Not if he's trying to get away; it would be ridiculous. He'd know that's the only place we'd look."

Ben reluctantly agreed. There was nothing for it but to get back to their apprenticeship and keep their eyes open for any sign of Joshua. After some persistence, Ben managed to get hold of Arnold again, and told him a slightly vague version of what had happened, and that Joshua had disappeared on them. Arnold promised to let them know the minute he turned up.

The rest of Wednesday passed without any sign of Joshua. Thursday and Friday came and went and Joshua remained absent from the Institute. Ben didn't often feel like tearing his hair out, but by 5pm on Friday, he came close to doing so.

"He'll turn up," Natalie said. "He can't stay away forever."

Ben let out a deep breath he hadn't realised he'd inhaled. "I know. And you know what? The more I think about the conversation I had with him, the more I realise that I jumped to conclusions in my desperation for answers. It just all seemed to fit. The dark elves seducing Barry, and having him try to get a powerful artefact that we know they want and my dad has. Everything fits, and yet I can't be sure until I speak to Joshua."

"Well, at least we've got something to do to take our minds off it tomorrow," Charlie said with a slightly ironic smile.

"Oh yes, I'm looking forward to that – I've always wanted to do metal detecting!" Natalie said with sudden enthusiasm.

Ben's sour mood faded without much effort, as it so often did. "I'm not sure what we'll find, but it will be a laugh."

"I bet your grandma has buried lots of things over the years," Charlie said. "I wouldn't be surprised if there were dead things under there, though she would have stripped them of precious objects first, of course."

"What time shall we meet?" Natalie asked.

"I'm picking the detectors up at 10am, so any time after that," Ben said.

The idea of metal detecting that Saturday morning was the catalyst for helping Ben forget about Joshua. He managed to kick his legs back, splash out on some fish and chips, and watch a movie, before heading to bed. His last thought was of his grandma, and what she was going to make of his friends coming round and metal detecting all over her garden. She wasn't going to sit there quietly, that was for sure.

*

Saturday morning dawned cold and fresh. Winter was fast approaching, and there was a crisp frost covering the back garden that the sun eventually dismissed. Ben loved winter – some people hated the cold, but it made Ben feel alive. Then there was all the football that was played and, on top of which, Christmas gave the place a certain atmosphere you just didn't find in any other season. Christmas with his grandma barely counted, but he still enjoyed recalling the more pleasant ones with his parents.

Getting the detectors was a bit of a chore, but he had plenty of time and made it home well before ten o'clock. He was just setting them up and testing each of them, when he heard a friendly voice.

"Hello, Ben!" Abigail said.

Ben wiped his hand on a cloth, and went to greet his friends. All three were walking together, decked out in winter clothes. Charlie had gone full-on, with a hat and scarf. The two girls both had their hair down, forsaking hats. Natalie and Abigail were smiling, but their pleasant auras didn't seem to extend to Charlie, who was looking at Ben's house with some concern.

"Is She Who Shall Not Be Named home?" Charlie asked.

Ben grinned. "Not yet; she's gone to a friend's."

"She has friends? I don't believe it. Have you seen these so-called friends? If not, I rather think she's popped down to hell to have a chat with her minions."

"Either way, she'll be back within the hour, so you can ask her yourself."

"Terrific."

"Are you finished?" Natalie asked Charlie with a half-hearted reproachful frown.

"Yeah, sorry. You haven't met her properly, though. You'll see what I mean."

"I'll judge that for myself. Now, before we get started, we need to resolve something very important. We need some hot drinks. What does everyone want? Tea, coffee or hot chocolate?"

Ben had made sure the kitchen was clean and that they had hot drink supplies, under specific instructions from Natalie the night before.

"Do you need a hand?" Ben asked.

"Oh no, Abigail's already agreed to help. You two get started; we'll join you in a few minutes," Natalie said.

The two girls promptly disappeared into the kitchen.

"Do you think they'll end up doing any actual metal detecting?" Charlie said, as the girls left.

"Don't know," Ben said. "But I'm happy I only hired out two

detectors. Come on, let's get these babies started."

It took them a little time to work out how to work the detectors, despite the instructions from the man at the shop, but they were soon up and running. The garden wasn't exactly big, but it had several tricky spots to reach, obscured by trees and bushes. Ben was determined to go everywhere thoroughly, by covering over the whole garden twice, once with each detector, just in case one was stronger than the other.

It seemed like they had barely started when the girls came out with the drinks plus a tin of biscuits. They took a quick break, Ben enjoying his hot tea and good company under the clear blue sky. The girls had a go with the detectors – they weren't as fast, but then they weren't exactly in a rush. Ben predicted that even if they went over the whole area twice, it wasn't going to take them more than a couple of hours.

"What the bloody hell is going on here?" a harsh voice said.

Grandma Anne's voice was so screechy it sounded like a bird squawking.

"Uh oh," Charlie said, looking with growing panic at the approaching lady. "Ben, she's here. Do something."

The four of them left the detectors where they were and walked back to the house – Charlie most reluctantly. Grandma Anne was standing on the patio, staring at them with a mixture of shock and outrage – a combination only she could pull off.

To Ben, Grandma Anne hadn't changed one bit since he was

young. Her white, permed hair was a little thinner perhaps, and there were a few more wrinkles, but those steely grey eyes looked as hard as ever, and the disapproving frown was something he had lived with all his life. Even her cane, with its silver tip, had been with her for as long as Ben could remember.

"Hi, Grandma," Ben said with a smile.

"Don't call me grandma," Anne snapped, poking him in the knee with her cane. Ben strongly suspected she didn't actually need the cane; she just carried it as a weapon. "Why are you using those things on my garden?"

"It's just for fun," Natalie said, knocking off one of her dazzling smiles.

"Was I talking to you?" Anne said sharply. "If I want your opinion, ditzy, I'll ask for it."

Ben thought he saw a subtle upturning of the lips from Charlie, as he worked to suppress a smile, though he disguised it well with a disapproving frown.

"We're using the metal detectors for the same reason anyone does," Ben said. "We're looking for metal objects."

"Coins? Treasure?" Anne said, suddenly becoming interested. "This is my land, remember. Anything you find is mine, by law. So don't even think about stealing from me."

"We wouldn't. It's just for fun, Grand— ...Anne," Ben said.

"Liar!" Anne said, giving Ben another poke. "Now, I'm going to go inside and watch you from my window. I want to see every treasure you find. If I deem it useless, you can have it. Got it?"

"Yes, we'll do that," Ben said, putting on a false act of disappointment, which seemed to satisfy Anne, for now.

The screeching noise came just as Grandma Anne turned to head inside.

"What on earth is that?" Anne said, instinctively looking up to the sky. "It sounds a bit like Charlie singing, but I could have sworn it came from—"

Half a dozen purple spots materialised in the distance, scything through the sky at a rapid pace, high enough so that the people below could see little more than a purple blur, yet the screeches reached them even at that altitude. As they got louder, the noise seemed to go right through every pore in Ben's body, hitting him with a sudden terror that made him want to collapse onto the floor and put his hands over his head.

"That noise, it's horrible," Grandma Anne said, her voice a little unsteady.

Ben shook his head, and turned to the others. The terror was starting to take hold, but they were battling it with varying degrees of success.

"Arm yourselves!" Ben said, whipping out his spellshooter. "Use the long-range ice arrows."

They were meant for the high-flying ptryads, but Ben figured they might also work for these things, whatever they were.

Ben raised his spellshooter, and took aim for the beast at the front. Even as he watched them approach, he saw several blue streaks fire up from somewhere in the distance, and the beast at the back went down. Ben gave a grim smile. There were other Institute members not far off, it seemed.

Ben risked a quick glance back at the others. Natalie and Charlie had joined their tips – they needed their combined strength to fire the arrow. Abigail was too young and inexperienced to warrant using her spellshooter outside the Institute, but she seemed least affected by the terror-inducing screeches. His grandma, by contrast, was now curled up in a ball, hands on ears.

The moment he turned back to the sky, the animals came into range. They looked like small wyverns, with their long necks and elongated jaws – except that their purple skin was spotted with green dots. On each of them was a dark elf, one hand holding the reins, the other a sword, extended skywards.

Ben focused on the beast at the front and, ignoring another piercing screech, pulled the trigger.

— CHAPTER ELEVEN —

Fight at Grandma's House

The spell that exploded from Ben's spellshooter quickly formed into a six-foot-long arrow made of rock-hard ice. Ben fired twice more, and two more arrows followed. They flew upwards like a rocket, so fast they were a blur, with a blue, icy tail. All three arrows hit their target, piercing the beast's neck and its underbelly with such force that it took out the rider as well. The beast and the elf died long before they hit the ground. Ben quickly turned to the beast behind, just in time to see Charlie and Natalie's smaller arrow pierce the beast's wing. The wyvern started spiralling down, but the dark elf on top managed to stop it diving out of control. Ben, Charlie and Natalie watched with a mixture of horror and amazement as it descended.

It quickly became obvious that the wyvern was going to

land very near them.

"Oh, crap," Charlie said, taking a step back.

The spotted wyvern was heading right for them.

"Get to the house!" Ben shouted.

He grabbed Anne, still curled up in a ball, and they sprinted to the back door.

The beast landed with an earth-shuddering crash in the garden, just as they dived into the kitchen. Ben put Grandma down and ran to the window, which overlooked the garden.

The wyvern was moving, but just barely. It was badly wounded, and curled up. Despite being a small breed, it took up a good portion of the space, flattening a couple of bushes in the process.

For a moment Ben thought the dark elf atop the wyvern had died in the crash, for he lay slumped on the beast's neck. But after a second Ben realised he was whispering into its ear. The wyvern seemed to relax, and stopped squirming.

The dark elf leapt off his steed, landing lightly on the grass. He was very much unharmed, and stood, back straight, sword in hand. He was tall and slender, with deep purple eyes that shone through his helmet. Those eyes slowly scanned the garden, until they arrived at the house and the kitchen window.

The four of them stared right at the dark elf. The dark elf stared back.

"I think he may have seen us," Charlie said.

Ben slapped the counter, and turned, barking out orders. "Abigail, you stay here and look after my grandma. You two, come with me."

"Outside?" Charlie asked faintly.

"No, we're going to go upstairs and play a bit of Xbox," Ben said, rolling his eyes.

Ben took a deep breath, and then opened the back door and stepped outside into the garden. He stopped on the small patio just before the grass and drew his spellshooter. Charlie and Natalie, either side of him, did the same.

"Stay behind me, but keep close," Ben said softly. "Remember, he can't harm me with his dark elf magic. And don't attack him – let me do that."

Ben moved onto the grass. He had several spells ready, but none were fatal. He wanted the dark elf alive.

The dark elf was already forming a ball of purple energy around his fist, which crackled and sparked with pent-up magic.

Ben kept walking forwards, undeterred. The dark elf raised his hand, and a purple ball of fire soared straight towards Ben's chest. Ignoring the spell coming right at him, Ben fired his spellshooter. What looked like a long piece of rope shot out of the barrel and spun towards the dark elf. So focused was the elf on his own attack, and so surprised was he that it deflected harmlessly off Ben, that he didn't think to defend himself. The rope wrapped itself firmly around the dark elf, pinning his arms and legs together so that he fell down. The dark elf tried to respond, and the rope seemed to glow, but it held fast. Just a couple of months ago, Ben knew the rope wouldn't have been strong enough, but he'd learnt a lot since then.

Ben stopped right in front of the dark elf, and extended his spellshooter, so that it was just inches from the dark elf's slender nose.

"What are you doing here?" Ben asked.

The dark elf stared back silently, full of malevolence, but clearly lacking any sort of fear.

Ben lowered the spellshooter. The dark elf clearly didn't care for his own life – perhaps he knew it was forfeit now that he had landed on enemy soil. Ben looked around, and spotted the wyvern. He changed his target from the dark elf to the wyvern.

"Tell me what you're doing here or the wyvern dies," Ben said.

The flicker of fear from the dark elf told Ben he'd made the right call. The fear lasted until Natalie gasped.

"Ben! You can't do that. I won't let you."

Ben watched in despair as relief replaced the dark elf's fear. He lowered his spellshooter, shoulders slumping.

"Natalie, please. I wasn't going to shoot him, but the dark elf didn't know that," Ben said.

"Oh, sorry," Natalie said, her hand going to her mouth as

she realised her mistake. "Try the threat again."

"Bit late now," Ben said, turning back to the dark elf. He was still secure, but there was little more that he could do. How else could he make the elf talk?

A swooshing sound cut short his thoughts. He turned, just in time to see a great eagle land next to them. Alex, the Trade Director, jumped off and landed on the grass.

Ben couldn't help smiling, despite the circumstances. He didn't get to see the Trade Director much, but Alex was just the sort of person Ben warmed to. He wore his customary Jedi-styled cloak, but this one was grey. His eyes were bright, and he somehow always looked like he was amused by something, no matter how dire things were. In one hand he held a spellshooter; in the other, he ran a gold coin between his fingers. Ben wasn't even sure Alex was aware of the coin anymore, it was such a habit.

"Good job, Ben," Alex said, flicking the coin up, and pocketing it, so he could give Ben a pat on the shoulder. "The others have all been shot down and dealt with. We're taking them back to the Institute for questioning. The clean-up operation is already underway. Fortunately, the wyverns were flying high, and most of the Seens who did spot them don't believe what they saw."

"What were the wyverns doing?"

Alex shrugged. "Oh, the usual. Trying to cause mayhem, in preparation for their invasion. Enough of those spotted wyverns, if left unchecked, could turn an entire population into a gibbering wreck."

Alex clapped and then rubbed his hands together. "Anyway, enough of that. How are you guys doing? Are you all okay? I can't imagine one meagre wyvern and a dark elf would cause you much trouble."

"We're fine," Ben said. "I need to handle my grandma, though."

"I'll leave that with you," Alex said. He turned towards the wyvern and, before Natalie could get a word in, he fired.

The wyvern vanished.

"What did you do?" Natalie asked aghast.

"Calm down," Alex said. "He's still there; he's just concealed. Our wyvern team will be here shortly to pick him up. Right, I'd better get back to work. These dark elves are really starting to annoy me. I'm not even supposed to be here. I had a long-awaited date with Julia, and was just flying over to pick her up, when these wyverns decided to ruin it."

Without further ado, Alex walked over, and hauled the dark elf onto his shoulder, before dumping him rather unceremoniously onto the eagle's back. Alex sat just behind, so that he could hold onto the elf with one hand and the reins with the other.

"Enjoy the rest of your weekend," Alex said with a grin and a jaunty salute.

The moment the eagle flapped its mighty wings and took

off, it vanished from view.

Ben's smile lasted until Natalie spoke up.

"He's a bit unorthodox, isn't he," Natalie said with a slightly disapproving frown. "Quite unusual for a director."

"I like him," Ben said. "He was really good friends with my parents."

"Oh, I like him too," Natalie said in an unconvincing voice.

"Shall we stop talking about who we like and don't like, and go check on your grandma?" Charlie suggested.

Ben cursed, thoughts of Alex forgotten, and immediately ran into the kitchen.

He stopped dead the moment he saw her.

She was standing upright, though Abigail was gently holding her elbow. To his surprise, she wasn't complaining, and she normally hated anyone touching her.

He saw immediately why. Her face was deathly white, her eyes wide.

"She's okay," Abigail said softly. "She just needs a moment to come out of shock."

Ben fingered his spellshooter. He knew what he had to do, but something stayed his hand.

"Those things," Grandma said. Her voice was soft, and it took a minute for Ben to realise why it sounded different – there was no antagonism attached. "That was an elf, wasn't it? I saw it through the window."

Lucidity was the absolute last thing Ben had expected from his grandma right now, but he found himself nodding.

Anne shook her head slowly, and a strange look crossed her face, one that Ben couldn't immediately place.

"Elves – that reminds me of—"

The spell hit Grandma, and she collapsed onto the floor.

Ben turned and, to his horror, saw Charlie with his spellshooter extended.

"I'm sorry, Ben, you were taking too long," Charlie said. "The memory wipe needs to be cast as early as possible. The longer you wait, the more damage it can have on their mind."

Ben knew Charlie was right. He should have fired it the moment he saw her.

And yet... and yet, Ben couldn't help feeling that his grandma was about to say something meaningful for once.

— CHAPTER TWELVE —

Grandma's Surprise

It was obvious nobody else had been paying attention to his grandma when she had spoken, and Ben decided not to tell anyone about it for now. He certainly didn't want to upset Charlie, who was just going by the book. He took his grandma upstairs and laid her gently on her bed, knowing she could be out for a while.

The wyvern clean-up crew arrived remarkably quickly and managed to get the animal back on her feet. They flew her back to the Institute to see if she could be re-trained.

"I suppose we should continue with the metal detecting," Charlie said without any enthusiasm.

The four of them were sitting on the patio, staring at the garden, their minds elsewhere. The good mood from the morning had vanished.

"Yeah, we should," Ben said. Nobody moved. Ben's mind was still on the raid, and he was certain the others were thinking about it too. Thanks to Dagmar, Ben knew how real the threat of the dark elf invasion was, and how soon it would happen, but until this sudden terror-filled flyover, the idea of a war still seemed unreal. Not anymore. The dark elves were coming, and they were getting increasingly bold about it.

"They won't openly show themselves yet," Charlie said, speaking to nobody in particular. "They still want to launch a surprise attack. If the dark elves revealed themselves now, the government would have time to prepare."

"But they'll still do nasty things like this," Abigail said.

"Yeah. Over the next couple of months, I bet they'll find all sorts of ways to scare people, without anyone having a clue what's happening."

"There has to be something we can do," Natalie said, tugging on her hair.

"I'm sure the Institute are working on it," Ben said. "Right now, they can only stop the raids as quickly as possible. But the prince and the executive council are trying to warn the government and the royal family, without freaking them out. I just hope they succeed in time."

Ben wandered over to one of the metal detectors and started it up. Charlie reluctantly followed suit, and they resumed their search. It took them a good hour, but they found nothing. Ben wasn't surprised. Looking back at all the ingenious ways in which the previous pieces of armour had been hidden, the garden seemed rather lame, especially for a couple as creative as his parents.

Anne finally woke from the memory spell the following morning. Ben was downstairs eating cornflakes when he heard the trademark clumping of her cane on the stairs. Ben looked up as she entered, and noticed immediately that she was wearing different clothes. Any look of shock or puzzlement that had existed yesterday was absent, replaced by her traditional scowl.

"Morning," Ben said with a smile.

"My head is hurting," Anne said. "I need you to make me some tea, and get me some painkillers."

"No problem," Ben said.

Anne gave a suspicious look around the kitchen. "Where are your friends?"

"They left last night."

"Good," Anne said. Then she scratched her long nose and a clouded look came over her. "What day is it?"

"Sunday. My friends were over here yesterday, on Saturday."

"I know what comes before Sunday, thank you," Anne said, though Ben could see the confusion in her expression. She left and wandered over to her favourite chair, sitting down in front of the TV.

Ben quickly finished up his cornflakes and grabbed his spellshooter. He focused, placing a hand on the orb. Yes! He had a couple of memory trances – only weak ones, but they might just do the trick. He glanced over at his grandma, who was almost hidden in the chair except for the top of her permed hair which stuck out above the seat.

A flash of doubt hit him. He knew he should leave his grandma's memory alone for a few days, to let it recover from the wiping spell Charlie cast. The Institute had been very firm about that when they handed out the spell. But Ben couldn't afford to wait that long; he had to know now. Yet uncertainty nagged at him. Were Grandma's odd comments really enough to act on? Ben had his doubts, but, at this point, he couldn't afford to turn away even the weakest lead. He was sure Anne had been about to say something relevant. He remembered her words exactly: *Elves – that reminds me of—* and then Charlie's spell had hit her. Reminded her of what? It could be something as silly as elves reminding her of Christmas or it could be something far more significant. Either way, he needed to know.

Ben walked quietly into the lounge. Anne was glued to the morning news, and probably wouldn't have noticed him if he had gone in doing star jumps, unless it blocked the TV. He skirted around Anne's armchair, until he was adjacent to her and had a target to aim at.

Ben had one final moment of doubt. He was being selfish

again, and he knew it – putting his own priorities in front of others. He hated himself for it, but he was committed now. More importantly, he was sure the spell wouldn't harm her. It was a weak one, and lasted only minutes. He knew all the rules to make the spell as gentle as possible, and wouldn't force anything his grandma didn't want to see.

Ben raised his spellshooter, focusing a little more than usual. Memory spells were not his strong suit, and he had little experience with them. Even though the spell was only level two, Ben still struggled to make it move down the orb, and he felt a small bead of sweat trickling along his forehead as he pulled the trigger. A small white spell hit Anne's chest, and she immediately zoned out, her eyes becoming distant.

Ben turned to face her head on, his heart suddenly moving up a gear. He didn't have long before the spell wore off, and he needed to act fast. At the same time, he couldn't go in with the difficult questions straight away; he needed to build up to them. Now he wished he had paid more attention to his Diplomacy lessons.

Ben took a deep breath, and started speaking in a soft, but authoritative voice. *Don't sound weak or they won't work with you.*

"Anne, have you heard of the Royal Institute of Magic?"

Anne nodded almost immediately. "Yes."

Ben did a silent fist pump. "From where?"

"Greg and Jane."

The answers were short, but then that was how it worked. The suspect in the trance would do no more than answer the question.

"What do you know about the Institute?" Ben asked.

"Greg and Jane claimed to work there. They said it was responsible for the kingdoms discovered by Queen Elizabeth that were hidden from ordinary people."

"Did you believe them?"

"No."

Ben was careful not to curse too loudly. Any noise during these sessions beyond the questions could be harmful to her memory.

Anne's eyes flickered and, for a moment, Ben thought the spell had ended, before she reverted back to the trance. He didn't have long, time perhaps for one or two final questions. He thought fast.

"You said the elf you saw recently reminded you of something. What did it remind you of?"

"The message."

Ben's heart quickened. "Did my parents leave any message for me?"

"No."

Her eyes flickered again, longer this time. Ben bit his lip and tried one more time.

"Did they leave anything with you? Any message or some object?"

"They left me a message."

Ben's eyes widened. "What was it?"

Anne shook her head immediately. "I cannot remember. I do not have access to that part of the memory bank – it is buried too deep."

Before Ben could even work out what she meant, Anne blinked, and stared up at Ben with surprise, and then anger.

"What do you think you're doing, Ben? You're blocking the TV." She started waving her hand. "Shoo! Get out the way."

Ben went up to his room and plonked himself on his bed, trying to process what had happened.

His parents had left Grandma a message.

It could be nothing, he told himself, but, as a natural optimist, he couldn't help thinking the message was significant. There was just one problem: the memory was buried deep, and wouldn't be easy to access. It was certainly beyond his abilities to retrieve it. He needed help. He needed Natalie.

— Chapter Thirteen —

Tricks of the Trade

Absolutely not," Natalie said firmly when they met the following morning.

Ben had fully expected that response, and he was prepared. The two of them had a few minutes to kill before they went on cleaning duties. Charlie was due to arrive a little later, as he spent some early mornings at Barrington's, studying his A-levels.

"Can I give you my reasons before you dismiss me out of hand?" Ben said with a smile he hoped would soften Natalie's hard stance. It did so. A little.

Ben went over to the tea corner, and quickly made them both cups of tea. He picked out her favourite sticky bun, which he was happy to see thawed her a little more.

"Honestly, you shouldn't have cast that memory spell in

the first place, Ben," Natalie said. "It's really dangerous to do something like that after a memory wipe."

"I know," Ben said, sitting down with his own cup of tea. "I just had a feeling my grandma might know something."

"It might be something completely insignificant," Natalie said, taking on Charlie's pessimistic role in his absence.

"You're right: it might be. It's certainly a long shot. I'll admit right now I'm desperate for clues. I've spent hours and hours looking for the sword, and I have nothing to show for it."

"We have Joshua," Natalie said.

"Yes, we have him, if he ever shows up. And even then, we have absolutely no idea what he's going to say. It might be a completely false lead. But now we have another lead: my grandma."

Natalie wasn't convinced. "Your grandma seems like an even more feeble lead than Joshua."

"Yes," Ben admitted, "and no. It could be something completely irrelevant – or it could be a clue to the location of the sword."

He leaned forwards, narrowing his eyes, as if he were about to reveal a secret. "Think about it for a minute – wouldn't it be clever, hiding a clue to the sword with the last person anyone would think of? Yet I see her every day. It's brilliant."

Natalie didn't respond, but Ben could see she was

struggling to maintain her scepticism. "I'll admit, it would be a good idea – if your parents planned it that way."

"They might have," Ben said with a smile. He had her. "But we won't know either way until we get the memory from my grandma."

"A week," Natalie said.

Ben's confidence took a sucker punch to the stomach. "A week until what? Until you'll do the memory spell?"

"It should be two," Natalie said. "Even a week is pushing it. If we tried it any earlier, your grandma would be in real danger of damage to her memory. It needs time to recover from the two spells we cast."

Ben was tempted to argue, but when Natalie dug in on something, she could be as stubborn as anyone, and any debate might just sour matters. So, with great reluctance, he nodded.

"A week," Ben said.

Ben thought the week would pass slowly, such was his impatience to access his grandma's memory, but he was wrong. First, there was the constant chatter from the apprentices about the terror-inducing raids. It appeared they had occurred all over the southeast of England, causing mayhem, and the apprentices couldn't stop talking about them, especially during lunch.

"I saw six fly over my old school," Amy said. She gave an evil smile. "I kind of hoped they would land there, but they didn't. I heard several of the teachers fainted, though. I wish I had been there."

"Only six, eh?" Simon said, his voice muffled as he downed a chicken leg. "I saw a dozen – managed to take down a couple myself."

"Only two?" William said with an amused smile. "I would have thought you would have taken the whole pack down."

"I probably could have, if the Institute had given me enough spells," Simon said with complete sincerity.

"Well, I don't think it's something to be chirpy about," Natalie said, giving Simon a disapproving look. "Hundreds of people were scared out of their skin without knowing why. Can you imagine what that feels like?"

Natalie's reprimand took them by surprise, given that it was so rarely done, and even Simon shut up after that.

Back on their apprenticeship, only Ben had managed to stay on target in Trade, as the challenges on the checklist became increasingly difficult. He decided to help out Natalie and Charlie on a couple of practical steps they were stuck on. Two days had passed since Natalie had stated a week's wait, and despite Ben's eagerness for the week to run its course, he found he was so busy that he was able to take his attention off Grandma, most of the time.

"So, tell me about these Trade practicals you guys are stuck on," Ben said, grinning and rubbing his hands.

"I've got a real deal I'm supposed to close in the Trade

room," Charlie said glumly. "I've tried twice this week already, and they offered me less than seventy percent of what I'm supposed to get. Every time I mention the asking price I need, they go into hysterics."

"Who are you dealing with, and what for?"

"Street goblin merchants representing Gorbon's Bank."

"Ah, yes, I can see why you're having difficulty," Ben said with a smile. "I'll come and have a look at how you're doing." He turned to Natalie. "How about you?"

"Not quite as bad," Natalie said. "But equally frustrating. I'm trying to place a small order with the *W* store Trade department for fifty levitation spells. The elf I'm dealing with says she has to stick to a price list, and will not budge. The price isn't terrible, but I need to somehow get it down ten percent."

"Everyone will budge, if you give them a reason," Ben said. "You just need to give them an incentive. Have you tried—"

Ben stopped talking the instant he saw Draven coming their way. With him was Joshua.

For once, Draven barely gave Ben a look as they passed; he was focused on Joshua, who looked considerably worse than when they last saw him, just a few days ago. His eyes were bloodshot and, if Ben didn't know better, he would have said it looked like Joshua had been crying. Ben tried to make eye contact, and was surprised when Joshua met his gaze, if only for a second.

It all happened quickly and, within a few heartbeats, Draven and Joshua were around the corner, and out of sight.

"My goodness, did you see Joshua?" Natalie said, whispering despite the fact that they were clearly out of earshot. "He looked terrible."

"Yeah – I'm almost starting to feel sorry for him," Charlie said. "Which is something I never thought I'd say. Do you think we should give him time to recover, before confronting him? He doesn't look in any state to talk."

Last week, when Joshua had made his escape from the antique shop, Ben was so desperate to track him down that he would have spoken to him in any state. But things had changed – time had served to calm Ben down a little, and his grandma had provided another possible lead.

"We probably should," Ben admitted. "Let's see if he's any better this afternoon."

With some reluctance, they continued on to the Trade floor, and attempted to take their minds off Joshua, if only for a few hours. The hustle and bustle of the main Trading room helped do the trick. Thanks to Ben, both Charlie and Natalie managed to get their prices down, and left the Trade room far happier than when they entered it.

"Have you thought about going into the Trade Department?" Charlie asked. "You're ridiculously good at it."

"It will be one of the departments I continue to study

when I graduate to the fourth grade. I have to admit, I do enjoy the thrill of Trade, but Spellsword is still my chosen choice, if they'll have me."

"I'm sure they'll have you," Natalie said.

"So, now what? How do we find Joshua?" Charlie asked.

"I think we should split up. He could be anywhere. Let's meet back in the common room in an hour. If we can't find him, we may need to start asking around. I bet Draven knows where he is."

"I hope it doesn't come to that," Charlie said, as they approached the apprentice floor.

Natalie came to a sudden halt, her green eyes widening in shock as she stared up at the doors leading to the apprentice department.

"I don't think it will," she said softly.

Standing on the landing just in front of the doors was Joshua. He was watching them. His eyes were considerably less bloodshot, and he looked almost respectable again.

"We need to talk," Joshua said, staring at Ben.

— CHAPTER FOURTEEN —

Joshua's Revelation

The four of them sat around the table in the Diplomacy conference room. Ben had been tempted to see if they could use the Crimson Tower again, but it would have taken time to arrange with Dagmar, and Joshua wasn't prepared to wait. As a compromise, Ben had cast the strongest shielding spell he had, a new one he had just learned how to cast last week with Volvek. That, combined with the magical security of the room, was enough to satisfy him.

"Well, we're here," Ben said, trying to inject a modicum of cheerfulness into the room. They had been sitting there for a couple of minutes, though it felt like longer, and Joshua had done nothing except stare at everyone.

"I need to speak to you alone," Joshua said.

"We've been over this," Ben replied, interlocking his

hands and placing them calmly on the table. "I told you – it's all of us or none. We work together. I have no secrets; they know everything."

Joshua shook his head firmly. "That is simply not acceptable. What I have to say is for your ears only. Furthermore, I need you to swear to me that you will never divulge it to anyone else."

Ben spread his hands, palms in the air, and gave a shrug. "Then we're at an impasse, Joshua. I'm not getting rid of Charlie and Natalie. So the choice is yours: do you want to talk or are we wasting our time here?"

Ben could see how desperate Joshua was to talk. Ben was just as desperate to hear what he had to say, but Ben hid it under an air of nonchalance. He watched Joshua carefully and, for one horrible moment, thought he was about to leave. Instead, he sunk his shoulders in defeat, and closed his eyes. In that one moment, he transformed – the stubborn insistence replaced by a frailty Ben had seen just a few hours earlier when Joshua had been with Draven. He took several deep, almost shuddering breaths. For a moment, Ben thought he was about to break down, and he exchanged a couple of concerned looks with Charlie and Natalie.

"My father disappeared last night," Joshua said.

Ben never thought he'd empathise with Joshua, but that one swift sentence almost did the trick. Natalie gave a little gasp, and even Charlie looked put out.

"I'm so sorry to hear that," Natalie said softly. She looked as though she wanted to reach out and touch Joshua's hand.

Ben could see that Joshua was uncomfortable with the sympathy – something Ben could relate to.

"Do you know what happened?" Ben asked.

"I do," Joshua said, taking a deep breath.

"You don't have to tell us if you're not ready," Natalie said, intervening.

"No, I need to," Joshua said. He took another deep breath, and then began. "The Institute's spy network got a tip that a strong unit of dark elves had taken over a small castle on the south coast of England, and were going to use it as a strategic stronghold for the invasion. My father led a team of top Wardens and Spellswords to raid the castle and take them down. There were over fifty members, chosen by Draven himself, all of them specialists in both magical and physical combat. They were confident that there were no more than thirty dark elves present. More were due to arrive the following day, so they needed to act quickly."

Joshua paused again, and placed his fingers on the bridge of his nose, needing another moment to compose himself. Ben, Charlie and Natalie gave him all the time he needed.

"There was just one problem," Joshua said, when he continued. "There were just thirty dark elves present, but leading them was Prince Ictid, son of King Suktar. Without him, Draven assures me, the Institute would have succeeded. With him there, they stood no chance. Ictid tore into them. The members fought bravely, I am told, and a few got away. My father wasn't among them."

Joshua finished talking, and was greeted with stunned silence. Natalie made a move to go over and give Joshua a hug, but Ben cut her off with a vigorous shake of the head.

"Did anyone actually see your father go down?" Ben asked.

"No," Joshua said, looking up, and giving them all a flash of vague hope. Ben pounced on it.

"If nobody saw him go down, he may still be alive. They take prisoners, especially important ones. Your dad is one of the top Wardens."

"That's what I keep telling myself," Joshua said. "And that is why I'm here. If there is any chance of finding my father, the dark elves need to be defeated. Suktar needs to be defeated."

Joshua seemed to gather himself, sitting up straighter, and giving them all a serious stare that, given the circumstances, both impressed and surprised Ben.

"How did the idea of toppling Suktar lead you to us?" Charlie asked with genuine confusion.

In response, Joshua glanced at Ben. "How strong is the shield you cast?"

"Level four. It's strong. Between the security of the room

and the shield, we are safe," Ben said.

"Good," Joshua said. "Now, do not interrupt what I'm about to say next. I know it will be difficult. You are going to be shocked."

"We won't interrupt," Natalie assured him.

Joshua nodded. "What I'm about to tell you, I learnt by casting dozens of memory spells on myself, and going back to several different incidents, including the one with my uncle and Greg. I was determined to find out the real reason behind my uncle's death. It all started with the dark elves. They were looking for a powerful artefact – in fact, the only artefact with enough power to thwart Suktar. It is called Elizabeth's Armour. You know about this, and you know of its history. So do I."

Ben very almost choked, and he wasn't the only one.

"You know about Elizabeth's Armour?" Ben said in whisper.

"I know about it, and much more," Joshua said, his face serious. "Shall I continue?"

Ben nodded, despite the questions bubbling inside his head.

"The dark elves believed that Barry was a Guardian, and therefore entitled to a piece of Elizabeth's Armour: the shield. They had the right family, but the wrong person."

Ben was suddenly finding it difficult to breathe. This wasn't going how he had imagined.

"The right family?" This time it was Charlie, eyes almost popping from his skull. "Your uncle? Are you saying that there is a Guardian in your family?"

Joshua tapped the table impatiently. "Yes, that's what I'm saying. Now, please let me finish."

"Sorry, go on," Natalie said with a weak smile.

Once Joshua was sure he wasn't going to get interrupted again, he continued.

"The dark elves' first mistake was getting the wrong family member. Their second was believing that your father had taken upon it himself as the Head Guardian to gather all pieces of armour for his own possession, shield included. They told Barry that Greg had the shield, which Barry was entitled to. This is what the argument between Greg and my uncle was about."

Joshua stopped, and it was just as well. Ben's head was spinning, and he wasn't the only one suffering. Charlie had gone completely red, and Natalie kept opening and closing her mouth, as if she were trying to speak.

It took a couple of minutes of extremely hard work, but Ben eventually finally managed to clear his head.

"Right family, wrong person," Ben said, repeating Joshua's words. "So who was the Guardian?"

"My grandfather," Joshua said. "He never told my father or my uncle. The knowledge passed directly to me just before he passed away."

Ben understood what Joshua was saying, but his brain was struggling to process it. "So, you're a Guardian?"

"Guardian of the Shield, yes," Joshua said.

"Impossible," Ben said, before he could stop himself.

If he expected anger from Joshua or outrage, he didn't get it.

"I expected you'd say as much," Joshua said. "The truth is, I have only known for a few weeks. My grandfather recently passed away, and it was only after everything he said and re-watching several memories in my life that I began to believe him. What I had a much harder time believing was you, Ben."

"Me?"

"Yes. While I may be a Guardian, you are the *Head Guardian*. My role is important, but yours is more so. I found this difficult to take in, given the historical importance of our families. I couldn't bring myself to believe that it is you, not me, who is responsible for uniting the Guardians and destroying Suktar."

Despite Joshua's fragile state, Ben couldn't help let slip a hint of disgust. "That's what all your comments were about before, then? *It cannot be. It's not meant to be.* You simply didn't want me in charge?"

"You have no idea of my family history," Joshua said, going slightly red. "Lord Samuel, my great ancestor, was an extremely important man. Michael Greenwood was a baker's boy. All this wouldn't matter, except when the queen chose Michael to be the Head Guardian, she was clearly unwell. Lord Samuel writes on multiple occasions that she was going a bit loopy, with what we know today as Alzheimer's disease. Samuel felt a grave mistake had been made, but he could not convince Michael Greenwood to relinquish the role. He felt Michael was putting the entire mission in danger. And when I discovered this, and watched you and your flippant, uncaring, spontaneous nature, I knew he was right."

"That's not fair," Natalie began, but Ben cut her off with a wave.

"I don't care what you think about me," Ben said truthfully. "If you are truly a Guardian, of which I'm yet to be convinced, then we have found everyone. Only two pieces of armour remain – mine and yours."

"You don't believe me?" Joshua asked, his upturned nose twitching.

"What proof do you have?"

"Plenty, actually," Joshua said. "I have letters from my grandfather, correspondence from Lord Samuel himself, as well as various precious items referenced by both these men to back my claim up."

Ben thought then of the key Joshua had retrieved from the antique store.

"What evidence do you have, though, Ben?" Joshua asked. "None, I bet. Thankfully for you, I happen to know your family history, probably better than you do, and I am satisfied."

"Thank god for that," Ben said, his voice laced with sarcasm.

Charlie, who had been uncommonly quiet, spoke up. "So, where does this leave us?"

"I need to find the shield, and Ben needs the sword," Joshua said without hesitation. "As I understand it, the rest have been found, along with their Guardians."

The transformation was quite remarkable. Something changed the moment Joshua got that titanic secret off his back – a weight had been lifted. Gone was the apathy, but the unfriendly arrogance had returned. Ben preferred the unfriendliness, as apathy often resulted in complete inaction, but it was definitely less pleasant.

"It might be easier if we work together," Natalie said.

"No," Joshua said. "I work alone. And the sword is your responsibility, Ben."

"Actually, they are both my responsibility," Ben said, giving Joshua a sudden smile. "I'm the Head Guardian. It is my job to re-unite each Guardian and their piece of armour, remember?"

Joshua bit his lip and cringed, looking as if he had just swallowed a lemon. To Joshua's credit, he didn't challenge the claim, though it looked like he dearly wanted to.

"I know where the shield is, but not how to get there,"

Joshua said finally. "The shield is located in Lord Samuel's house on Vanishing Street, in London."

Ben gave Joshua a blank stare, but both Charlie and Natalie gasped.

"He has a house there?" was Charlie's immediate response.

"It's the one at the end of the street, rumoured to be larger even than Lord Nelson's," Joshua said, thrusting his chest out a little.

"I'm guessing by its name, Vanishing Street isn't the easiest place to get to?" Ben said.

"You've not heard of it?" Joshua asked with just a fraction of a smirk that reminded Ben of old times.

"I'm not from around here, remember?" Ben said. "Natalie knows of it, and Charlie knows more or less everything. So fill me in."

"It's the most famous, grandest, most expensive street in all of London – and that includes both the Seen and Unseen districts. The only problem is that it's so exclusive, it's extremely difficult to find."

"Even for you?" Ben asked. "I mean, it's your ancestor's house."

"Especially for me, most likely," Joshua said. "Each piece of armour is supposed to be well hidden, and I believe Lord Samuel took it upon himself to make the shield the hardest piece of all to find."

"You need an invitation, right?" Charlie said.

"Yes," Joshua said, giving a small but approving nod to Charlie. "To get to Vanishing Street, you need an invitation to one of the residents' houses, on a certain day, at a certain time. Miss that, and you've missed your window. There is no other way to get there."

"So, we need to find someone else who lives on that street, assuming nobody in your family still lives there?"

"The house is empty," Joshua said. "That much I know. So, yes, we need to find some other family who live there. I have some prospects that I have been working on, but it is taking longer than I hoped."

"Charlie can help you," Ben said.

Joshua immediately shook his head. "I'm doing fine by myself. I do not need help."

Ben's eyes narrowed, and he leaned forwards. "You just said it is taking longer than you hoped. That doesn't sound like you are doing fine."

Joshua had no immediate response to this, so Ben pressed on.

"Time is of the essence, remember? We can't afford to be self-righteous about this. We've found three Guardians and their pieces of armour already, and it takes a lot of time and work – time we don't have. You are going to need all the help you can get."

Joshua's expression darkened for a moment, as he took

in Charlie, who stared pleasantly back at him.

"Fine. I will use Charlie to help me find Vanishing Street," Joshua said eventually. "But while we are doing that, you need to find your sword. Have you got anywhere?"

Ben detected a clear challenge in Joshua's voice, but he refused to rise to the bait.

"Yes, we have actually," Ben said, thinking of his grandma. Suddenly, she became important, now that his lead with Joshua had gone nowhere, for the sword at least. "You find Vanishing Street, and I'll concentrate on the sword."

— CHAPTER FIFTEEN —

The Prince's Offer

No," Natalie said firmly.

Joshua and Charlie had left, both looking rather uncomfortable with each other. Ben wasn't concerned – they'd be fine the moment they hit the library. Charlie might be anti-social, but when in the library, he could work with anyone.

"So you still want to wait five more days before casting the memory spell, even after everything that just happened?" Ben asked.

"Your grandma needs that recovery time," Natalie said with forced patience. "You don't seriously want to put her in danger, do you?"

"No," Ben said, sighing. "You're right. It's just that she's my only lead. I really thought Joshua would provide me with a clue to the sword. I got that wrong."

"It still worked out, though," Natalie said. "He's the last Guardian, and he and Charlie are hot on the trail of the shield." She smiled. "We're almost there, Ben. We're almost ready."

Ben didn't show quite as much enthusiasm as Natalie, for two obvious reasons. First, he still hadn't decided if she and Charlie should come on the final journey – a decision that was going to cause pain no matter what he chose. But, more significantly, the thought of setting off to try to kill the most powerful living being on the planet was terrifying.

They brainstormed for a little while longer about the sword, but got nowhere. Ben was left with no option but to wait the five days, unless something else came up.

Even with the apprenticeship, the extra Spellsword lessons, and the havoc the dark elves continued to wreak, those five days did not pass quickly. Joshua took every opportunity he had to ask about the sword's progress whenever they met.

"What leads do you have?" Joshua said.

Joshua had taken to having lunch with them occasionally, much to Ben's displeasure. Natalie, being Natalie, was quickly getting used to the old Joshua, but Ben was having difficulty, especially with all the digs about the sword.

"I have a few," Ben said vaguely. "Don't worry about me.

How are you guys doing?"

"Pretty good," Charlie piped up, before Joshua could intervene. "We have three families we think might own properties on Vanishing Street. Two are royal families from significant Unseen Kingdoms, and the third owns half the magic industry. The trick is to locate someone who is currently living there, as that is a criteria to getting an invite. London isn't exactly the safest place right now."

A part of Ben was delighted Charlie and Joshua were making progress, but a smaller, selfish part was just a little upset that they were doing so well, while he was striking out. He knew it was ridiculous, but he couldn't shake the thought away.

That night, before he went to bed, Ben caught himself staring at his grandma, who was eating dinner while watching the news. He was thinking about the memory spell, and trying to gauge a critical eye over her progress. She certainly seemed back to her normal self. Were five more days really necessary?

"Did you see that?" Anne said, stabbing a fork perilously close to Ben's private area. "The country is going to pieces. I knew it was going to happen; it was just a matter of time."

"Why, what's going on?" Ben asked. He had been paying attention to his grandma, not the TV.

"You should be watching this, Ben; it's important. People are dropping dead all over the place."

"Dead?" Ben said, turning to the TV in alarm.

"Well, as good as. They're going unconscious, and the medical people are having a hell of a time waking them up. Happened to my friend Caroline just the other day. White as a ghost she looked, as if she'd just seen one."

Ben was careful to show just the right level of concern. "That's terrible. I hope they find out what's happening."

"They will or they won't," his grandma said. "I've never had much faith in the NHS, to be honest. Waste of money."

Ben decided to let her continue her rant alone – she probably wouldn't realise he was gone, and when she did, she definitely wouldn't care.

Ben was sure the Institute knew what was happening, but the fact that it seemed to be going unchecked was alarming.

That night it took a little longer than usual for Ben to get to sleep.

Ben woke to a room that was vast and looked strangely familiar. The floor was entirely marble, and there were huge columns running along the walls that rose up to a ceiling Ben could barely see, such was its height. A cold breeze ran through the room, though its origin was uncertain, as was the faint light that permeated the place.

He was dreaming, that much was obvious. It was an odd dream, though; he felt more aware than usual, yet there was no other explanation. He looked around once more – there wasn't much happening in this particular dream.

"Are you sure you're dreaming?" a deep, powerful voice said. Ben couldn't place its origin – the voice seemed to come from everywhere.

Out from one of the columns stepped a dark elf that made Ben shudder. Prince Ictid looked exactly as he had the last time they met. He wore a purple cloak with sparkling gold hieroglyphs. For an elf, he was huge, well over six feet, with broad shoulders. His eyes glowed purple, and on his head was a small crown. The only difference to their last meet was that in this dream place Ben was able to stare at the prince without his eyes burning.

"I fell asleep a moment ago, and I woke here," Ben said. "I can't see how I'm not dreaming."

"There are many different types of dreams," Prince Ictid said, walking slowly towards Ben. "Some are harmless – others aren't."

With a casual flick, Ictid threw a small ball of energy at Ben. It hit him and seared his shoulder. Ben cried out, and rubbed the injured area – the skin was red and burnt.

"See what I mean?" Ictid said with a smile. "Elizabeth's magic won't protect you here."

Ben took an involuntary step back, fear rushing through his body and freezing his veins.

"What do you want?" Ben asked, trying to inject some

defiance into his voice.

"Do not be scared," Ictid said. "I have only come to talk. I have a proposition for you that comes straight from my father. It is not one you should ignore."

"I'm listening," Ben said, simply because it bought him more time to try to work out what was happening. He'd never read anything about this semi-dream world; it wasn't covered in his studies – at least not yet. Could he die here? Surely not.

"You must know by now that our invasion on your Seen Kingdoms is inevitable, as is our success," Ictid said. "It is only a matter of time; your government will fall."

Ben knew there was more coming, so he remained silent.

"However, my father is a curious man. Despite his incredible power, he is always seeking more. That is where Elizabeth's Armour comes in. He wants it."

Ben had heard this before. "In order for him to utilise its power, you need our blood – all of it. I remember you saying that."

"I was wrong," Prince Ictid said with a casual shrug. "I thought we did, but having spoken to my father, he assures me that only one pint per Guardian is required for the spell that is needed to harness Elizabeth's Armour."

It didn't matter if Ictid was telling the truth or not, Ben had no intention of handing over a droplet of blood, let alone a pint. But he kept that to himself.

"If we give him the armour, he will truly be immortal," Ben said.

"That state has practically already been achieved," Prince Ictid said. "Believe me, there is nothing that can stop him. Your Institute is your last hope, and it is a feeble one."

Prince Ictid spoke as though the war had already been fought. The frankness scared Ben more than any threats could have.

"So you are asking us not to use Elizabeth's Armour to try to take down Suktar? What do we get in return?"

"If you willingly relinquish the armour, we will let your parents go, unharmed, and guarantee your safety."

"Is that it?" Ben asked, trying for a nonchalance he did not feel.

"No," the prince replied. "We will give you one of the Unseen Kingdoms that we see fit, and allow one thousand Seens of your choosing to live there in peace, thus preserving your otherwise dying race."

Ben was silent. Did Prince Ictid really think they would be able to wipe out all of humanity? It appeared so. That was impossible, surely?

"I need to think on it," Ben said, trying to sound convincing. "It is a decision that involves all the Guardians, not just myself."

"I understand," the prince said. "You have twenty-four

hours. We will meet here again. I will hope for good news, for both our sakes."

Ben raised a hand. "Wait, I—"

His eyes shot open, and Ben found himself staring at his bedroom ceiling. The morning light was creeping through the curtains.

Ben sat up, rubbing the fine stubble that was starting to accumulate on his face. His drowsiness, which normally took a few minutes to wear off after waking, vanished the moment he recalled his dream.

"Oh shit," was all he said.

— Chapter Sixteen —

A Decision to Make

Well, that's a hell of an offer," Charlie said, the following morning.

The two of them were on the Dragonway, which was typically busy and noisy at this time of morning, giving them a bit of time to talk without fear of being overheard.

"Yeah. The good news is that we could get your family into the kingdom. Then we could hand pick all the families with the most attractive daughters, and create a kind of paradise."

"You're making it a difficult proposition to turn down," Charlie said. "Other than the small matter that we would have to sacrifice millions of lives, as there would be no creditable opponent to Suktar with the armour in his hands."

"Yes, there is that," Ben said. "Damn it, I guess that's a

deal breaker. What a pity."

The humour didn't last long, as they both considered Prince Ictid's offer in all its seriousness.

"What are you going to do?" Charlie asked.

"Speak to Dagmar," Ben said immediately. "I need to work out how to avoid going into that place. He must have pulled me in; there has to be a way to stop that."

"And if there isn't?"

"Then I need to find out what that place is, and how I can defend myself."

"From someone as powerful as Prince Ictid?" Charlie said doubtfully.

"I can't believe he could just pull me in there and kill me. If that was possible, we would all be dead already."

"Not if he wanted your blood," Charlie said. "Not if their plan all along was to harness Elizabeth's Armour for themselves, as we now believe it might be."

"So, what do you suggest, then?" Ben asked with irritation.

Charlie shrugged. "I think your idea is a good one. Ask Dagmar. If she can't help, I think it's important enough to take all the way to Wren."

Ben went to Dagmar straight after muster, ignoring Aaron's orders for more cleaning. Despite everything, Aaron still tried to fit in at least thirty minutes most mornings and hadn't stopped giving them the worst jobs on offer.

"By yourself, this time?" Dagmar said as Ben entered. As usual, she was sitting at her desk, writing away at the sort of dazzling speed necessitated by the amount of paperwork on her table.

"Yeah. It doesn't really involve Charlie or Natalie," Ben said. "It does involve you, though, and all the other Guardians."

Dagmar put down the pen, and gave Ben her undivided attention, a rarity that Ben was keen to make use of. He didn't waste time, and recalled the events of last night's "dream". Dagmar didn't interrupt him, but Ben could see a rare look of concern on her face once he'd finished. Her brow was furrowed, not enough for a normal person to look concerned, but, with Dagmar, such subtleties spoke volumes.

"He pulled you into the draymas," Dagmar said.

"The what?"

"Draymas. It is a semi-dream world that sits between the real world, the dream world, and some other undefined mystical world that few people know of. Within the draymas, certain rules of the other worlds apply. For example, pain is real, and you can think and use your mind – traits of the real world. At the same time, the world can twist and change without your intention – traits of the dream world. And then there is magic, which works much like it does in the void – traits of the other, mystical world."

"Magic works like it does in the void?" Ben asked, his

face lighting up.

"Yes, but don't for a moment think that's easy," Dagmar said. "Magic in the void is a very difficult thing."

Of course, Dagmar didn't know about their trip to the void, and the time and energy they put into learning its rules. He was careful to conceal his delight at the news.

"So, what can I do?" Ben said.

"The easiest solution is to not get sucked in," Dagmar said. "Do you dream a lot?"

"Yes," Ben admitted. "Almost every night."

"That's the first thing we need to work on," Dagmar said. "It is far easier for Ictid to drag you into the draymas from the dream world. I will give you some techniques to work on, and a tonic to help you sleep without dreams."

"Okay, but what if that doesn't work and I get pulled in? I don't have much time to learn anything, as I plan on going to sleep tonight."

"There is a way to get out," Dagmar said. "It requires practice, patience, and focus. You have to concentrate on where you fell asleep, and will yourself back there. You must use each of your senses, until you feel like you are there again. Only then will you return."

"Great," Ben said. "And what if, while I'm doing that, Prince Ictid is busy trying to kill me? That's going to be a bit off-putting."

"You cannot die in the draymas," Dagmar said. "But he

can make you experience a world of pain."

Ben ran a hand through his hair, which suddenly felt a little damp. "I have to admit, I'm not looking forward to going to bed as much as I normally do."

Ben hadn't thought that much could take his attention off the hunt for the sword, especially with the constant jabbing from Joshua, but he was wrong. It wasn't just the potential meeting with Prince Ictid, but also the talk from the apprentices, and even the members, of people at home suddenly falling unconscious. Several friends of Ben's had their own family members fall victim to the phenomenon, and there was a glum, dispiriting feel at muster that afternoon.

Only Dagmar remained unaffected – though Ben suspected she wouldn't bat an eye if the entire dark elf army landed on their doorstep.

"The Institute have their best Scholars working on a cure with some of the finest magic users in the Unseen Kingdoms," Dagmar said. "They are already working on prototype bullets for the spellshooter, and are confident that within forty-eight hours they'll have something. So, my advice to you is to stop worrying and get on with your studies. Dismissed."

Ben didn't even bother telling the other Guardians about Prince Ictid's proposition. He could see Joshua possibly giving it some thought, but even he wouldn't seriously consider it. Joshua might be a pain, but he was on the side for good as much as any of them.

"Why don't you brush up on your void knowledge?" Charlie suggested. The two of them were in the library, studying historic battles against the dark elves. Charlie was eating through the pages, but Ben had read the same page three times, and still couldn't remember what it said.

"Yeah, that's not a bad idea," Ben said.

Charlie bounded off and returned a few minutes later with a couple of small black books.

"Get through those bad boys and you'll have a much better chance against Ictid tonight," Charlie said.

Ben spent the rest of the afternoon devouring the books while Charlie went off to help Joshua continue their research for the families that could get them into Vanishing Street.

By the time evening came, Ben felt a little more confident about meeting the prince.

"Remember, he can't kill you," Charlie said, as the two of them left the Institute and headed to the Dragonway, back home.

"But he can cause me a world of pain," Ben said.

"What's pain compared to death?" Charlie said with a cheerful smile.

"What's pain?" Ben raised an arm. "Do you want me to show you? It's really not that enjoyable."

"Point made," Charlie said hastily.

It took a lot to make Ben anxious, but that evening before bed, Ben found his body constantly shaking, and his breath slightly laboured. Several times his grandma tried talking to him about a new person she knew who had conked out, but it just went in one ear and out the other.

The last thing Ben felt like doing was going to bed early, but at the same time he was eager to get the meeting with Prince Ictid out the way. The best way to confront a problem was always to attack it, not drag it out. It was for that reason that Ben didn't even bother trying to avoid the draymas. The meeting was inevitable, whether it happened tonight or in a week's time. There was no point drawing it out.

Ben was in bed by 8pm. But forcing himself to get to sleep proved harder than he anticipated. Every time he felt himself drifting off, he would have a surge of adrenaline, and have to start the cycle again. It wasn't until ten o'clock that he finally drifted off.

— CHAPTER SEVENTEEN —

The Meaning of Pain

The room was identical to the one he'd arrived in last night, with its impossibly high ceiling, pristine marble floor and mighty columns. Ben still couldn't tell what the place reminded him of, but it would come.

"Welcome back," a powerful, familiar voice said

Prince Ictid stepped out from the columns. He looked identical to yesterday, though Ben thought his purple eyes looked a little brighter.

"I liked it so much here I couldn't stay away," Ben said.

Unlike last time, where fear of the unknown had taken hold, Ben was now prepared, and stepped forwards to meet Prince Ictid's slow advance. He was determined not to stop until Ictid did. No more than twenty feet separated them by the time they came to a halt. Very little time to stop a magic bolt, *Ben thought.*

"Have you thought about the proposal?" Ictid said.

"I have," Ben said. "This might sound hard to believe, but we have declined your generous offer. We're going to fight."

If Ben expected surprise or disappointment, he didn't get it. Indeed, the only acknowledgement he got was a knowing nod from the prince.

"I did not think you would accept," the prince said. "The idea was my father's. He has this notion that you are survivors, willing to do anything to prolong yourselves and your species. The idea of honour, of fighting for your race and sacrificing yourselves, is alien to him. I have to say, I don't understand it either, but I recognise its existence in you humans."

Prince Ictid stopped talking, and Ben saw his fists start to glow purple. His eyes, likewise, started glowing.

"I'm afraid this is the end of the line for you, Mr. Greenwood," Ictid said. "Just remember, you brought this upon yourself."

Ben knew in that fleeting moment that he could have tried returning home – a place without pain, a place of safety, where he didn't have to fight one of the most powerful enemies that existed. But he turned the chance down. He hated running. If this confrontation didn't happen now, it would happen tomorrow. If not tomorrow, then the next day.

Ben focused, pulling everything he remembered from the void, on top of everything he had spent reading. This wasn't the real world – physics didn't apply. Your mind was in charge, limited only by what you had the confidence to envisage and conceive.

Prince Ictid raised both his hands, and a pair of purple fireballs seared towards him.

>Ben flicked a hand, and both fireballs veered away, smashing into the walls.

The surprise on Prince Ictid's face was a joy to behold. His eyes widened, and the glow in his purple eyes seemed to dull for a second. But the surprise lasted only a moment, and was replaced with a thin smile.

"I will admit, I was not expecting that," Prince Ictid said with a small, but respectful nod. "Where did you—?"

Prince Ictid was still blabbering on when Ben launched his counter attack, throwing an ice-made disc with serrated edges right into Ictid's chest. It sunk deep, and the prince cried out. He yanked the disc clear, and threw it aside, his chest healing almost instantaneously.

Most enemies, even the most powerful ones, would have let their anger take over, giving Ben one or possibly even two more chances at a surprise attack. But Prince Ictid was not your ordinary enemy. He rubbed his chest, dusted himself off, and even managed a smile.

"Clever and cunning," Prince Ictid said. "I respect that. But the time for games is now over."

A sword materialised in the prince's hand, and he stepped forwards. Ben wanted to keep some distance, but the prince was too quick. He visualised his own sword just in time to block the first attack. Ben would have been cut to shreds within the first thirty seconds had it not been for the lessons with Volvek. As it was, he was immediately on the back foot, blocking and dodging at a furious pace. The prince's sword was a purple blur, and Ben could barely keep up. He received a nick to the shoulder, and another on the side of his ribs. The pain was excruciating, but with supreme effort, he refused to accept the sensation, and it dulled immediately.

Ben knew unless he did something audacious he was going to be overrun in a matter of moments. Fuelled by the knowledge that he couldn't die, only suffer a world of pain, Ben ducked under a slice, losing a few hairs in the process, and launched a blistering counter attack. He threw absolutely everything he had into it, his own swordsmanship enhanced by his knowledge and skill in the void.

There was a flicker – just a flicker – of alarm from Prince Ictid, as he back-pedalled for a couple of steps. But to Ben's horror, the prince had another gear, and he used it. Before Ben was even aware what was going on, Prince Ictid spun and something struck him in the stomach, throwing him into the air. He landed hard on his back. To his relief, Prince Ictid hadn't followed up, but remained standing some twenty feet back. He looked almost as fresh as when the battle started.

"Rest a little," the prince said, when Ben tried to rise. "I want to draw this out. It's no good if you go unconscious on me within minutes."

Ben focused on his stomach, and tried to eliminate the wound. The blood stopped flowing, but it still stung like hell. He managed to squirm his back up against the wall, and tried to calm his ragged breathing, while he gathered what energy he had left. It's just the void, *he told himself.* Take all the energy you want. *But it was difficult when your body was screaming at you, telling you it was done for.*

Still Prince Ictid did not advance. True to his word, he appeared in no hurry.

"I have to confess, I'm a bit of an expert when it comes to pain. I enjoy inflicting it and watching the reaction. It's quite a marvellous thing, observing the way different people respond. You, I suspect, will be a particularly interesting case. You are strong, determined and, as a Guardian and protector of Elizabeth's Armour, I am very keen to see what happens when you reach your threshold."

Prince Ictid idly inspected his sword as he spoke, giving it a completely unnecessary clean with a pristine white napkin he had summoned.

"I'm sorry, I'm rattling on. Were you not so exhausted, you probably could have surprised me with another one of your clever attacks. Are you ready or would you like a few more minutes?"

"A few more hours would be good," Ben said. With supreme effort, he used the wall to drag himself upright.

"We have hours, but not to be idle," the prince said with a smile. "Now, let's get on with it, shall we?"

The prince was in no hurry, and stepped forwards at a leisurely pace. Ben was exhausted and hurting in more areas than he could count. He could barely lift his sword, let alone fight. He thought about his room at home, but knew he'd never be able to focus properly on that while he was getting sliced to pieces.

Fear flowed through his body, providing him with a fillip of adrenaline. He raised his sword, in an effort to delay the explosion of pain that was about to come.

A sheet of white energy materialised from nowhere, forming a barrier between the advancing prince and Ben. Ictid's sword sliced into the barrier, and rebounded harmlessly away, just inches from Ben's face.

The prince stepped back, staring at the barrier with undisguised shock.

"How did you do that?" Ictid asked, tapping the barrier with his sword.

"He didn't. I did," a soft, almost child-like voice said.

Abigail materialised next to Ben and gave him a smile. She wore nothing but a dressing gown, but it was her head that caught Ben's eye. She was wearing Elizabeth's Helm.

"Hi, Ben," she said, giving him another smile, her soft eyes sparkling through the helm.

Ben reached out, tentatively touching the helm. "Is that the real thing?"

"Yeah, it is," Abigail said, looking rather proud of herself.

"I know you," Prince Ictid said, staring keenly at Abigail. "Or rather my father does. You have been most troublesome lately."

"Thank you," Abigail said, her eyes sparkling with pride. "It's taken a lot of hard work, but I think I'm almost ready."

Prince Ictid gave an almost amused smile. "We'll see."

Ben hadn't quite come to terms with the fact that he hadn't been diced into little pieces, but his body relished in the lack of pain he was still experiencing.

"So, what happens now?" Ben asked.

"Now, we shall ask Prince Ictid to no longer bother you," Abigail said, staring pointedly at the prince.

"You think you can stop me?" the prince asked.

"I know I can," Abigail said, nodding. "Watch."

She did nothing that Ben could see, simply staring at the

prince, and perhaps focusing a little.

The prince disappeared in a flash.

Ben stared in disbelief, and then turned to Abigail who was grinning from ear to ear.

"I did it! Dagmar's going to be so impressed."

"Forget Dagmar, my mind has just been blown. How did you do that?" Ben asked. "That wasn't any old dark elf – that was Prince Ictid, one of the most powerful elves that exists."

"In the real world, yes," Abigail said. "But not in here. In fact, in here I am the only one with real power, and that is because of Elizabeth's Helm. Everything else is just imagination. That is how I was able to trump him. He won't be coming back here, because he knows I'll be waiting for him, and I can cause him pain."

Ben stared at Abigail as if he was seeing her for the very first time. The sweet, innocent girl still remained, but the steel and determination Ben had guessed at when he first saw her were now shining through, and it was an incredible sight to behold.

"You've made a lot of progress," Ben said.

"I couldn't have done it without Dagmar," Abigail said. "However, I'm still not ready."

"Ready for what?"

"To confront Suktar's mind," Abigail said with a remarkably straight face.

"*Do you think you'll need to do that?*"

"*I hope not, but I need to be prepared,*" Abigail said. She smiled again, the momentary gravity on her face disappearing. "*Anyway, don't worry about me. You have to find your sword and start learning too. I know you'll be faster than me, but it's still a lot of work.*"

"*I'll be ready,*" Ben said.

"*I know you will,*" Abigail said. "*Now, do you want to go home? I'm kind of tired myself, and the body doesn't sleep so well when in the draymas. Do you remember what to do to get back?*"

"*Yeah, I think so,*" Ben said.

Ben closed his eyes, and immediately thought of his bedroom. Without the threat of Prince Ictid, the imagery came easily. He visualised his bed, the computer desk, and the slightly dirty carpet. He smelled the pizza that hadn't fully cleared from the night everyone came over, and he listened to the soft flapping of the curtains created by the open window.

Ben felt a strange, not unpleasant shift, and he felt himself move in some transcendent, almost spiritual way. Suddenly, he was aware that he was no longer standing, but lying down.

He opened his eyes.

Ben was lying in bed, back home.

— CHAPTER EIGHTEEN —

The Kingdom of Casteria

He calls himself Baron Vongrath," Charlie said with a perfectly straight face. "And he's our man."

Ben, Charlie, Natalie and Joshua were sitting in the secure conference room the morning following Ben's exertions with Prince Ictid. It was a Saturday, but the Institute had been on a seven-day-a-week schedule since the escalation of the dark elf threat, and apprentices were encouraged to do the same.

"He has a house on Vanishing Street?" Natalie asked.

"He does," Joshua confirmed. "He is a hard man to track down, but we found the house of his choice for this particular month. If we can meet him, I am confident I can get an invitation to Vanishing Street."

"How many houses does this man have?" Ben asked.

"He has one for each month," Charlie replied. "In each of the primary Unseen Kingdoms."

Ben sat up. "Who is this guy? He sounds richer than Bill Gates."

"He comes close," Charlie said. "And therein lies our first problem."

"What's wrong with being rich?"

"Nothing," Joshua said immediately.

"No, there is nothing wrong with being rich," Charlie said, giving Joshua a pointed stare. "However, there are a few things wrong with running the largest illegal magic trade in the Unseen Kingdoms."

"It's not all illegal," Joshua said. "He has a perfectly legitimate business, which the Institute deals with on a regular basis."

"They are either ignorant or turn a blind eye," Charlie said. "Anyway, the point is, as befits someone dealing beneath the law, he has a bit of a thing on security. And he's also a bit mad."

"So I guess walking up to his house for a quick hello is out of the question?" Ben said.

"Right. Think castles, moats, and all sorts of weird and exotic creatures protecting entry," Charlie said.

Joshua cleared his throat. "The plan is to go tonight. We need to assemble a team, but I will be the only one visiting him. My family credentials will get me an audience."

"Fine with me," Ben said. "I'm not a big fan of barons anyway, to be honest."

Joshua ignored Ben's comment. "I only want you, Krobeg and me on the mission."

Ben frowned at exactly the same time Natalie voiced a fairly vocal complaint.

Joshua raised a hand. "Krobeg with his armour is like a one-man fighting machine. You are also useful in combat, Ben. Charlie and Natalie are surplus to requirements."

"That is unfair," Natalie said angrily. "Charlie and I are now well above third-grade level."

Joshua gave an unimpressed smirk, and turned to Ben. Natalie and Charlie did likewise. Ben noted that Charlie wasn't really complaining.

"Okay, first of all, Krobeg isn't coming," Ben said. "At least not with the breastplate. And though he's a great fighter without it, he would be too noisy at a time when I believe we need stealth."

"Why can't he bring the breastplate?" Joshua asked. "What is the point of these artefacts, if not to use them?"

"The point in them," Ben said, emphasising every word, "is to defeat Suktar. I won't risk them for anything else. If anything were to happen to them, we'd be in right trouble. On this I will not argue."

To Ben's surprise, Joshua didn't complain. He might have been a complete pain in the backside, but at least he could see reason when it was staring him in the face.

"Secondly, Charlie and Natalie are coming with," Ben said.

If Joshua took the first ruling without complaint, this time he was the complete opposite. "Why bring them? What do they add to the mission?"

"Friendship," Ben said simply. "You might not value it, but it helps, especially if things get sticky."

"Nonsense," Joshua said, shaking his head vigorously. "You're letting your heart get in the way of reason. I will not stand for it. This is my shield, remember? I am responsible for finding it, and I won't have you messing it up."

Ben knew Joshua was right, but he didn't care, and he certainly didn't show it. He needed Charlie and Natalie, and it wasn't for friendship, but for something else, though he wasn't about to tell anyone quite yet.

"They are coming," Ben repeated. "Yes, it's your shield, but I'm the one responsible for gathering them all, not you. Trust me, Charlie and Natalie will be needed."

As far as arguments went, Ben knew it was pretty lame, and he had to supplement it with a conviction and anger he didn't really feel.

Joshua stood up. "If they mess this up, I'm blaming you." He marched to the door, and turned around just as he was about to leave. "This is *exactly* what Lord Samuel feared."

The door slammed, leaving the three of them alone once

more.

"Well, that was unnecessary," Natalie said, flashing an angry glance at the door. "Still, it might be good for him to see how well we work together. Then he'll realise how ridiculous he's being."

"That's the idea," Ben said.

He avoided looking at Charlie. Even from his peripheral vision, he could read his friend's scepticism and he knew without asking that Charlie suspected another motive. Ben had long since given up trying to get anything past him, but he wasn't going to explain himself – not while Natalie was around.

Joshua avoided them most of the day, which suited Ben just fine. At least that meant he got no more badgering about his own search for the sword. There were only a couple of days left until Natalie was willing to use the memory spell on his grandma. Ben tried not to think about what would happen if that resulted in a dead end, and instead focused on their mission tonight. On impulse, he stopped off at Dagmar's office.

"Baron Vongrath?" she said, when Ben imparted the news.

Ben noticed that Dagmar no longer took to working when he stopped by, a sign that she was becoming increasingly involved.

"He is a peculiar man," Dagmar said. "Certainly not a

man to be trifled with. Alex knows more about him than I do, but he is not around at present, or else I would send you straight to him."

"Is he a good sort or a bad sort?" Ben asked.

"Both, and neither," Dagmar said. "He is extremely wealthy and owns half the magic industry. We are aware that some of it is not ethical, and he sells to both sides. But we are his biggest customer, and are usually able to keep him in check. His industry has become so big now that if we wanted to shut him down, it would be almost as difficult as stopping the dark elves."

"He sounds interesting," Ben said.

"Eccentric would be a better word," Dagmar said. "But Joshua is right: the baron will be impressed with his family history, and the fact that they own a house on Vanishing Street. It is best that Joshua visits him alone."

"Will he be easy to reach?" Ben asked.

"We have never had to face his security, because Alex would always go on invitation," Dagmar said. "I don't doubt security will be interesting, but you are no slouch anymore, Ben. You should be able to cope."

"Joshua wanted me to take Krobeg and his armour."

Dagmar nodded. "You were right to say no. The armour should not be risked."

Ben smiled, then, thinking of last night. "Abigail found and saved me in the draymas last night."

To Ben's surprise, Dagmar returned the smile – it was only a flash, but it lit up her stern face quite remarkably.

"That was a necessary risk, and a good test for Abigail. I am happy with her progress."

"She's doing amazing," Ben said with feeling. "Thank you for taking her on. I wouldn't have had a clue what to do."

"You have enough on your hands," Dagmar said, swiftly returning to her more familiar impassiveness. "Now, you should get going. You have a lot to prepare for tonight."

Ben knew when he was being asked to leave, and went to find Charlie and Natalie. They were forced to spend a little time on their apprenticeship, lest they attract attention again from Draven for falling behind, but as soon as they were able, they dived back into the library to continue their research on Baron Vongrath.

"Where's Joshua?" Ben asked, not displeased to see that he wasn't around.

"He wanted to work alone," Charlie said. "We are to meet him at the Dragonway at seven o'clock."

Ben knew he shouldn't have been excited, as it was a dangerous mission and an important one, but he found that by the time seven o'clock came, his heart was beating that little bit faster, in a good way. After the frustration of the sword, it felt good to be doing something pro-active towards finding the next piece of armour.

Joshua met them with the mutest of acknowledgements

and a barely concealed withering glance at Charlie and Natalie, though he held his tongue.

"The kingdom of Casteria, right?" Charlie asked, glancing towards Joshua.

"Yes. Platform four, at 7:13pm."

"He owns the whole island, doesn't he?" Ben asked, as they boarded the Dragonway not ten minutes later.

"One of many," Joshua said with an authoritative nod. "This one in particular is one of his smaller, more exclusive islands."

"Isn't security going to be tight?" Natalie said.

"Yes, but not in the way you think," Joshua replied. "You'll see when we get there."

Casteria lay a hundred miles off the west coast of Ireland, and the dragon made the journey in good time. Ben always got a little thrill when he ascended to a station he'd never been to before. It was well into the evening and Ben feared they might not see much, but Casteria station did not disappoint.

It was located inside what looked like an old stone fort, built during mediaeval times, and had been sympathetically restored. The Dragonway track ran right through the middle of the fort, and they stepped out onto the platform, feeling as if they'd just gone back five hundred years. Old suits of armour sat in small recesses, and narrow window slits ran up and down the fort. The only real concession to magic was the chandeliers that hung from the ceiling, lit by scores of candles.

The place wasn't empty, but there couldn't have been more than a couple dozen people around, and most of them seemed to be leaving. Ben noted they wore green uniforms, and were most likely employed at Baron Vongrath's main residence.

They tore their eyes away from the inside of the fort, and made their way to the exit, which consisted of nothing more than an open archway. The cool breeze hit them as they stepped outside, and their eyes adjusted to the moonlight.

"Well, I guess we know where to go," Natalie said.

That much was obvious the moment they stepped outside. Before them stood a forest, with a large path running through its centre. The forest rose on a gentle incline, and beyond it was a mighty rock, towering over the trees. On top of the rock was a castle.

"I don't suppose they have a taxi service," Charlie said, as he stared into the distance at the castle. It was an impressive sight, but Ben guessed it to be at least a couple of hours' walking, and that was without interference.

"I'm sure there is some sort of transport for people who work here," Joshua said. "But we are not here by invitation. We must walk."

Charlie sighed. "Has anyone else noticed how many of these islands are basically just forests and hills?"

"England used to be one big forest," Ben said, as they started walking. "That's what it's like around here, I guess."

As soon as they entered the main entrance into the forest, the trees obstructed much of the moonlight, and all four of them lit their spellshooters. The pathway itself was wide and well used and, for the first twenty minutes, they had little difficulty navigating their way through. They saw a few employees coming their way, but nobody glanced at them with much suspicion, and it wasn't long before they walked alone.

As far as forests went, there was nothing particularly unique about it. In his recent adventures, Ben had been to bigger ones, scarier ones, and certainly many that were less inviting.

"This isn't too bad," Ben said, giving them all an encouraging smile. "I'm starting to wonder why we bothered with all that research. I don't see anything that—"

"There," Natalie said, cutting him off suddenly. She was looking ahead right down the path, and pointing.

Her part-elven eyes were so keen that it was another minute before Ben saw what she was pointing at.

"What on earth is that thing?" Ben asked.

— CHAPTER NINETEEN —

A Dangerous Journey

A rhinosaur," Charlie whispered with a mixture of fascination and anxiety.

The description was apt. Ahead of them was something that looked like a small troll, with the head of a rhino, complete with mud-grey skin and a huge, pointed horn.

"Now what?" Joshua asked, looking at the rhinosaur with alarm.

Ben enjoyed the anxiety on Joshua's face. He might have shared it, if not for the rhinosaur's demeanour. In his hand was a clipboard, and he was writing on it, his short, stubby tongue sticking out in the process. There was no weapon that Ben could see, though Ben was fairly certain he rarely needed one.

"We talk," Ben said.

Without waiting for a response, Ben walked right up to the rhinosaur. He must have been at least seven feet, with muscles that threatened to rip his shirt. His skin looked so hard that Ben wasn't sure if an ordinary sword would penetrate it.

"ID cards please," the rhinosaur said in a deep voice without looking up.

Ben gave a quick look at his friends, who shrugged at him with varying levels of concern. With a subtle motion of his hand, Ben slowly eased his way down to his spellshooter.

"We were in a bit of a rush this evening, and left them at home," Ben said.

The rhinosaur gave a bored shrug, still more interested in his clipboard than in them. "No card, no passage. You know the rules."

Ben quietly searched his orb for a spell he thought might be suitable and get them past. He didn't want to make too much of a scene. He was still searching, when Joshua's voice rung out.

"I have a meeting with the baron. I cannot be detained any longer."

The rhinosaur stopped being interested in his clipboard, and looked up, suddenly a lot more intimidating than he had been a moment ago. "Say that again?"

Joshua seemed to lose his voice. The rhinosaur clenched his fists, and lowered his head. He was going to charge, Ben realised with sudden horror, all because of Joshua's idiotic demand.

A flash of light exploded, and something hit the rhinosaur right in the chest. He froze in place, his eyes glazing over.

"Go – now!" Natalie said. "We've got less than thirty seconds."

She dashed past the rhinosaur, spellshooter in hand, and started running down the path. Ben followed immediately, with Joshua and Charlie close behind. They ran hard until the rhinosaur was long out of sight.

"Are we safe? What did you cast?" Charlie asked, his hands on his knees, as he struggled for breath.

"Memory wipe. It cleans the last minute of his life, so the only thing he will remember is working on his clipboard, just before we turned up. It's only really effective against enemies with low IQ, but I thought he fit the bill."

"Good job," Ben said, smiling at Natalie. He turned to Charlie. "Might be time to dish out the gear, don't you think?"

Charlie nodded, and undid the backpack he had been wearing. He opened it up and started doling out large pouches for each of them.

"After doing the research, these are the spells I think will best suit us here. The baron doesn't like us killing his 'pets', as he calls them, so there are a lot of stunning and sleeping spells in the pouches. There are also a few specialised spells, for certain enemies we might run into."

"Good stuff," Ben said. He turned to Joshua, and gave his pouch a wave. "Good thing Charlie and Natalie came along, eh? We'd already be in trouble without them."

Joshua rose his chin a little. "I would have done the research myself, but I was too busy learning all about the baron."

Ben rolled his eyes. "Let's keep going. It's only going to get darker and colder, and I don't fancy spending the night here."

The path continued onwards, going ever upwards, but still at a gentle pace, and without danger. After all, this was still the route to the castle taken by the employees every day. Half an hour of gentle trekking passed, when the path came to an abrupt end. In its place, they spotted a railroad track that dug itself into the hill through a tunnel that had a pair of double doors barring entry. Just outside the doors was a miniature car that sat on the track, and was pointed right at the double doors that blocked the tunnel's entrance.

"Good evening, folks," a cheerful voice said. From the shadows a small dwarf emerged, wearing green overalls and a matching green cap. "ID cards please; then we'll get going."

He dropped himself into the driving seat without even waiting for a reply, and stuck a hand out, waiting for the cards.

Ben thought about coming up with some clever story, but he started to feel like it wouldn't matter.

"We don't have them today," Ben said.

"What?" the dwarf said, his head whipping round, though he stayed in the front seat. "How did you get past Reggie, then?"

"We zapped him," Ben said, holding out his spellshooter with a grin. "Which is, I'm afraid, what I'm going to have to do to you unless you give us a lift in that delightful car of yours."

"Won't matter," the dwarf said, staring anxiously at the spellshooter. "Can't start the car or open the tunnel without the ID cards."

"There's no other way to get in?" Natalie said intervening.

"Afraid not, miss," the dwarf said.

Ben glanced beyond the tunnel. The main path had ended, but the shrubbery and forest beyond were light enough so that they could continue their journey up towards the castle.

"Not a good idea," the dwarf said, stepping out of the car. "Don't go up there, trust me."

"We don't have an option," Joshua said, his voice stern, as if it was the dwarf's problem that they couldn't progress. "I have an appointment with the baron."

"Yeah, right," the dwarf said with a sudden burst of

laughter. "If that were true, he'd fly you up in one of his carriages. You wouldn't be scrapping your way through the forest."

Joshua paled a little. "It's an unusual sort of appointment."

The dwarf laughed again, a hearty sound that defied his size. "Of course it is. Now, you should head home before it gets too dark. It gets cold out here at night."

"Can't do that, I'm afraid," Ben said. "My arrogant friend is right – we need to see the baron. If we can't use your car, we'll just have to walk."

The dwarf's humour evaporated, replaced by what looked to Ben like genuine concern. "I'm warning you. There are creatures up there – things that the baron likes to collect. He lets them roam the castle grounds, and they don't respond well to intruders."

"We'll worry about those," Ben said, injecting a cheerfulness he didn't feel. "Unless you fancy changing your mind?"

"I wish I could," the dwarf said, spreading his hands. "But it's not under my control."

"A pity," Ben said. He waved to the others, and started his climb around the tunnel, continuing up through the forest.

There wasn't much of a path, but, with their spellshooters lit, they were able to pick their way through the shrubbery and undergrowth. It was slow going, as they often had to lift their legs over gorse and pine, but slowly the giant rock in the distance became larger.

A sudden rustling noise halted their advance.

"What was that?" Charlie asked.

They aimed their spellshooters over the undergrowth, like searchlights.

There, less than twenty paces away, something was writhing its way towards them. It looked like a snake, but it was far larger than anything Ben had ever seen before. The moment the light hit its eyes, the snake leapt up, and snapped its sharp jaws into the open air, before diving back down again.

"Stunning spells!" Ben said, pointing his spellshooter at the enemy.

Ben's aim was true, and his spell knocked the snake out cold. But the moment he did so, the entire undergrowth seemed to shudder and move of its own accord.

More snakes. Lots of them.

Hissing, snarling and even leaping, they slithered forwards from all angles.

"Oh my!" Natalie said with a gasp.

The four of them started firing at anything that moved.

"There are too many of them," Charlie said. He had to scream to be heard over the hissing and shooting.

"We should retreat and find another way forwards,"

167

Joshua said in rare agreement, as he took down a large red snake that had got a little close.

"No," Ben said firmly. "We push forwards."

Overcoming all natural desire, Ben put one foot in front of the other. Unlike the others, he had the composure to aim and shoot, without scatter firing.

"Stop wasting pellets!" he ordered. "It only takes one head shot to take these things down. You don't need to hit them a dozen times."

"You do if your aim is as bad as mine is," Charlie muttered. He had crept up behind Ben, using him as a human shield.

Progress was slow, but Ben could see, less than fifty yards ahead, the forest opened up to a clearing, and the snakes seemed absent there.

"Keep going forwards," he urged. Natalie and Joshua were several paces behind, but both were making slow progress. The snakes were starting to thin, and Ben was able to pick and choose his shots. But it was dark, and difficult to see, which was why he didn't notice the snake that slipped past him.

Charlie cried out suddenly and he fell, disappearing into the undergrowth. Ben could just about see the tail of a snake whipping around Charlie's legs. With a cry of pain and horror, Charlie was dragged along at a frightening pace, deep into the forest.

Ben whipped his spellshooter round and squinted at the rapidly departing Charlie, whose arms and legs were flailing, making the snake an impossible shot. Ben had but seconds before they would be out of sight. He aimed as best he could, and fired. The snake stopped dead, as did Charlie. To Ben's dismay, Charlie didn't get up, but instead lay prostrate in the undergrowth. Ignoring his own advice about not rapidly firing, Ben shot left and right like a mad man, forging a path before any more snakes could grab Charlie. One almost reached him, but a good kick to its jaw sent it packing. Ben reached down, grabbed Charlie as best he could, and then, still firing at anything that moved, somehow managed to run to the end of the undergrowth, and threw himself into the clearing beyond. To his great relief, the snakes shied away from the bare ground, and Ben was left alone with an unconscious Charlie.

"Is he okay?" Natalie said.

She and Joshua arrived moments later, panting and grimacing.

"I shot him," Ben said, wiping sweat from his brow. "I can't believe it. He was being dragged away, and I didn't have much to aim at. My spell must have hit both the snake and Charlie."

"Well, it was just a stunning spell, right?" Natalie said. "There is no lasting damage."

"How long will it take for him to come to?" Joshua asked.

"Half an hour, maybe," Ben said, trying to remember what Charlie had told him earlier. "But I don't know if the effect is reduced because the spell was spread between him and the snake."

Joshua looked unhappy about the waiting, but he didn't complain. They moved Charlie further into the clearing, and placed his backpack under his head as a cushion. Natalie had a basic healing spell that she fired at Charlie. His colour started to look better immediately, but they had an anxious twenty-minute wait before he started to stir, and finally opened his eyes. He sat up gingerly, rubbing his face. Finally, he turned to Ben.

"You shot me, didn't you," he said.

"Yeah. Sorry about that," Ben replied with a sheepish grin.

"Are you okay to continue?" Joshua said. "We still have a lot of walking to do."

"Don't have much of a choice, really, do I," Charlie said. He stood up with a grunt of pain, clutching his back.

"We'll go slow," Natalie said, giving Charlie's shoulder a squeeze. "At least the ground is easier now; it's just dirt."

"I'll manage," Charlie said. Ben couldn't help noticing the way Charlie glanced up warily at the night sky. Was there something else out there? Ben decided now wasn't the best time to ask.

Charlie battled gamely with his aches and pains, but

though the ground now made for easy walking, it was still uphill, and the huge rock on which the castle was mounted seemed to be taking an awfully long time to get within reach. They were very exposed now, and though that meant they should have been able to see anything coming, there was also nowhere to run. Charlie had taken to looking skywards every few minutes, and it was starting to unnerve Ben.

"What is it?" he asked eventually.

"I think we should hurry up," Charlie said out of the blue.

"Why?" Joshua asked.

"The open air and the cliff – it's perfect for one of the creatures I read about, and they're not pleasant."

"What are they?" Joshua asked a little impatiently.

A horrible screeching noise rent the air, making them all jump.

"Harpies," Charlie said, glancing up at the night sky.

Dozens of the most peculiar creatures Ben had ever seen dropped out of the sky, diving right for them. They were far more terrifying than the harpies he'd seen in video games. Their upper bodies were that of a witch, with matted black hair and malevolent green eyes. The rest resembled a savage bird of prey, with sharp claws that looked ready to rip something to shreds.

"Fire spells!" Ben cried, aiming his spellshooter above his head.

He unleashed swirling balls of heat, but the harpies were remarkably nimble, and they dodged many of the spells with deft manoeuvres, barely losing speed as they did so. Suddenly, Ben was staring up at half a dozen sets of claws, about to rain down on him. He had a split second to prepare for impact, and then, with a mighty crash, they collided. Ben felt claws grapple on his wrists. The harpies hissed and spat at him, their green eyes full of hatred. Ben gave one a mighty whack round the head, but another immediately took her place. He unleashed a spell from point-blank range, which even the nimble harpy could do nothing about.

It was a mass of confusion, with limbs and talons everywhere, on top of the screams of both pain and glee from the harpies. Ben was vaguely aware that there were now several harpies lying motionless on the floor, and one or two had beat a retreat.

A cry of horror cut through the screeching harpies.

Natalie was airborne. Two harpies had gripped either wrist, and were flying away with her, or trying to – Natalie was kicking and screaming with such frenzy that the harpies were having a hard time gaining air. Ben attempted to batter his way through to her, but the harpies seemed to guess his intent, and they snapped at him, even attempting to lift him from the ground. Ben suddenly found he was surrounded by three harpies who had vice grips on his wrists. Joshua was attempting to reach Natalie, but he was also pinned down.

Another scream, this one of defiance, ripped through the air. Charlie powered through the harpies as if they were nothing more than teddies and, with a mighty leap, jumped and grabbed Natalie's ankles as the harpies made to do away with her.

"I've got you!" Charlie cried.

The harpies, suddenly inundated with weight, almost dropped both of them. Charlie started wagging and kicking. The harpies screamed in protest. Their grip was loosening, but all the while they were gaining altitude. Five feet. Ten feet. Fifteen.

The harpies gave one final scream, and then dropped Natalie and Charlie. Ben watched in horror as they fell, and hit the ground with a bone-crunching thud.

"They're fleeing!" Joshua said, kicking out at a harpy that was trying to escape.

The harpies had had enough, and those that still could took to the skies, promptly disappearing into the night, still screeching.

Ben and Joshua ran over to Charlie and Natalie. Charlie was moving; Natalie wasn't.

"Shit," Ben said, staring despairingly at Natalie. There was blood pooling down her forehead. Ben wanted to do something, anything, but he felt powerless.

"Out the way," Charlie said, pulling free his spellshooter. He closed his eyes, and focused. Ben watched as his breathing slowed and the frown on his face receded, replaced by a calmness of sorts. Ben waited impatiently, but was careful not to make the slightest of sounds. After what seemed like an age, Charlie pointed his spellshooter at Natalie's head. Eyes still closed, he pulled the trigger. A white mist flowed from the barrel and over Natalie, covering her like a blanket. Ben watched in silent apprehension, almost forgetting to breathe. After what seemed like an eternity, Natalie gave a soft groan, and her eyes flickered open.

Charlie sat back, and wiped his brow, as if he'd just run a marathon. "I've never cast anything as powerful as that before. I almost lost it."

"You did great," Ben said. He turned to Natalie. "How are you feeling?"

"Tired," Natalie said with a weak smile.

"Can you make it to the rock?" Joshua asked.

Ben was about to mutter an angry reply about giving Natalie a minute, but Charlie intervened.

"Joshua is right. The cover of the rock will be safer than being exposed out here."

"I can walk," Natalie said.

It took Ben on one side and Joshua on the other to help her up. Charlie wasn't that much better off, but he managed to get to his feet. Together, the four of them hobbled their way to the sheer rock. Ben kept looking up at the night sky, but the ominous presence of the harpies, or anything else for that matter, remained absent.

The closer they got, the more imposing the rock became, until the mighty structure loomed over them. Charlie and Natalie collapsed against it, both groaning as they sunk to the floor.

Ben and Joshua immediately stepped back to inspect the rock. There were plenty of footholds and crevices, should climbing be required, but Ben knew instinctively that they wouldn't all be able to make it.

"Over here," Joshua called with a wave.

Joshua was staring at a piece of the cliff, not twenty paces away. The moment Ben approached, he could see what Joshua was referring to. It was a door, cut into the rock. There was no handle, but there was a small slit.

"Let me guess, that's for the ID card," Ben said, running his hand over the slit.

"I believe so," Joshua said.

Ben stepped back again, and stared up at the cliff. He turned to Joshua, and gave him a small smile.

"Well, looks like we're climbing."

— CHAPTER TWENTY —

The Stone Soldier

There has to be another way," Natalie said

Her green eyes were determined, but Ben noticed that neither she nor Charlie had moved from their sitting position.

"There isn't," Joshua said. "We have to climb."

Despite everything, Natalie tried to get to her feet. She made lots of noises, but very little upward motion occurred. Eventually, she slumped back down, visibly crestfallen.

"I can't do it," she said, her voice soft. "I'm in too much pain."

"I don't expect you to," Ben said with a gentle smile. "You've done quite enough already. The cliff is hard enough to scale when fully fit, and then there is the small matter of what lies at the top, right, Charlie?"

Charlie nodded. "If my research is correct – and it normally is – you'll have to face a stone soldier to gain entry."

"A stone soldier?" Joshua asked. "Who is that?"

"Not a 'who', but a 'what'," Charlie said. "It is a soldier crafted of stone – one of the baron's most prized possessions."

"Won't he get upset if we destroy it, then?"

"Possibly, if he didn't have a whole unit of them. He's quite a collector." Charlie's face turned grave. "Be careful up there. The stone soldier will not be easy to take down."

"Don't worry about us," Ben said. "You guys just stay low, and we'll be back shortly."

Ben and Joshua left Charlie and Natalie lying against the rock – Natalie looking considerably more miserable than Charlie – and they turned their attention to the climb. It took them a good fifteen minutes to find the best place to ascend, and another five to prepare themselves.

Ben took one look at the sheer cliff, then turned to Joshua, who was still staring up at the daunting challenge.

"Good luck," Ben said on impulse. "See you at the top."

Joshua appeared surprised by the wish, but not displeased, and returned it with a nod.

Ben always liked to climb. He had plenty of experience, and counted himself competent at it. He was athletic, his limbs were strong, and football had given him a fair amount of stamina. But five minutes into this ascent, and Ben quickly realised this wasn't like anything he'd done before. For starters, there was no safety net. He made the mistake of looking down once, and almost fell from the shock. It was also several times higher than anything he'd ever encountered and almost impossible to see the top.

Concentrate on one foothold at a time, he kept repeating to himself. It was slow going, but it forced him to focus. When his limbs started to ache, he would hold his position and attempt to relax for a moment, before taking a deep breath, and ploughing on. By the time he could see the top, his arms felt like they were about to come off; every inch gained took supreme effort and his mouth was dry from the constant grunting. What would happen when he reached the top? Would the stone soldier be there waiting to chop him down? It didn't matter now – he was spent, and all he could think of was lying down at the top of the rock.

Ben's heart jumped when he finally sought out a hand slot, and found only air. With a final surge of energy, he scrambled up and onto the rock. He turned onto his back, and lay there, panting, as his limbs were finally able to catch a break.

Ben saw a hand in his peripheral vision and, a moment later, Joshua scrambled up and lay prostrate on the ground, his chest heaving.

"Soldier?" Joshua whispered, unable to do anything

more than use his eyeballs to indicate direction.

Ben sat himself up, and gasped at the sight that beheld him. Set back some hundred yards from the rockface was a castle that looked like something out of a story book. It wasn't large, more like a house, but every stone and battlement was perfectly cast, with turrets and towers that gleamed in the moonlight. It looked as though it had been constructed just yesterday, and yet still had an age about it lacking in most theme park reproductions.

The stone soldier wasn't immediately obvious, for he was made from exactly the same grey stone as the castle. But Ben could just detect a faint outline, in front of a gated entrance.

The figure moved forwards, and suddenly the stone soldier became very real indeed. Both Ben and Joshua scrambled to their feet, taking in deep breaths of air in an effort to recover. Thankfully, the stone soldier appeared to be in no hurry, giving them both time to inspect their adversary as he approached.

"I see why he's called the stone soldier," Ben said.

Even from a distance, it was clear he was made entirely from stone. He wore short-plated armour and breeches, though it was clearly cosmetic because, armour or not, everything was stone, even the feather that protruded from his helmet. He wore a short sword and a small circular shield. There was something about the way he held it that spoke of both experience and skill.

Ben felt the first surge of adrenaline course through his body, fuelling his tired limbs. He focused, and fired a complex spell into his hand. A glowing blue-tinted sword materialised in his hand, just as Joshua fired the same.

"You realise we are going to have to work together here?" Ben said, glancing at Joshua.

"I'm aware of that," Joshua said. Ben was pleased to see the way Joshua held his own weapon. He had also received lessons from Volvek.

"You circle left; I'll circle right," Ben said. "Don't launch into an attack – let's measure him first. I've got a feeling he's going to be quick. He might be made of stone, but he's pure magic, not restricted by normal material limitations."

"I'll be fine," Joshua said. "You just make sure you stay alive long enough so I can take him down."

"Fine by me," Ben said.

The stone soldier stopped, twenty paces from them. His eyes were grey, and there was a life, of sorts, in them, though Ben knew it wasn't real.

"This way is barred," the stone soldier said in a monotone that reminded Ben of an old computer. "Please return from whence you came."

"I've come to see Baron Vongrath," Joshua declared. "It is of utmost importance."

Ben wasn't even sure the stone soldier heard Joshua. He waited a moment, without batting an eyelid, before speaking again.

"This way is barred. Please return from whence you came."

The stone soldier spoke in exactly the same tone, with precisely the same inflection, his eyes showing the same casual, impassive expression.

"I'm not sure he's listening to you," Ben said.

Joshua tried again, taking a step forwards to emphasise his point. The stone soldier didn't react at all, and replied again.

"This way is barred. Please return from whence you came. *This is your last warning.*"

Ben felt his stomach threaten to exit through his mouth. He brought his sword to bear. "Get ready – he's—"

The stone soldier launched forwards in a grey blur, his short sword sweeping in an arc, and forcing both Ben and Joshua into an immediate block. Ben went right and Joshua left in an attempt to surround him. But the soldier was not human, and it became immediately clear he wasn't subject to things like the resistance of gravity. Ben and Joshua attacked at the same time, but somehow the stone soldier was able to block both advances, twisting and turning with stunning speed. Ben pressed forwards, cutting and thrusting, but his every move was blocked with the shield. The soldier jumped back suddenly, and Ben and Joshua almost collided into each other.

To Joshua's credit, there was no fear in his eyes, just single-minded determination.

"Can this thing be killed?" he asked.

"Yes," Ben said. "We just need to cut its head off."

"Is that a joke?"

"No."

The stone soldier attacked again, cutting off their chatter. They were both forced backwards until Joshua launched a risky counter thrust, and grazed the soldier's underbelly. The soldier stopped, and looked at his stomach with an expression of mild interest.

"Has to be the head," Ben repeated, panting slightly. "Our only chance is routine 3A."

Joshua barely had time to give him a look, before the soldier came again. Ben tried another audacious move, but the soldier was ready, and ducked, stabbing at Joshua, who cried out in pain, clutching his shoulder.

Again, the stone soldier stepped back, after the brief flurry.

"Why doesn't he just finish us?" Joshua asked.

"I think he's doing what he's programmed to do," Ben said. "He's giving us a chance to escape. You were right: the baron isn't all that bad, it seems. But I can't take many more of these attacks. We need to execute routine 3A before—"

Ben got no further before the stone soldier attacked again, nicking Ben's wrist and Joshua's arm, before backing away again, and inspecting them both with that same expressionless stare. The soldier showed no sign of weariness – indeed, he had no lungs.

"Who's going to be the victim?" Joshua asked.

The two of them were now only just about holding on to their swords, and Ben's vision was starting to blur.

"Me, of course. You need to speak to the baron."

"Are you sure about—?"

"Yes!"

Ben didn't wait. It was now or never. He lurched forwards, and gave an exaggerated stumble. The stone soldier stepped in and launched a stab right into Ben's stomach. Ben twisted as best he could, but the sword still found its mark, driving into Ben's ribs. He screamed and fell, but even as he did so, he was aware that Joshua had leapt high, and got a clean strike on the stone soldier. With a mighty sweep, he carved right into the stone soldier's neck, and took the head clean off.

Ben was vaguely aware of Joshua's face in front of his, and that he was mumbling something urgently.

Everything went black.

— CHAPTER TWENTY-ONE —

Caught Red-Handed

Ben woke to the smell of strong herbs and the throbbing of his ribs. He was lying on a chaise longue in a small but comfortable room, filled with jackets, coats and scarves that hung on the wall.

Ben sat up, groaned, and promptly lay down again, his head spinning. He inspected his chest, and saw a tight bandage, stained red, strapped tightly around his torso. The memory came flooding back, bringing renewed pain that made him clench his teeth. He took several deep breaths, and was about to take another attempt at getting up, when he heard voices.

"...One can never be too careful in this day and age, and there are just so many fascinating creatures to see, especially in the lesser-known Unseen Kingdoms. I have an expedition going to Tripmandu next week, you know. Hoping to find some genuine capriats. I know they're only supposed to be a rumour, but I have it on good authority that they really do exist."

The voice was clear and well spoken, reminding Ben of nobility.

"That sounds fascinating," Joshua said.

"Oh, it will be. And I can arrange for you to come. You will see some remarkable things."

"Thank you, I would like that."

"Right. We'd better wake your friend up. I expect he will be eager to get home and get that nasty gash seen to. My doctors aren't a touch on the Institute's."

Ben managed to get to his feet just as Joshua and Baron Vongrath entered the room.

"Ah, you're up already, I see. Well, out with you, boy. Can't have you clogging up my cloakroom now, can I?"

The baron wasn't quite what Ben expected. He was small, with a receding hairline and a hooked nose. His mouth was so large it seemed to encompass half his face, and there was a cheerful air about him that Ben took to, despite his blunt manner.

"Yes, sir," Ben said. Any attempt at walking with haste was put to bed, as his ribs started aching upon movement.

"Steady on, I don't want you dropping dead before you reach the front door," the baron said with a little chuckle.

Ben didn't want to make a scene, and steadied himself. He could feel Joshua and the baron walking behind him, and desperately wanted to know whether Joshua had received the invitation to Vanishing Street. The temptation to stop and ask was overwhelming, but he knew it would be silly. It was clear that the baron placed a good deal of emphasis on class, and Ben didn't exactly score well on those stakes, so he kept his mouth shut.

"Give my regards to the council," the baron said, as a butler moved to open the front door. To Ben's surprise, the baron turned once more to him, and gave him an approving nod.

"I watched your fight with my stone soldier," the baron said. "You performed admirably. It's been some time since I've had genuine intruders, and it was amusing to select a few of my playthings to come and greet you. Count yourself lucky that you piqued my curiosity, else I might have sent some of my more formidable pets, which would have left you in pieces long before you reached the cliff."

"Thank you," Ben said, managing to keep his voice respectful with some effort.

"Don't forget the date!" the baron said with a cheerful wave, as they left. "You won't get another one."

"I won't," Joshua said with a smile, patting his pocket.

Ben and Joshua followed the butler outside into the frosty night air. The butler had a torchlight, allowing the rather unpleasant view of the rock's edge in the distance.

"Please tell me we're not going down there," Ben said with a shiver.

"Absolutely not," Joshua said with feeling.

They followed the butler a little way, until he suddenly stopped, and pointed the torchlight on the ground below.

"Please stand inside the circle, masters," the butler instructed.

The circle was formed of stone slabs that were marginally different from the rest of the cliff's surface. Ben and Joshua tucked themselves into the centre. There was a sudden shudder and a jolt, almost throwing the two of them off balance. The butler remained unmoved and unconcerned as the circular platform started descending into the cliff, with slow, mechanical whirring noises. They emerged several minutes later from the door that had been barred to them without the ID card.

"You made it!"

Natalie's voice had regained some of its vigour and energy, though she and Charlie were still sitting against the cliff wall. She struggled to her feet and was about to give Ben a hug, but stopped the moment she saw his blood-stained top.

"I'm fine," Ben said, raising a hand. "Well, fine-ish. I just need a bed, and maybe some heavy painkillers."

"Well, it won't take us long to get home," Charlie said. He

pointed to a small chariot pulled by a couple of grey Pegasi that stood nearby. "We knew you'd succeeded the moment this carriage arrived," Charlie said.

"The chariot will take you back to the station," the butler said. He glanced at his watch. "If you leave promptly, you can catch the 12:07am back to Taecia."

"Thank you," Ben said.

The butler gave a bow, and then disappeared back through the door.

"So, did you get the invitation?" Charlie asked.

Joshua pulled out a lavish card with the baron's insignia and a clear date and time printed on it.

"A fortnight on Monday, 10:45am. Directions included. If we don't get there right on time, we lose our chance to get to Vanishing Street."

"Just over two weeks. We'll be there," Ben said.

The journey back to the Dragonway seemed to take just minutes compared to their arduous trek up to the castle, as the pegasi flew them effortlessly over the dark forest below. It wasn't long before the fort comprising the Dragonway station came into view, and they landed lightly in front of it.

Ben's ribs were aching like crazy, and he wanted nothing more than to get onto the dragon and rest, without having to worry about being killed or bitten or stabbed again.

His sixth sense flared seconds before he entered the Dragonway and stepped onto the platform. A flash of red diamonds and a terrifyingly familiar face made his stomach lurch. Ben barely had time to stop and stare.

"There he is!"

Standing on the platform was a thunderous-looking Draven and a delighted-looking Aaron, pointing at them like an excited child.

Ben and the others stood there, stunned, as Draven and Aaron approached them.

"You have been colluding with the baron without Institute authority," Draven announced. "You are all in serious trouble."

"Wait, Director—" Joshua began, but was cut off by a furious gaze.

"Ben Greenwood, you are to come with me. The prince wants to see you immediately. The rest of you, home. The council will see you in the morning."

— CHAPTER TWENTY-TWO —

A Tight Spot

Ben was too weary to argue. He followed Draven and a smiling Aaron onto the dragon, sitting in between the two to prevent any further mischief, according to Draven.

"We'll sort this out," Natalie said from behind. "Don't worry about it, Ben."

"No talking," Draven ordered. "You don't want to make things even worse on yourselves."

Despite the pain and the injustice roaring inside his head, Ben still found himself drifting off on the journey back to Taecia. Dreams of the prince, of being stabbed by the stone soldier and even old memories of his parents filled his head until, after what seemed like just minutes, the dragon started its slow ascent up to Taecia station.

Ben stumbled out of the train and almost fell onto the

platform.

"He can barely walk!" Natalie said. She had remained on the Dragonway with Charlie and Joshua.

"He'll be fine," Draven said, though there was a flicker of concern when he saw the red-stained bandage. "You should be more concerned about your own predicament."

Ben wasn't sure how he made it up the hill to the Institute, but he was certain Aaron played an unwitting part by fuelling his anger with constant chatter.

"I knew you were up to something," Aaron said, shaking his head and giving a soft chuckle. "I just couldn't work out what, and I have to admit, it was starting to distract me from the apprenticeship. After you kept slipping my colleagues, I realised I had to up my game. It cost me a fair bit of money, but the pixie spies I employed worked a charm. They followed you to Casteria. As soon as I realised where you'd gone, I realised the severity of the situation. It wasn't hard to enrol Draven. He's smart, and has long suspected you were up to something."

Confusion momentarily shone through Ben's anger. "What situation? What are you talking about?"

"Colluding with the baron, of course," Aaron said, as if it were the most obvious thing in the world. "I don't know what your intentions were, but dealing with the baron without Institute authorisation is tantamount to treason." Aaron chuckled again. "To think that I worried about you being a potential rival for the Spellsword Director. Now you'll be lucky if the Institute doesn't dismiss you."

Ben gave Aaron a withering look. "You're mad, you know that?"

"No, not mad," Aaron said, wagging his finger. His grey eyes looked almost eerily bright. "I'm just intelligent – and sometimes the boundary between the two can seem slim."

Their arrival at the Institute cut short their conversation. Ben estimated it to be somewhere around three in the morning, and yet the Institute looked almost as busy as usual, with members flying up and down the stairs, and talking as if it were three in the afternoon.

"I will take it from here," Draven said.

The deflated look on Aaron's face was almost amusing. "Are you sure, Director? Is there nothing I can do to help? I may have some useful information."

"No," Draven said. "You've done enough. Get some sleep."

Ben's smile at Joshua's disappointment lasted until he turned his attention to the grand staircase.

"I can't make it up there," Ben said. "I'm exhausted."

Ben expected the inevitable rebuff, but Draven looked at Ben's chest, and nodded. "We take the executive lift, just this once."

Ben never got to see much of the ground floor, except the atrium, and he would have shown more interest had he not been on the verge of collapse. Draven led him through a secure door, along a hallway, and into a large shaft that ran all the way up the building. A soft spray hit Ben from overhead as he entered.

"You've done this before, right?" Draven said. "The spray is a basic levitation spell."

It seemed an age ago when he first experienced the levitation at Hotel Jigona, but he remembered exactly what to do. Ben visualised being weightless, and his body started rising. It was far quicker than taking the stairs and, in less than a minute, they had floated to a door near the top of the building, upon which were the words *Executive Floor*.

Draven led them through into the rarely visited floor. Ben was now finding breathing difficult, and he barely noticed the expensively appointed décor, the plush red carpet or the gold trimmings on the wooden panels. He walked along in a daze, until Draven stopped by another door. This one said: *Throne Room*.

Draven grabbed the gold handle, and turned to Ben, his face even sterner than usual. "I'm only going to say this once: no funny business. The prince is under a great deal of pressure, and he wants answers. Do not mess around. Got it?"

"Answers to what?" Ben said, cringing as he spoke. He had a sudden desire to lie down. Anything to stop the throbbing.

Draven was either oblivious to or uncaring of Ben's agony, for he ignored Ben's pained face and opened the door with uncommon diffidence.

Ben followed Draven into the most lavish room he had ever seen, immediately reminding Ben of one of the royal palaces in London. There was so much gold, in the form of decorations and furniture, that Ben's eyes hurt. Expensive paintings lined the walls, and at the back was a large window that Ben imagined flooded the room with natural light during the day.

Despite the room's extravagance, it was the throne chair bang in the middle of the room and the man sitting on it that grabbed Ben's attention. The prince had his eyes closed, and looked to be sleeping, the five coloured diamonds floating serenely over his shoulder. He wore a weathered brown cloak and his hair looked a little ruffled, as if he had not long come back from some travelling.

"Ben Greenwood," Prince Robert said, opening his eyes.

Ben had forgotten just how peculiar the prince's eyes were, with their gold-flecked tint that seemed even more noticeable than normal.

"Your Highness," Draven said with a bow. "I have, as instructed, Ben Greenwood. The young boy, Aaron, was correct – I found him at Casteria, colluding with Baron Vongrath."

Prince Robert's calm demeanour disappeared the

moment he spotted the red bandage on Ben's waist.

"Draven, can you explain to me why Ben Greenwood looks as though he's bleeding to death and hasn't been treated?"

"I'm sorry, Your Highness," Draven said, his voice flustered. "I assumed getting Greenwood was the priority, and his medical situation could be handled presently."

"You thought wrong," the prince said, giving Draven a stern look. "Go and get Wren, now."

Ben had never heard anyone order Draven in such a manner, and he would have savoured the moment if he hadn't been ready to collapse.

Draven gave a stiff bow. "At once, Your Highness."

He gave Ben a murderous stare, before disappearing through the door. Ben could hear him muttering down the hallway.

The moment Draven left, Prince Robert stood up, and pulled a sofa over to the middle of the room, unconcerned about the marks it was leaving on the plush gold carpet.

"Here, Ben, lie down, before you fall over," the prince said. "I'm sorry about Draven."

"That's okay," Ben said. He sat down gingerly, careful to ease himself onto the couch; his ribs still hurt like the devil.

The prince sat back down on his chair, but he leant forwards, hands on his thighs, watching Ben carefully. There was something in those gold-flecked eyes that made Ben stir uncomfortably.

Of course. Elizabeth's Armour. It wasn't long ago that Ben had been convinced that the prince was searching for it. Ben remembered only too well Queen Elizabeth's warning about her descendants being drawn to the armour. Was Prince Robert feeling the pull?

"I know you are in great pain," Prince Robert said, breaking the silence. "However, there are some questions I would very much like to ask you while we are alone. Are you okay to talk?"

Ben was tempted to say no, which would have been the truth. Wren would be here in a moment, and he felt better around her. But then, what was to stop the prince sending Wren away so they could talk in private? And more significantly, Ben was curious. What did the prince want to talk about? Those gold-flecked eyes looked dangerous, like they could explode one way or the other. Ben decided to gamble, and nodded his assent.

The prince sat back. Now that he had Ben's agreement, he suddenly seemed unsure what to say. Ben waited, anticipation temporarily easing the pain.

"The pressure is immense," Prince Robert began. He said it in a very matter-of-fact way, and even managed a rueful smile, but Ben could sense the emotion behind those simple words.

"The Institute is the only thing lying between Suktar and

a war the like of which England has not seen in many decades," the prince said. "Only this time, we have no Winston Churchill to save us. I fear I may not be up to the job."

Ben waited, patiently. He knew the questions were coming.

"You are probably wondering why I am telling you this," the prince said.

"The thought crossed my mind," Ben admitted.

The prince took a moment to compose his words. "You may remember, I spent a lot of time looking for your parents, in the hope that they might provide some clue to thwarting Suktar. I have never revealed why I believed this was so."

Ben guessed what was coming, but hearing it from the prince made his stomach flutter.

"Queen Elizabeth left something, I believe, that might just prove vital in stopping Suktar," Prince Robert said. His eyes suddenly narrowed into golden slits. "For reasons I could never discover, she did not leave said artefact with her family line, but instead passed it on. I have reason to believe your family may have been one of the benefactors."

Ben had never worked harder to keep a straight face in his life, as the prince's keen golden stare cut into him, measuring him, looking for the subtlest sign of reaction.

Ben was struggling to think amongst the pain, but one thought shone through: *the prince must not get hold of*

Elizabeth's Armour, no matter the cost. Not now, not when we are so close.

"Have you asked my parents about this?" Ben asked, striving desperately to sound like he was ignorant to the prince's revelation.

"I have been unable to reach them," the prince said. "That is not their fault, of course. But with the dark elf invasion now imminent, I can no longer delay. I must act, which is where you come in."

"How?" Ben asked slowly.

The prince leaned forwards. "I believe the artefact, whatever it may be, passes through the family to the youngest member. That member is you, Ben Greenwood. I have watched you intently the last few months, but I have been careful never to get involved. But now, I can say with some conviction that you know exactly what I'm talking about. So, my question to you is – do you know where this artefact is?"

Ben was almost grateful that he didn't have to lie.

"I don't," Ben said.

It was immediately obvious that the prince didn't believe him, so Ben decided to carefully elaborate.

"You are right: my parents were given a responsibility to safeguard an artefact, and as the youngest member of the family that responsibility should have passed to me. But my parents didn't think I was ready. They never revealed the

Royal Institute of Magic to me. Perhaps they would have, but they were forced to go on the run, as you may remember."

The prince was looking at him very carefully. His expression seemed to darken, and Ben suddenly felt he was in a very precarious position. He took another gamble.

"Do you know why Queen Elizabeth would have decided against handing it down to her descendants for safeguarding?"

To Ben's relief, the question got the prince thinking. "I have thought much upon this, but read little. I can only assume it is dangerous, somehow. Occasionally, when I think about this artefact, I find myself feeling a little peculiar, and I wonder if this artefact somehow affects my mind."

Ben wanted to scream "yes" and somehow confirm the fact, but he had nothing to back it up, so instead, he gave a sage nod.

"That sounds like it might be possible."

"And yet..." The prince covered a hand over his forehead. He closed his eyes. When he re-opened them, there was an undisguised longing – or was it greed? – that chilled Ben to the bone. "I need that artefact," Prince Robert said. "Do you understand? I need it if we are to have any chance of thwarting Suktar. His power is simply too great."

For a moment, Ben thought the prince might get violent. Ben prepared to defend himself, though he wasn't sure he could even lift an arm, let alone summon a spell.

The door flew open as if it had been blasted outwards.

"Ben!" Wren said.

Ben had never seen Wren looking anything but serenely composed before, so her pale, shocked face looked almost alien. She dashed up to him, and bent down, immediately touching her hands on his chest.

"Ow!" Ben said, grimacing.

"Sorry, Ben."

Others had followed Wren in. A couple of Scholars, both with four white diamonds, were hovering behind her. Draven was there too, looking decidedly unhappy about proceedings.

"Do you want me to take him to the sick bay?" Wren said, looking up at the prince.

The prince's intensity had vanished the moment Wren entered. He shook himself, and waved a hand. "No, no. Do what you need to here."

The prince had barely finished speaking when Wren got to work, carefully unravelling the red bandage.

"I'm sorry, Ben," Wren said softly. "I will be as gentle as possible, but this may hurt a little."

By "a little", Ben quickly realised she meant a lot. Twenty minutes of agony followed, as Wren and her Scholars used a mixture of old and new treatments, combined with some of the most powerful healing spells, until, exhausted and ready to collapse, Ben had a new, clean bandage that showed no sign of getting soaked with blood.

"You need sleep," Wren said. "I don't want you going home. Use the sleeping quarters on the Diplomacy floor."

Draven, who had been watching the ordeal with a great deal of impatience, frowned. "What about his unauthorised visit to the baron's estate? I didn't travel all the way to Casteria with that idiot boy Aaron for nothing. Why would they go there in the first place? We need answers."

"There is nothing illegal about it," Wren said. "I will speak to Alex; he will smooth things over with the baron, though I doubt that will even be necessary."

"What?" Draven said, his voice rising. "Is that it? You are willing to let them get away with that? They are withholding something from us. I know it, and you know it too, Your Highness. We have talked about this relentlessly. It is time Ben Greenwood came clean."

Draven spoke with such intensity and belief that the prince wavered, and he turned back to Ben, giving him another searching look. Ben felt hounded, trapped on all sides. The Institute were perilously close to discovering the secret of Elizabeth's Legacy. But they weren't going to get it out of him. Ben met the prince's stare with as much sincerity as he could muster.

"There are many unanswered questions," the prince said finally. "However, right now, with the dark elf threat, we cannot afford to waste any more time, so it will have to be addressed later. In the meantime, Ben, I order you to sleep for at least ten hours. Is that understood?"

"Yes, Your Highness," Ben said, attempting unsuccessfully to hide his relief.

Wren smiled. Draven did not.

— CHAPTER TWENTY-THREE —

Grandma's Memories

How did you get us off the hook?" Charlie asked.

Ben, Charlie, Natalie and Joshua sat in the Diplomacy conference room on a brisk Sunday morning. They had come in early, expecting the worst, only to be told at the door by a senior member that there would be no disciplinary action, and to continue with their apprenticeship as normal. Ben had spent a good hour searching for Aaron to impart the good news, but he was nowhere to be found.

Ben retold them everything that had happened in the throne room, including, most important of all, the prince's revelation.

"So, he knows," Charlie said. "Or at least he knows some of it."

"Some," agreed Ben. "But only bits. For example, he

doesn't know that Elizabeth's Armour is five separate pieces, and is to be used by each Guardian. He thinks the armour is intended for himself, though he admits he can't understand why he didn't inherit it."

"You said he can feel the pull," Joshua said. "Maybe he realises that it's dangerous."

"Possibly," Ben said. "At least he managed to resist it."

"For now," Charlie said. "But what about tomorrow? What about next week? I bet as the pressure builds, the pull will get stronger, especially with Draven bugging him about it. Will he be able to hold out? And if not, will he come for you, Ben?"

"Not if he thinks I don't have it," Ben said. "Which I don't, by the way."

He was thankful Joshua didn't give him a nudge about the sword. Perhaps he felt that after everything Ben had been thrown, he deserved a little respite.

"So, where does that leave us?" Natalie asked. "We have just over two weeks until our date on Vanishing Street. Once we are there, how easy will it be to get into Lord Samuel's house and get the shield?"

"It won't be easy at all," Joshua said. "In fact, I have no idea what will be waiting for us."

"Can we research it?" Ben asked.

"I have tried," Joshua said. His face went just slightly red. "I would like to get Charlie's help, in case he can dig anything else up."

It was the perfect opportunity to have a dig at Joshua for claiming he didn't need assistance, but Ben resisted the urge. Charlie nodded enthusiastically.

"Natalie and I have a lead with the sword that we're going to follow up tomorrow morning. Let's meet up after that," Ben said.

It would be stretching things to say the four of them were starting to get on, but as they parted ways, Ben couldn't help noticing that Joshua's sniping seemed to be less frequent. But Ben wasn't naive – he knew that if the memory spell on Grandma produced nothing, their temporary peace would be shattered.

Ben spent the rest of the day trying to prepare Natalie for the memory spell. They spent hours in the Diplomacy Department, practising on magically formed creatures. They had chosen a level-four spell, as it had greater potential to dig deeper into the mind. But it was far harder to cast as well as being more dangerous, should anything go wrong. After two hours of solid work, Natalie slumped down, exhausted.

"I'm done," she announced. "God, I need a shower; I'm sweating like Charlie."

"You're doing great," Ben said. "You don't want to do one more round? I feel we should try it again with me attempting to distract you, as the spell wavered just a fraction the last time we tried that."

Natalie gave Ben an evil frown, but with great reluctance they put in another hour's work, before even Ben declared himself satisfied.

"You're going to nail it," Ben said with a smile. "I bet you could take my grandma all the way back to her birth without a hitch."

"Let's hope it doesn't come to that," Natalie said.

It felt peculiar, going to sleep that night, knowing that the challenge ahead wasn't his, but Natalie's. As he lay in bed, he kept running over the memory spell she had been practising, wondering if there was anything more they could have worked on or any further refinements that might have helped. He fell asleep satisfied that they'd not missed anything, but at the same time unable to shake off the concern that they may not have done enough.

*

Another cup of tea?" Ben asked.

Natalie smiled. "No, I'm fine, thanks. I've had enough caffeine to last the whole day, and it's only ten o'clock."

Ben busied himself in the kitchen and finished up the dishes from breakfast, while Natalie sat down, cup of tea in hand.

"I don't think your grandma knows I'm even here," Natalie said, glancing into the lounge.

"That's the idea," Ben said, scrubbing a dirty cup. "I purposefully had you come over at ten o'clock, as she often drifts off in front of the TV after the news. If we can catch her just before she dozes, that will make the spell that much more effective."

Ben finished up the dishes and dried his hands, before turning to Natalie with an encouraging smile.

"Are you ready? Is there anything you want to go over one last time?"

Ben knew he was being uncommonly pedantic, almost bordering on neurotic, but he didn't care. This was their only lead to the sword, and if it went wrong, they would be at a dead end. The thought was inconceivable, and he'd kick himself if it was for lack of preparation.

"I'm ready," Natalie said. "Shall we use the TV like we discussed?"

"Yeah, I think that would look cool."

Ben and Natalie headed into the lounge. He knew it hardly mattered, but he kept the noise to a minimum anyway. His grandma was locked onto the TV. Her eyes already looked heavy, and Ben knew it wouldn't be long before she dozed off. They had to get her before that happened. Ben nodded to Natalie, who slipped her spellshooter silently from her holster. She stood directly behind Grandma's chair, leaving her with just one shot – to the back of Grandma's head, which jutted above the chair's back.

Ben watched silently as Natalie begun a routine he had

witnessed dozens of times yesterday. She took three relaxing breaths, and then aimed the spellshooter, her finger resting lightly on the trigger. A large blue pellet started floating serenely down the orb. Ben watched in anticipation as the spell stopped, just for a moment, and then slipped into the barrel.

Natalie pulled the trigger.

A flash of light lit the room and a tiny speck of a spell hit, and entered Anne's head, illuminating her perm for a second. Anne's head immediately flopped back, resting on the top of the chair.

Ben grabbed the TV remote and quickly turned it off. Natalie sat herself down on the carpet, cross-legged, eyes shut, looking very much like she was performing yoga. Ben sat down silently next to her and turned his attention to the TV.

Nothing happened.

Ben felt a flicker of concern, until he saw a sudden flash of colour on the screen.

"Going back three years," Natalie said. Her voice was soft, but focused. "Nothing. Going back five years. Nothing. Going back ten years."

The TV flickered again, and Ben saw a flash of something and the picture came into focus. His grandma! She looked far younger, and was outside, tending the garden.

"Ten years, overshot," Natalie said. "Going back eight

years."

Another visual appeared on the TV, one more familiar to Ben, of Anne watching TV, but she also had a crossword puzzle on her lap.

"Getting closer, I can feel it," Natalie said, her voice rising a fraction with intensity.

The TV flickered and Ben's stomach gave an almighty leap. There, right on the TV, were his parents, playing with a young version of himself in their garden. Ben stared in astonishment, momentarily forgetting what their objective was. To his dismay, the visual lasted only seconds, before flickering again.

The scenes continued to change with increasing frequency. Ben was transfixed by each one, as Natalie continued to narrow down the time to more exact units. Occasionally Ben would flick his gaze towards Natalie to make sure she was okay. Her forehead was gleaming with sweat, but he was reassured by the intensity and focus of her expression.

"I think I have it," Natalie said with such exclamation that Ben jumped. He turned back to the TV so quickly his neck gave an almighty crack.

His parents were sitting in their lounge with his grandma, who was knitting. Ben himself was nowhere to be seen. There was an uncommonly serious expression on his parents' faces that made Ben frown. This was it, he realised.

Natalie had found it.

"We need to talk," Greg said.

Greg had a comforting arm on Jane's leg, but was staring intently at Anne.

"We are talking," Anne said. "Did you see that? Another gaffe by our PM. I'll try to contain my surprise."

Greg grabbed the remote and turned the TV off.

Anne's head whipped round in a look of confusion. "What the—? What just happened?"

"I turned the TV off, Anne," Greg said calmly.

"That was uncalled for," Anne replied angrily. "Turn it back on."

Greg retained his calm demeanour in the face of Anne's hostility. "Not until we are done talking."

"Okay, well, get on with it," Anne said impatiently, venting her frustration on her knitting; her hands moved furiously.

"Jane and I have some news," Greg said. "Some of it you will probably have difficulty believing. It relates to our employment."

Anne frowned. "You're not unemployed, are you? I had a feeling you might be, when I saw the pitiful car you recently downgraded to. Don't expect any handouts from me, Greg – my pension barely covers my expenses as it is, what with weekly bingo and the national lottery."

"We're not unemployed," Greg said. Jane was frowning

with disapproval at Anne, but Greg kept his patience. "But we have deceived you about the nature of our employment, for your safety, as you will soon understand."

"You're not going to tell me you work for MI5 are you?" Anne said with a sudden laugh. "You? MI5? That would be a joke."

"Not quite," Greg said. "But nor do we work for Greenpeace. In fact, we never have."

Anne stopped the knitting, and for the first time gave them her undivided attention. "I never trusted that place. So, where do you work?"

Greg exchanged a look with Jane, before giving a little shrug, and turning back to Anne. "There is no possible way to tell you this in a manner that you will believe me, so I will just come out with it. How is your history? Do you know who Queen Elizabeth I is?"

"Of course I do," Anne snapped. "I grew up in a time when they actually taught you history. Queen Elizabeth, the 'Virgin Queen'. Born 1533, died 1603." Anne gave a thin smile. "They made us recite the monarchy, word for word. Still remember most of it."

"That's handy," Greg said. "During that time, there was great expansion for the British Empire, with many wars around Europe, including the Spanish Armada. However, her most noticeable discovery was never recorded in history."

"What are you talking about?" Anne asked with typical abruptness.

Greg took a deep breath, and spoke softly, as if this might somehow help do the impossible and convince Anne of what he was about to say.

"Queen Elizabeth discovered certain islands, or kingdoms, that were different. These kingdoms didn't conform to the normal physical universe laws that ours do. In fact, they were entirely invisible to most normal people, which is why they went unseen for so long."

Anne frowned, her mouth half-opening. "I'm not following."

"Unseen Kingdoms," Greg said. "Islands populated by humans and non-humans alike: dwarves, elves, ogres and dozens of other magical creatures."

Anne stared at Greg as if he had just lost the plot. "You're joking, right?"

"He's not," Jane said with a firmness Greg had thus far avoided. "We work for an institute that governs these kingdoms and makes sure they stay hidden. We work for the Royal Institute of Magic."

Anne looked at Greg. Then she looked at Jane. Then she burst out laughing, throwing her head back with glee.

"That's got to be the most ridiculous thing I've ever heard. Do you think I'm stupid? You really expect me to believe that?"

"No," Greg said simply.

This sobered Anne a little, and some of her resentment swiftly returned. "Then why waste silly stories on me? I'm not a child."

"Excellent point," Greg said. "The answer is simple: we need to hide some information somewhere nobody would think to find it. After much debate, we decided that your mind would be the safest place. Nobody would think to look there, and your natural disbelief in everything will act as a remarkable defence. Couple that with a memory-locking spell, and I think the information I am about to tell you will be safe."

Anne shook her head. "I'm seriously considering calling emergency services. You've both clearly gone nuts."

"Possible," Greg said with a shrug.

He pulled out a spellshooter, previously hidden by an invisibility spell, from his waist, and pointed it at Anne.

Anne went almost cross-eyed looking at the weapon. "What on earth is that? You're not going to—"

"Afraid so," Greg said.

He fired.

The TV went black.

"What just happened?" Ben said, turning to Natalie. To his surprise, and dismay, he found her frowning and sweating profusely, though she still maintained her yoga position. Anne, too, was sweating, and Ben became aware that she was moaning softly to herself.

"Memory-locking spell," Natalie said, her voice strained. "It has blocked your grandma from accessing whatever Greg was about to say."

"Can you unlock it?" Ben asked.

Natalie grunted in reply. "Trying to."

Ben turned to the TV, willing it to flicker back to life. Everything they had just seen was worthless unless they could access this last piece of memory. Ben wanted to say something, to urge Natalie on, but any noise would just distract her. The chance for Natalie to work in peace was swiftly ruined by his grandma, who started groaning louder and shifting her head left and right.

Ben checked his watch. How long had they been in the memory spell? Five minutes? Ten? The theoretical maximum was no longer than twelve minutes, before irreparable damage could be incurred.

Ben cursed inwardly, and felt his own spellshooter. He had the power to break the spell, but he wouldn't do it until the last minute, to give Natalie every chance of finding what they needed. His grandma cried out loud, and Ben grimaced. *Come on, Natalie.* He checked his watch again. He would give it ninety seconds, no more, and then he would have to end it.

Natalie's hands suddenly bunched into balls, and she bit her lip.

Eighty seconds.

Ben watched helplessly. His grandma cried out and threw her head forwards.

Seventy seconds.

Ben fingered his spellshooter. Should he end it now?

Sixty seconds.

Ben focused on the orb, and moved the cancelling spell forwards, ready to launch.

Fifty seconds.

"Twenty-three—"

The TV! Ben whipped his head round. It was still black, but he could hear a faint audio coming from the speakers.

"Twenty-three – seventy-one."

Was that his dad's voice? It sounded like it, but he couldn't be sure.

Forty seconds.

" Twenty-three – seventy-one. Find me last. I am not hidden."

Ben frowned. What the hell did that mean?

Thirty seconds.

"Twenty-three – seventy-one. Find me last. I am not hidden."

That was it, Ben realised. There was nothing else coming, and no pictures at all. His grandma let out an almighty groan, and Natalie shuddered.

Ben lifted his spellshooter, and fired.

— CHAPTER TWENTY-FOUR —

Ominous Signs

Ben sat on the floor, leaning against the chair. He was exhausted, even though he'd not been directly involved. Anne was now safely tucked away in bed, and Natalie lay on the couch, staring at the ceiling.

"Damn it," Ben said for the tenth time in the last half-hour.

"Would you stop saying that?" Natalie said. "We found what we needed."

"Did we?" Ben kicked a leg in frustration. "We got a couple of numbers, and a riddle that makes no sense: *Find me last. I am not hidden.*"

"Well, your parents hid that memory for a reason, so it must be important. We just need to work out its significance."

Ben had thought of little else, but he kept drawing a blank. The numbers could mean anything, and the riddle had no reference. It felt like a lost cause, and the feeling made Ben want to slam his fists against the carpet. His grandma had been his last chance to find the sword, and now that had led to another dead end. Where did that leave him? The thought that all the Guardians bar him would have their pieces of armour made him cringe.

His one faint hope was Charlie. If anyone could solve riddles, it was him.

They met up at the Institute later that day, and found Joshua and Charlie busy in the library, heads buried in books.

"How'd it go?" Charlie asked, dragging his eyes away from the book.

Ben told them everything that had occurred, careful not to miss anything out, no matter how small it seemed; sometimes Charlie picked up clues from the most insignificant facts. Ben wasn't surprised when Charlie's face lit up when he heard about the riddle; even Joshua showed interest, momentarily forgetting his own mission with the sword.

"Very interesting," Charlie mused, tapping his cheeks. "The question is – did you glean everything from the memory or did you miss something?"

"Well, we got no pictures," Natalie said, biting her lip.

"Do you think that mattered?"

"Possibly. If you were supposed to see something and didn't, we may be missing a piece of the puzzle, which will make it that much harder." Charlie seemed pleased by the thought. "But, honestly, the numbers and riddle seem complete by themselves. We just need to link them up to something."

"What, though?" Ben asked. "The numbers could relate to anything."

"That's what we have to find out."

Natalie twirled a strand of hair around her finger. "What about the riddle?"

"No clue," Charlie said with a cheerful smile. "But we can work on that. I'm sure we can come up with some ideas, but it might take a bit of patience."

"Not my strong suit," Ben admitted, flicking an idle page on the book. "Especially given the whole dark elf attack thing."

Joshua gave Ben the sort of frown he'd not seen in a while. "You will just have to work it out. Charlie and I have our hands full already, trying to figure out what awaits us at Lord Samuel's house."

To Ben's surprise, Charlie nodded in agreement. "There are going to be some nasty surprises there, and unless we're prepared, we haven't got a chance."

Ben couldn't argue with the reasoning, but he still felt a

little hurt that Charlie had sided with Joshua.

"Don't worry about Charlie," Natalie said, giving Ben a sympathetic smile as the two of them left the library. "You know how he is when he's knee deep in research. I'm sure he'll help us when he's got a minute."

"I'm fine," Ben said, surprised Natalie had read his thoughts so well. "So, I guess it's me and you for now."

"It's not just us," Natalie said. "There's also Dagmar, Abigail and even Krobeg, if we need them. Between us we'll find something."

Ben nodded, throwing away the doubts that had been nagging him. "Well, we've got two weeks until our date on Vanishing Street, so we need to have the sword before then."

*

The next few days were some of the hardest and most frustrating of Ben's Institute life. With no leads, and no Charlie to help, searching for the sword was even harder than the Diplomacy practical he was stuck on, involving a seriously dysfunctional sprite family. For three days he'd visited their house and he'd got nowhere.

"Enough!" Ben shouted.

The family of six looked at him with a mixture of shock and anger. Raising his voice was one of the many things not to do when dealing with sprites, but Ben didn't care.

"I'm sick of this," Ben said. "You know what the Institute wants. As crystal sprites, you are one of the few of your kind that has the ability to venture into dark elf land without being detected. Now, are you interested in helping or not?"

"We're interested, but not for the pathetic terms you offer, apprentice," the largest sprite, Thell, said. "The danger alone should be worth twice what you offer."

Ben ground his teeth. "I've told you already, the Institute's resources are stretched to the limit, and that includes their coffers. I can offer you thirty percent more, but you will have to take it on credit, providing we win the war."

"Thirty percent?" Thell said, balling his tiny hands theatrically. "That's an insult. Our very lives will be at risk!"

"Thirty percent," Ben repeated with a shrug. "Take it or leave it."

"Leave it!" Thell cried.

Ben knew he should care – the crystal sprites were a crucial part of the Institute's spy network, and Thell was right – it was a dangerous mission; many had already fallen to the enemy – but he was struggling to really care about anything except finding Elizabeth's Sword. It was now three days since they had searched Grandma's memory, and they had got nowhere.

"Thirty-five percent and you have a deal."

It was the soft, calculating voice of Tressa, Thell's wife, who was eyeing Ben with a good deal more intelligence than her husband.

"Done," Ben said emphatically. He extended his hand

and interlocked it with Tressa's to seal the deal. "Report to the Institute when you are ready. I will have a Warden waiting at the door for you."

Ben left the sprites' house feeling a little better. At least he'd done something worthwhile today, even if it had nothing to do with Elizabeth's Armour. But his good mood didn't last, as the rest of the week passed without any development on the sword, with Natalie having no luck either. He even tried Dagmar, but though she had an opinion, none of it was particularly helpful.

"You know your parents better than me," Dagmar said. "Where do you think they would hide it?"

"Somewhere nobody would think to look," Ben said glumly. "That's the problem."

"Well, that's where I suggest you start."

He knew he'd searched his grandma's house a hundred times, but Ben couldn't shake off the idea that somehow his parents had hidden it there. And so, on Thursday, he, Natalie and Abigail left the Institute after lunch, and headed to his home.

"Do you have any new ideas where it might be or are we going to look in the same places?" Abigail asked in an innocent voice that was devoid of accusation.

"Same places," Ben said. "But I'm thinking we should look at them differently."

"What do you mean?" Natalie asked.

221

They left the Croydon station and started the walk through town. It was grey and there was a trickle of rain that England was famous for, though Ben barely noticed it.

"There are lots of ways to hide the sword, if you use magic," Ben said. "For example, what if they are using time, not space, to hide it?"

"You mean, hiding it in a different time?" Abigail said. She smiled. "That would be neat."

"Neat, but not easy to find. How do you find something that's always in the past?" Natalie said.

"No idea," Ben said with a shrug. "I'm just guessing here, but, knowing my parents, they've thought of something clever but so simple nobody would ever think of it."

"Well, why don't we split up this time," Natalie said. "I'll check the house today; you checked it yesterday."

Ben was nodding in agreement when he spotted the strange object on the pavement ahead of them. "What on earth is that?"

The street was busy, with kids and adults making their way home from school and work, yet nobody saw the purple pod sitting right in the middle of the pavement. It must have been at least six feet tall, and was covered with peculiar writing etched in black. Ben recognised the writing immediately and his blood froze.

It was the dark elf tongue.

"Don't touch it, Ben!" Natalie warned.

But Ben's hand was already reaching out, before realising it might not be a good idea. The pod felt warm, almost alive. It was certainly hollow. There was a soft pulsing that came from within, making the pod blink every few seconds.

"Are you okay?" Natalie asked.

"Yeah. It feels like it's alive."

"Maybe it is," Abigail said. She started looking around at the people passing by. "Why is nobody else looking at it? See that man there? He just swerved right round it without realising what he was doing."

"It must be protected by a glamour spell," Natalie said. "It must be a weak one, only strong enough to work on people oblivious to the Unseen Kingdoms."

Ben squinted his eyes. "The question is – what's inside?"

"And when is it going to come out?" Abigail asked.

The three of them exchanged looks of increasing alarm.

Suddenly, Elizabeth's Sword didn't seem like the most pressing issue.

"We need to tell the Institute," Ben said.

"You think they don't know?"

"I'm not sure, but if they don't, we need to tell them."

Neither Natalie nor Abigail argued the point, and they immediately turned round.

Ben spotted three more pods. Two across the street and a big one that must have been at least ten feet high dead ahead.

"That wasn't there a minute ago!" Abigail said, stating the obvious.

"No, it wasn't," Ben said, his voice tight. "Come on, we need to hurry."

They passed a further six pods on their way back to the Dragonway. As soon as they stepped into the station, it became obvious that the pods were already known about. The members were talking about nothing else, and there was a worrying anxiety on their faces.

"At least they're aware of it," Natalie said. "Do you still want to go back to the Institute?"

"Yes," Ben said. "I want to find out what's going on. The constant chatter here isn't exactly reliable. I want to speak to Dagmar."

As they took the Dragonway back to the Institute, Ben couldn't stop thinking about the pods. They looked alien, and yet throbbed with life and magic. The thought that they were accumulating all over the place, with the population completely ignorant, sent a shiver down his spine.

Ben headed straight for Dagmar's office upon arrival, and had to exercise considerable restraint in the vigour of his knocking.

"She's not there," Abigail said after several unanswered knocks. "If she was, she'd answer. She always does."

"She's probably in a meeting," Natalie said. "Especially if

the pod thing just started happening."

He tried once more, and then decided on the next best thing: the library. He headed downstairs, but came to a shuddering halt the moment he passed through the library doors.

Ben had never seen it this busy before. Institute members, mainly Scholars, dashed about, grabbing books, and talking with rare animation, obliterating the usual quiet, peaceful aura. Ben searched for Joshua and Charlie and eventually found them shunted to the end of a table at the far side of the main reading hall. Both were staring with complete bewilderment at the Scholars.

"Charlie!" Ben said, relishing the chance to shout and not get punished inside the library.

Charlie turned, startled. "What's going on? Ten minutes ago we were reading in peace, and then this happened." Charlie waved at the number of Institute members who had stormed in.

"Pods," Ben said breathlessly. And he proceeded to recount exactly what they had seen on the streets of Croydon.

Charlie and, more particularly, Joshua listened with increasing worry as Ben finished the story.

"So that's why they're all here," Joshua said. He turned to Charlie, but found he had scampered off into the shelves. He returned a few minutes later, with a couple of tattered books.

"Unsurprisingly, nearly all the books on dark elf war tactics have been raided. But I hid these two books a while ago because I wanted to come back to them later."

Charlie sat down, and opened a book that looked as though it had been used as a play thing by a dog.

"The Institute already knows a lot about dark elf pods, of course," Charlie said, not looking up. "They have used them several times before in battles, though not as much in the Unseen Kingdoms, because people spot them, and chop them down before they can mature. But in the Seen world, they go unnoticed."

"I know I don't know as much as everyone else, but I'm confused," Abigail said.

Ben gave her a reassuring look. "You're not the only one. What are you talking about, Charlie? How do pods mature? What's inside them?"

"Front line dark elf troops, known as Bloodbringers. They are maniacs, whose only real purpose is to cause mayhem. The bigger pods you may have seen will contain their steeds."

"But how did they get there?" Ben asked.

Charlie shrugged. "Magic, of course. Nobody really knows. But if you can open the pods before they are ready, you can sometimes stop the dark elf from ever materialising. Sort of like a premature birth, I guess."

Natalie glanced around at the Scholars who were

everywhere. "So what are they doing here now?"

"Trying to work out how to open the pods," Joshua said. "Each pod has a certain pattern, and can only be opened by a very specific magic source."

"That's right," Charlie said, pointing at a paragraph he was staring at. "It says here that if you try to break the pod by force, it will explode. You have to hit it with exactly the right type of magic. I bet the Scholars are scrambling to find how to 'read' each pod. They can only do that by looking at historical records, to see what worked the last time this happened."

Ben ran a hand through his hair. It was finally starting to make sense.

"So how long until these pods mature? How long do we have?"

Charlie looked up, his face grave. "Not long. Days."

Ben's legs felt strangely weak, and he slumped onto a chair.

"Days? So the dark elves could potentially launch their attack in days?"

"According to past records, yes," Charlie said.

Ben felt sick. No wonder the Scholars were running around like crazy people. "We still have ten days until we can get to Vanishing Street and find the shield. Let's hope war doesn't break out before then."

— CHAPTER TWENTY-FIVE —

Elizabeth's Museum

Ten days. Ten days to find the last two pieces of armour and hope the dark elves didn't declare war.

If Ben thought the Royal Institute of Magic was busy before, that was nothing compared to now. Members had been called in from every corner of the Unseen Kingdoms, as well as dozens of royal families, all with the aim of stopping the dark elf attack.

The severity of the situation was summed up the very day after the discovery of the pods, during morning muster. Dagmar breezed in, an unmoving rock amongst the storm, and rattled off their names in double-quick time.

"I have just one announcement, but it's an important one," Dagmar said, addressing them all. "The apprenticeship has been temporarily suspended for the third grade and up."

There was a shocked gasp, which Dagmar silenced with a subtle movement of her hand.

"First and second grades will continue as normal. The rest will report to the department you have been assigned to. As soon as the dark elf threat has been dealt with, your apprenticeship will resume."

The way Dagmar spoke made it sound as though the dark elf situation was a minor inconvenience the Institute would brush off in a few days' time. Though completely misleading, Ben could understand the need not to alarm the younger apprentices. He almost felt a little better himself the way she said it.

Unsurprisingly, Ben had been assigned to the Spellsword Department, Charlie to the Scholars, and Natalie, Diplomacy. As the Wardens had taken Joshua, the four of them had little time together.

Every day that Ben went home, he would stare at the pods with growing frustration. There were now at least two dozen between the Dragonway station in Croydon and his grandma's house. He often saw Institute members inspecting some of them, and a few had been successfully destroyed, but there were still plenty around.

Ten days became nine. Nine became eight. Ben spent every available second continuing his search for the sword, and working on deciphering the message hidden in his grandma's mind, but he made little progress.

With just a week to go until their date on Vanishing Street, Ben found that he had a rare morning free from the constant demands of the Spellswords. He went to look for Charlie, to see if they could do any more brainstorming for the sword, and found him heading out of the Institute.

"I need to get some documents from Elizabeth's museum," Charlie said. "Layla thinks there are some old records of the original war with Suktar that might give us some more information on the pods."

"I'll come with," Ben said. "I've got nothing better to do, and it will be nice to get out. We can walk and talk."

Elizabeth's museum was right in the heart of central Taecia. Ben had never been inside, though he had passed it several times. It was one of the first buildings the Institute had built upon Elizabeth's death, and stored many of her artefacts and treasures from her early conquests into the Unseen Kingdoms.

The fact that the dark elves were intent on invading England made Taecia more of a safe haven, and that was reflected by how busy the place had become. The wide roads were packed with traffic, and Ben and Charlie were constantly having to dodge old cars and citizens of every race. Taecia had always been known as the multicultural capital of the Unseen Kingdoms, and now it was even more so.

"Have you made any progress on the sword?" Charlie

asked. "Either with the riddle or the numbers?"

"No," Ben said. "In fact, it's doing my head in. I keep going round in circles. Have you had any time to think about it?"

"I've barely had time to breathe with the Scholars' constant demands. And I'm still trying to research what's inside Lord Samuel's house, remember? That's proving more difficult than expected."

Ben wished, not for the first time, that Charlie hadn't committed himself to researching Lord Samuel's house. He felt lost without him.

"I haven't a clue about the riddle," Ben admitted. "To be honest, it's the numbers I've been more focused on. Twenty-three, seventy-one. I thought maybe they could be a pass code to a safe box in a bank. I've spent hours hitting up all the banks, but so far I've not got anywhere."

"That's a start," Charlie said, as he just about avoided running into a couple of young elf children. "You need to be methodical about it, though. The library has a good reference book of all the banks and safe houses in Taecia. When we get back to the Institute, let's check it against the banks you've already tried, and make a list of those that you have left to visit."

They spent the rest of the walk brainstorming other possible answers to the pass code, until they reached Elizabeth's museum. It didn't have the grandeur or size of some of the London museums, but it was still a sight to behold, with turrets and towers, built with impressive stone craftsmanship. There were two large doors, both ajar, which let a steady stream of people in and out.

Ben had always wanted to visit the museum and, with time to kill, he had intended to join Charlie. But during their walk, they had come up with several banks Ben had yet to visit, and he thought it a better use of his time to continue his search.

Ben turned to go, when he spotted a flash of something on the museum door that caught his eye. It wasn't immediately obvious what attracted him, and he stepped up to the door to inspect it further. It was a huge thing, befitting a museum or a small palace. Like most buildings in Taecia, the building was numbered; in this case there was a small panel on the door, on which were four iron-cast numbers: one seven three two.

One seven three two.

Ben frowned. He frowned some more. Then he gasped.

"What is it?" Charlie said, spotting Ben staring with an open mouth at the door. "One seven three two," Charlie said, inspecting the number on the door. His eyes lit up. "That's it! Twenty-three seventy-one backwards."

Ben's head was spinning, but he tried to stem his excitement. "Is it? Or is it just a coincidence?"

Charlie stepped back to get a better look at the museum.

"It could be a coincidence, but think about where we are. We're at *Elizabeth's museum*."

That is exactly what Ben had been thinking: Elizabeth's museum, where some of her oldest treasures, diaries and discoveries were housed. Could it really be that simple? Could his parents have hidden the sword in Elizabeth's own museum?

"There's one way to find out," Ben said.

Ben hadn't been to many museums, but this one seemed very similar to the few he had visited. There were endless hallways lined with glass cabinets that housed everything from ancient documents and maps to old coins and larger treasures. Ben noticed a lot of nautical equipment, including parts of old ships, oars, even seemingly worthless pieces of rotting wood. Linking the hallways were vast rooms, with yet more treasures, and many had paintings of Elizabeth herself. What interested Ben most, though, was the early Royal Institute of Magic stuff. There were old-fashioned spellshooters with orbs that could house only a handful of spells, enchanted items and jewellery given to the queen from powerful members of the Unseen Kingdoms, and much more.

"Where do we go?" Charlie said. Now that they were on the trail of the sword, his own task was temporarily forgotten. "Surely your parents wouldn't have stored Elizabeth's Sword in plain sight?"

"I'm not so sure," Ben said. "We should expect the unexpected. Let's work our way to the armoury section."

The museum was well signposted and it didn't take them long to find the armoury section, which occupied most of the second floor. Rows of armour, weapons and shields from the seventeenth century covered the walls and central display units. It was busier here, with much of the younger generation clamouring over the weaponry.

Ben walked slowly, inspecting every sword closely. Though the museum was named after Elizabeth, it was clearly about the time period, and not just the queen. They were methodical, taking in every hallway and room. Ben wasn't exactly sure how he would spot the sword, but so far Elizabeth's Armour all looked relatively similar, and he was hoping the sword would be the same.

The adrenaline that had first fuelled Ben when they entered started to wear off a little after half an hour of searching the second floor. There were many fine weapons, but nothing came close to striking Ben as Elizabeth's Sword.

"It was a long shot," Charlie said. "Though I have to admit, the fact that the numbers matched the door did excite me."

"And that it's Elizabeth's museum," Ben said, clenching his fists in frustration. "Have we been over there?"

"Yeah."

"What about there?"

"Twice. Remember, we saw that giant ogling over that crossbow?"

Ben was almost ready to concede defeat, when he saw it. The room was small and easy to miss, but not for lack of interest. There was a queue running outside into the hallway. But it was the sign atop the doorway that set his heart racing.

Queen Elizabeth's Personal Possessions.

"We've not been in there," Charlie said.

Ben and Charlie joined the queue. It moved slowly, and they eased forwards at a painfully slow rate, which only heightened their anticipation. Ben had run into so many dead ends he tried not to get his hopes up. After all, what were the chances that his parents would leave the sword here? It was clever, but surely far too obvious?

It took fifteen minutes before they found themselves under the doorway, and moving into a small square room.

"One at a time, no pushing," a guard said.

The back of the room was roped off, and people were huddled behind the rope, making it impossible to see anything. Ben spent several more minutes waiting for someone to leave, before he could replace them, and get a proper view.

What he saw took his breath away.

The queen's original chair that she used in the Institute's throne room dominated the small space. There were several tables, with her possessions from the days she ruled the

Institute. Everything from her own spellshooter to old unused spells she had taken to battle during the first war with Suktar. There were clothes and jewellery from some of the most powerful Unseen Kingdom families, sent as gifts to appease the British Empire and hopefully stop the Queen's aggressive conquering campaign in her early years. Meticulous notes were made for each item, right down to the scrap of wood that came from the ship she had first discovered the Unseen Kingdoms in. There was an almost reverential atmosphere in the room, as if Elizabeth herself was watching over it.

But there was no sword. Indeed, there was no armour at all.

Ben tried to not feel too disappointed. He had known it was a long shot. Instead, he re-examined every item and its corresponding note, in the hope that he might learn something.

Ben almost missed the item resting against the throne chair.

It was a scabbard for a sword. Ben couldn't believe he hadn't spotted it before. Despite its age, the scabbard gleamed a polished silver and looked every bit as elegant as the throne chair it rested upon.

Ben's heart almost jumped out of his mouth.

It was undeniably the scabbard for her sword. Elizabeth's Sword.

"What is it?" Charlie asked irritably. Ben was attempting to tap his shoulder while still looking at the scabbard, and ended up jabbing him in the cheek.

"Look," Ben said, redirecting his finger towards the scabbard.

Charlie blinked. "That's funny, I didn't even notice it. You don't think—?"

"That's the scabbard for her sword," Ben said softly. "The design, the elegance and the craftsmanship are the same as the other pieces."

They both stared at the scabbard silently. Ben couldn't take his eyes away from it.

"So, now what?" Charlie asked. "It's the sword we're after, not the scabbard."

"I know," Ben said. "But the two belong together."

Ben felt a sudden urge to jump over the rope, and grab the scabbard. In a way he couldn't describe, the sword felt incomplete without the scabbard.

"No," Charlie said sternly, seeming to read Ben's mind. "It's too risky. You can't just go into a museum and take something; people will notice, especially a museum like this one."

But the more Ben thought about it, the more certain he became that somehow the scabbard was the clue they needed.

The riddle came to him almost unbidden.

"Find me last. I am not hidden," Ben said softly.

Charlie's expression softened, replaced by a sense of curiosity, and he rubbed his cheeks. "I had forgotten about the riddle."

The more Ben thought about it, the more excited he became, until it felt like his entire body was buzzing. He turned to Charlie, and found his friend similarly animated.

"I think you might have something," Charlie said softly. "Maybe the sword will only reveal itself when we have all the other pieces."

"And somehow we need the scabbard for the sword to appear," Ben said. "Which is why my dad's numbers in the memory led us here."

"I have to admit, it's possible," Charlie said with surprising reluctance.

Ben wanted to leap in the air and high-five something, but he was put off by Charlie's pessimism. "What's the problem? We just made a major breakthrough."

"The problem, Ben," Charlie said, whispering, "is that now we have to steal that damn scabbard."

— CHAPTER TWENTY-SIX —

Night-Time Break-in

So, tell me about the museum's security," Ben said, sipping a cup of tea.

Ben, Charlie, Natalie and Joshua had escaped to Fuddleswell tea room to talk. The Institute was so busy the Diplomacy conference room was seldom free, and Ben was sick of spending so much time there. Plus, the tea room had the added benefit of serving up some of the finest desserts in Taecia. Ben had become so good at casting silencer spells, the table they sat on was almost as secure as the Institute.

"The Old Guard," Charlie said. "You might have seen a few when we were there. They wear a blue uniform with a diagonal gold stripe across their chest and gold lapels on their shoulders. They were Elizabeth's personal guards and were picked for their loyalty and intelligence by the queen

239

herself."

"What do they do now?" Natalie asked. "Queen Elizabeth has been dead five hundred years, after all."

"They are responsible for guarding her property. She has many different residences throughout the Unseen Kingdoms. And there is the museum, of course."

"So we need to work out how to get past them in order to steal the scabbard," Ben said, taking another sip of tea.

"Not just them," Charlie said, "but also the museum's magical defences. Alarms, spells, that sort of thing. It's not going to be easy."

"How will you get inside?" Joshua said. He had initially refused tea and cake, but had changed his mind at the last minute and was now onto his second slice of carrot cake. "If I remember rightly, the doors are pretty solid. I've heard they are also resistant to magic."

Ben waved a sticky bun. "Don't worry about the doors; I've got a plan."

Charlie put a hand over his eyes. "I had hoped never to hear those words uttered from your mouth again."

"You don't mean that," Ben said. He rapped the table, and gave them all a smile; he had been smiling a lot since they had discovered the scabbard. "So, who wants the honour of coming with me to pick up the scabbard?"

"I will," Natalie said immediately. Charlie somewhat reluctantly raised his hand.

"I can, if you need me," Joshua said. Ben was surprised and pleased to hear the sincerity in his voice. "However, I'm supposed to be helping the Wardens with border patrol, so I'd have to make some excuse to get out of that."

"No, don't do that," Ben said. "The last thing we want is to draw attention to ourselves. Charlie and Natalie will be fine."

"So, when do we go?" Charlie asked. "It should be done at night, when at least we don't have to deal with the crowds."

"I need a day to put my plan into action," Ben said. "So let's plan for tomorrow night. In the meantime, let's get everything we need for the break-in. We're going to need some spells, for starters."

They spent the next hour devouring cups of tea and planning exactly what they would need and how to get in and out. Eventually, they headed back to the Institute and returned to their respective departments. Ben, however, had other plans. He took the grand staircase all the way up to the roof. The cold air hit him as he emerged amongst the paddocks. It was windy, and the smell was unusually strong, owing to the fact that there were far more steeds about than usual. There were dozens of apprentices managing the animals, cleaning them, feeding them, and occasionally preparing them for flight.

Ben walked along the path that ran next to the arched

roof, his eyes searching for one particular apprentice. It didn't take him long to spot his ginger hair, and his manic laugh could be heard even over the animal noises.

Simon was busy attempting to feed a griffin that was clearly not hungry.

"Take the food, you silly animal!" Simon said, trying to get a spoonful of something into the griffin's mouth.

"Simon!" Ben shouted, raising a hand in greeting.

Simon turned, gave a wave, and immediately dumped the spoon on the floor with obvious relief. "Ben! Please tell me you're here to relieve me. These animals are driving me crazy. My talents are being wasted. I should be with you, in the Spellsword Department, honing my skills."

Simon made a few sword-fighting motions to emphasise his point.

"Afraid not," Ben said, giving Simon a consolatory slap on the shoulder. "However, I do need your help with something." He lowered his voice a fraction. "I need to get in somewhere."

Simon's demeanour changed immediately. He grinned, and rubbed his hands together. "You've come to the right guy. That's what I do best. Did I tell you that me and Anthony managed to break into *Gimble's Sweet Store* last week? That place makes even the dwarven banks' security look pathetic."

"Impressive," Ben said. "My particular problem is getting

through some magic-resistant doors," Ben said.

This seemed to delight Simon further. "A tricky customer, eh? What are you trying to break into?"

"Can't tell you that," Ben said smoothly. "Can you help?"

"Of course," Simon said. His eyes narrowed. "For the right price."

"I'm on a budget," Ben said. "Two hundred and fifty quid."

"Oh, I don't want money," Simon said. "I've got enough of that with my thriving businesses. No, I want you to replace me here."

"How long for?" Ben asked.

"Ten hours."

"Seven."

"Eight and a half," Simon said stubbornly.

Ben glanced up at the griffins, and finally nodded. "Done. What have you got for me?"

"I have a few ideas," Simon said. "I need to speak to one of my contacts. I know a gnome who specialises in getting round magical defences."

They talked possibilities until Simon was caught slacking and ordered back to work. They agreed to meet again tomorrow morning to make the transaction.

Ben spent the rest of the day working in the Spellsword Department, but left as early as possible with Charlie and Natalie later that evening. They headed back to Elizabeth's museum to get a better look at the outside and also become more familiar with the layout inside. Ben spotted several members of the Old Guard, with their blue and gold uniform. Given the size of the museum, there weren't that many of them, but they were strategically placed at all the main exit points, and it was clear they knew the place inside out.

"Do you think they'll all be here when we come?" Natalie asked.

"They'll probably have a night shift," Ben said. "But I don't think it will consist of that many. We may have to knock a few of them out."

On the way home they talked about the best way to get in and out, until Ben felt pretty confident that they had some sort of plan. They just needed Simon to come good tomorrow and they might have a chance of pulling it off.

*

The following morning, Ben went straight up to the roof after muster, searching for Simon. Despite the fact that it was barely nine o'clock, the paddocks were already busy. Ben spotted half a dozen Wardens mounting pegasi and flying off on some mission.

"Would you stop doing that, please!"

Simon's voice was hard to miss, and Ben quickly followed it to the panther's paddock. Ben had always been fascinated by the black cats, though the Unseen variety was somewhat different to those that Ben had seen at the zoos at home. They were larger, and had the ability to disappear completely at night.

The panther Simon was tending to kept trying to lick Simon's face. The moment he spotted Ben, Simon leapt out of the paddock in double-quick time, heedless of the supervisors watching.

"I should have got the full ten hours from you," Simon said, trying to wipe the saliva from his face.

"Did you find me something?" Ben asked.

Simon took out a small, octagonal-shaped piece of metal, no bigger than a tennis ball, and handed it to Ben.

"Space displacement," Simon said. His voice dropped and he looked around to make sure they weren't being overheard, before continuing. "Experimental, cutting edge stuff the gnomes have been working on."

"What does it do?"

"It's called a portaler. It's basically like a really short portal," Simon said. "But it's unique as it can theoretically pass through anything, including your magical doors."

"Perfect," Ben said, smiling and pocketing the item.

"There is only one drawback," Simon said, sounding unconcerned. "It has never been successfully tested on humans, only gnomes."

"What?" Ben said a little too loudly.

"Calm down," Simon said. "They said there was no reason it shouldn't work. Gnomes and humans are quite genetically similar, apparently."

"Wonderful," Ben said, running a hand through his hair. He gave Simon an angry look. "If this doesn't work, I'm not wasting a second cleaning your animals."

"It'll be fine," Simon said with one of his insolent grins. "Trust me."

Ben, however, trusted Simon as far as he could throw him. The problem was, they couldn't try out the portaler on the museum's doors during the day, as it was too busy. They would just have to hope that it worked when they tried it that night.

"Typical Simon," Charlie muttered, as they sat down for dinner that evening. "If it doesn't work, we're screwed."

"Let's not think about that," Natalie said. "Have we got everything we need?"

"I think so," Charlie said. He pulled out a piece of paper on which was a rough floorplan. "I found this in the library – it's a full layout of the museum."

"Good," Ben said. "Did you get the spells, Natalie?"

"Yeah, it wasn't difficult," Natalie said. "I get almost free rein in the spell repository these days, as long as I don't take anything above a level-three spell."

The plan was to break in to the museum after midnight, so they had several hours to kill that evening. None of them felt like working, but the Institute roped them into various duties until eleven o'clock, when they were finally let go.

It was a typically cold winter's night when the three of them stepped out of the Institute gates. Ben zipped up his jacket and tightened his scarf. Charlie adjusted his large, furry earmuffs and huffed into the air, producing condensation. Ben was pleased to see the sky was overcast, hiding the moon.

There were still plenty of people around, and several of the pubs were doing a roaring trade, especially with the dwarves. Thankfully, as they wandered aimlessly around Taecia for the next hour or so, most of the crowds slowly disappeared, until they found they were alone even in the busier thoroughfares.

It was a little past midnight when Ben, Charlie and Natalie finally headed for the museum.

"What do we do if there are guards outside?" Charlie asked.

"We knock them out," Ben said. "And we do it quickly, so they can't call for back-up."

"Oh, good," Charlie said, sounding decidedly unhappy about it.

The road to the museum was a wide one, to cater for the high amount of traffic in what was one of Taecia's most popular tourist destinations. Unfortunately, there was a lot of open space around the museum, making it difficult to hide at a moment's notice. Ben eased his spellshooter out of his holster, aware that his hands suddenly felt sweaty despite the cold. The front of the museum would come into view any moment, and they would have only seconds to act if the Old Guard were stationed outside. The minute he sighted the museum entrance, Ben scanned the area, spellshooter ready. He gave a sigh of relief. The place was empty. The ground lights surrounding the museum enabled Ben to sweep the area without squinting. Nevertheless, he kept his spellshooter in his hand as the three of them climbed the gentle steps up to the front door. When he was certain they were alone, he put his spellshooter away, and took out the portaler. It was a reassuringly heavy piece, crafted of a dark metal.

"Now what?" Natalie said. The three of them were staring at the piece in Ben's hands.

"Let's see if this bad boy works," Ben said.

Ben placed the portaler on the door, and pressed a button in the middle of the device. There was a loud click that made them jump, and the object latched onto the door, like a magnet.

"I'm going to press the button again; then we stand back."

"Why? What's going to happen?" Charlie said. "I need some sort of warning."

"I honestly don't know," Ben said with a shrug. "Let's see."

Ignoring Charlie's protests, Ben pressed the button in

further, and then stepped back.

The door that materialised looked so real it could have come from Ikea. It was plain white, with a handle, and stood just in front of the museum's doors, floating in mid-air, inches above the ground.

Ben grabbed the handle and carefully pulled the door open, half-expecting the whole thing to fall down. Instead, the door swung open on invisible hinges.

"Oh wow," Natalie gasped.

The open door revealed the museum inside, as if the museum's doors had been cut away.

"Can we just walk through?" Charlie asked tentatively.

"I think so," Ben said.

The portaler was still stuck on the door, and Ben could just about reach it.

"The portal will only last seconds after I remove the portaler from the door," Ben said. "After you two have gone in, I'm going to remove it, and follow you in. Remember, if you see any Old Guard, stun them. You will have the advantage of surprise."

Natalie gave a determined nod; Charlie less so. Ben watched as they prepared themselves, and then stepped through the door. The moment they passed through, Ben pressed the central button on the portaler. There was a click, the portaler detached itself, and the white door immediately started to fade. Ben darted round, and leapt through.

— CHAPTER TWENTY-SEVEN —

A Brief Reunion

Ben's skin tingled as he passed through and there was a rush of cold, before emerging just inside the museum doors.

Natalie and Charlie stood staring at an Old Guard lying unconscious on the floor.

"He was there as soon as we entered," Charlie said, looking almost as stunned as the unconscious guard. "I think I might have overdone it by firing three stunning spells."

"You reacted quicker than I did," Natalie said.

Ben nudged the man, and was relieved to discover that he was still breathing. He looked around, and spotted the cloakroom.

"We can't have him lying here like this. Let's move him out the way."

They dragged the guard into the small cloakroom and,

after some effort, managed to shut the door.

Ben drew his spellshooter, and quickly scanned the area again, half-expecting more guards to materialise. After a minute of standing rigidly, waiting, it became apparent they were alone, at least for now.

"I think we're in the clear," Ben said, though he didn't holster his spellshooter.

Charlie pulled out the floorplan. "We need to take the stairs."

They walked quickly, but silently through the grand museum. Charlie concentrated on leading them in the right direction, while Natalie and Ben were on the alert, searching for any sign of movement. To his surprise, and relief, they met no more guards as they took the stairs to the second floor.

"Not that I'm complaining, but the place seems awfully quiet," Natalie said, as they passed through yet another magnificent room, detailing Elizabeth's sea adventures.

Ben had been thinking the same thing, but there was no point worrying about it. It was one o'clock in the morning, after all, and the front doors of the museum were normally enough to put most people off.

"There it is," Charlie said.

He was pointing at the small room they had spent so much time in just yesterday. *Queen Elizabeth's Personal Possessions.* Unlike last time, where there had been a huge queue to get in, it was now empty, with not even a guard in sight.

Ben, Charlie and Natalie entered the small room, and Natalie immediately gasped, as she feasted her eyes on the same exhibition Ben and Charlie had recently witnessed. Ben's eyes went straight to the scabbard, still innocently leaning on the throne chair. Ben found himself admiring the item all over again, from its simple, understated design to the quality of craftsmanship of the silver.

"It's beautiful," Natalie said. "I can see the similarities to the other pieces."

"Yeah, it's a perfect match," Ben said.

Charlie's attention kept flicking to the room's only exit, rather than the scabbard. "So, what now? Pick up the piece and go? I'm sure you'll set off some sort of magical alarm."

"Maybe," Ben said. "Maybe not."

But he didn't move. The scabbard seemed so precious, he suddenly felt strangely reluctant to sully it with his dirty hands.

"Am I the only one worrying about the guards?" Charlie said, oblivious to Ben's fascination with the scabbard. "We've only met one. Where are all the others? I can't believe they'll just let us take something and walk out."

"Maybe there was only a handful here to start with," Natalie said. "After all, most people wouldn't be able to get through those magical doors."

"Really? We didn't have much difficulty."

"We had the portaler from Simon," Natalie said. "He said it was the latest thing on the market."

"Which, coming from Simon, doesn't mean anything," Charlie said. "I'm just saying, we're about to steal one of Elizabeth's personal possessions, and it seems a bit too easy."

Ben shook himself out of the trance the scabbard seemed to have on him. "You're right. It does seem all a bit too easy. But does that mean we shouldn't take the scabbard?"

"No, I'm just scared of what's going to happen when you do."

Ben grinned suddenly. "We'll find out soon enough, won't we? Maybe nothing happens or maybe we get ambushed by fifty Old Guards. Most likely something in between. The trick is to be ready."

"I'm ready," Natalie said, drawing her spellshooter. Charlie followed suit with a little less conviction.

Ben rubbed his hands together, and then carefully stepped over the blue rope barrier. He froze, waiting for some sort of magical alarm. Nothing happened. He shuffled forwards in pigeon steps, easing his way just to the left of the throne chair, until he was standing directly over the scabbard. He could feel his whole body shaking as he stared down at the magnificent sheath. The previous pieces of armour they found flashed across his mind – the helm, the boots and the breastplate. Each had provided significant obstacles right up until they were claimed. Was there some last trick or spell, just waiting to go off when he picked up the scabbard? Or was it really as easy as picking it up? After all, this wasn't the sword itself, only its sheath.

There was only one way to find out.

Ben bent down and picked up the scabbard.

The icy shock was so powerful it forced his mind from his body. He sailed upwards, towards the ceiling, through it, and outside into the night air. It was the most bizarre feeling – he could still sense his body, but he was no longer inside it, nor was he in control of where he was going. The world below whizzed by. He felt terrified, but also strangely exhilarated by the experience of being free. Faster and higher he went, until he became aware of a small red spot in the distance. It looked like a ring of fire, floating in space, with flames licking around its edges. It couldn't have been more than six feet in diameter – not that it mattered, as he didn't have a physical form. He was being pulled towards the ring, he realised. For the first time, Ben felt a rush of fear, for he could feel evil emanating from the ring. He didn't want to go in there, but he couldn't gain any sort of control over his direction. He cried out, or tried to, as he sailed right through the fiery circle.

Blackness hit him and, for a moment, he had no point of reference in space or time. He felt sick and dizzy. He touched his stomach to stop it from heaving.

He frowned. His stomach. He had a stomach! Which meant he had a body again.

A soft, dry wind whipped around his legs, and he opened his eyes.

He hadn't expected to be back in the museum, and he wasn't. He wasn't even in Taecia, and he was fairly certain he wasn't even in the same spiritual dimension.

He was on a hilltop. The grass he stood on was brown and dead, but it was the sky above that made his body tremble. It was a blood red, with streaks of black ink staining the sky.

He was in the void.

The hilltop was just a clearing, a respite from a dead forest that surrounded him. The trees seemed to sway and make soft groaning noises, as if calling him, daring him to enter. It was clear there was nowhere to go without facing the very real prospect of death.

But Ben had no plans on going anywhere, not until he could work out what was going on. Why was he here? How had he got here? He took several deep breaths to calm himself, but he couldn't even begin to get his mind in gear. He was still trying to come up with some sort of explanation, when he heard a rustle in the trees below. He spotted a flash of colour amongst the dead tree trunks.

Someone, or something, was coming.

Ben was far from defenceless in the void, and he

immediately summoned a sword and prepared himself to cast whatever element of magic might suit the oncoming beast. At least he had the advantage of elevation. He waited for the creature to arrive on the hilltop.

Two forms strode into the clearing.

They weren't beasts. They weren't creatures, and they definitely weren't enemies.

Ben lost control of the sword, and momentarily lost control of his legs. His heart, such as it was inside the void, almost gave out.

It was his parents.

Despite the time – had it been years? – they looked exactly as he remembered. His dad still had that same ridiculous moustache and raised eyebrows giving the impression he knew something you didn't. His mum was smiling, her blue eyes sparkling. She broke into a run the moment she saw him. Ben wanted to run too, but his legs felt too wobbly.

Given the size of the hill, his mum covered the distance impressively quickly, including the final few leaps that would normally be possible only on the moon.

"Ben!" his mum said, throwing her arms around him and almost knocking him over. She sobbed unashamedly, and squeezed him so tight that Ben found it difficult to breathe. For his part, Ben struggled to keep himself together. His body was shaking, and he kept thinking he must be dreaming. After arguably the longest hug in history, she stepped back, her eyes wet and with a smile from ear to ear.

"You've grown," she said, holding him at the shoulders.

"It happens to teenagers, dear," his father said. "Now step aside, woman."

Greg gave him a slightly more manly hug, though no less affectionate.

"What is going on?" Ben said. He was finding it difficult to speak. "Am I really here? Is this really you?"

"Yes, you are really here," Greg said. "Though your body is not. You are in the void, though I suspect you already know that. You are here because you activated my admittedly brilliant spell that was connected to the scabbard."

"The spell summoned you to us," Jane explained. "Of course it would only work for the sword's Guardian. You have no idea how long we've been waiting for you."

"Two years, give or take," Ben said with a rueful smile. "But why now?"

"We could only harness the magic from Elizabeth's Sword through the scabbard, and you had to have physical contact with it," Greg said. "Believe me, the spell we used to summon you here wasn't an easy one. But it was worth it."

Ben was just starting to come to terms with what was happening, and he found he couldn't stop smiling. He knew there wasn't really any such thing as weight in the void, but he still suddenly felt fifty pounds lighter. He was with his parents. The thought kept revolving round his head, making him feel a little giddy.

"We don't have long," Greg said, puncturing Ben's elation. "The spell we used to pull you here required an enormous amount of magic."

"So why am I here?" Ben asked.

Greg's expression turned serious, or as serious as one could imagine with his quirky moustache and permanently upturned lips. "Do you have all the Guardians and their pieces of armour?"

"All except the sword and the shield," Ben said.

"Don't worry about the sword," Greg said with a wave. "You'll work out what to do. The shield will be difficult. Lord Samuel will be determined to prove that his piece was the most secure of them all."

"We know where the shield is," Ben said. "And we are going to retrieve it soon."

"You will need all the Guardians to find the shield," Greg said.

"That's not a problem."

Greg nodded, and clasped Ben's arm. "You've done so well, son. I cannot even begin to describe how proud I am of you."

Ben tried to smile, but his lips suddenly started

quivering of their own accord. "I wish you had told me about all this earlier."

"That's my fault, not your mother's," Greg said. "I mistakenly thought you weren't ready to take on the role of a Guardian. Whether that is true or not, I should have at least introduced you to the Unseen Kingdoms and the Royal Institute of Magic, to give you time to prepare. I know it's a cliché, but we were trying to give you a normal life."

Ben couldn't think of a suitable response to that. He wasn't one to dwell on regrets of the past, and so much water had flowed under the bridge. Nevertheless, he couldn't help thinking how his life might have been if he had known about the Royal Institute of Magic, and his parents' real jobs.

Jane stepped back up to Ben, pushing Greg aside. Her eyes looked almost pleading. "We weren't made aware that the role of a Guardian was passed down to the youngest member of the family until after you were born. The thought of you going to face King Suktar was one we simply could not tolerate. It still terrifies me."

"I'm not mad about it either, but with the other Guardians, and Elizabeth's Armour, I think we have a chance."

"You'll be fine," Greg said, his eyes burning with rare sincerity. "I know that now. I just wish I'd known it two years ago."

There was a momentary silence. His parents seemed content to stare at him, and Ben revelled in just being in their presence. He was so lost in the moment that he almost forgot about his parents' own plight.

"I'm going to rescue you," Ben said. "Once we've taken out Suktar, of course."

"Of course," Greg said with one of his trademark smiles. "We're just waiting for you, and getting rather impatient about it, I might add."

"Are you doing okay here?" Ben said. "I know the void is pretty harsh."

"We're doing fine," Jane assured him. "It's not that bad, once you know the right people. Your father has seen to that. Do not worry about us."

Ben never thought he'd want to stay in the void, but at this moment, he dreaded leaving. He wanted nothing more than to stay with his parents.

"Eight minutes," Greg said, glancing at Jane.

"What's eight minutes?"

"It's been eight minutes since you arrived. The spell is only able to last a maximum of ten."

Even as Greg spoke, Ben felt a pull from his insides, as if someone had hooked him from behind and was trying to lift him up.

"No," Ben said, clenching his fists. He ground his feet into the hilltop, and willed himself to stay put. The pull *lessened, but only a fraction.*

Greg and Jane recognised what was happening immediately. As one, they grabbed him in a three-way hug. The combined willpower of the three of them lessened the pull for a blessed minute, and Ben stood there, revelling in the proximity of his parents, trying to take in every last moment.

But the pulling power soon increased, getting stronger each time. Ben struggled in vain, putting everything he had into staying.

"Don't worry, Ben," Jane said softly. She had a tear running down her cheek. "We'll see you soon, okay?"

A hard yank almost jerked Ben away completely, and he became airborne, but Greg caught his hand, and looked up. He gave a roguish smile, one that Ben had been so familiar with.

"Go kick some dark elf backside, Ben," Greg said with a wink. "We'll be waiting for you."

— CHAPTER TWENTY-EIGHT —

Steel Shield, Level Four

"Ben!"

Natalie's voice came from a distance. It sounded like a faint echo. He heard shuffling footsteps, and then someone grabbed him. He became aware that he was lying on his back, and his head hurt. Had he fallen down?

Ben opened his eyes, and found himself looking into the concerned faces of Natalie and Charlie.

"Are you okay?" Natalie asked.

Charlie extended a hand and helped him up.

"How long was I out?" Ben asked, rubbing the back of his head. He felt groggy, like he'd just been rudely woken from a deep sleep.

"Just seconds," Charlie said.

Ben suddenly became very awake. "Seconds? That can't

be right."

But then Ben remembered that time in the void acted very differently to the real world. Hours there could be just moments here.

"You touched the scabbard, then slipped and fell. The bang on your head must have knocked you out," Natalie said, looking at him anxiously. "Are you okay? Do you need to sit down?"

Ben rubbed a hand over his face. Thoughts of his parents were still wonderfully vivid, though the pain of leaving them hurt far more than the bang on his head. He wanted to tell Charlie and Natalie what had happened, but now wasn't the time. He glanced at the scabbard in his hand, feeling the small engravings on the fine silver.

"So, I guess no alarm went off, then?" Ben asked.

"Not so far," Charlie said. He gave a tentative look at the exit. "But I think we should get out of here before our luck changes."

Ben stepped over the rope, scabbard in hand, and Natalie and Charlie followed. Now that he had the scabbard, he was as eager as Charlie to leave the museum.

He was about to exit the small room, when he heard a faint noise in the distance.

He stopped, and pulled out his spellshooter. "Did either of you hear that?"

Their rapidly paling faces were all the answer he needed.

Ben cursed softly. They stood still, ears perked, but no more noise was forthcoming. Was someone out there, waiting for them the moment they left the room? Suddenly, the museum seemed a dark, dangerous place.

"Arm yourselves," Ben said.

"Wait!" Charlie whispered, grabbing Ben's arm as he made to leave the room. "What's our plan? We should have a plan if there are guards out there, right?"

Ben nodded. "The plan is simple. If there are guards, shoot them."

"What if we get separated?"

"Meet back at the Institute," Ben said. "If any of us doesn't make it, we'll come back when the scabbard is secure."

"What if you don't make it?" Natalie said.

"Then we're in trouble," Ben admitted with a grim smile. "But we're getting ahead of ourselves. There might not be any guards out there at all. Now, you guys ready?"

Ben took a deep breath and stepped out of the small room and into one of the grand exhibition rooms.

Lined up at the end of the room, almost hand in hand, were the Old Guard, blocking their path. Their blue uniforms with diagonal sashes were impossible to miss. They stood calmly, clearly waiting for them with quiet composure.

Ben whipped his head round. The same scene greeted him at the other end of the room.

"Let's surrender," Charlie said, staring at the Old Guard. "We've got no other choice."

"No," Ben said firmly. "We surrender and we lose the scabbard."

"We don't exactly have a choice," Charlie said, motioning vigorously at the Old Guard with his hand. "Look at them! There's a dozen each side."

"The odds aren't great," Natalie said. Her green eyes blazed with a determination that matched Ben's. "But Ben's right – we need that scabbard, and I don't think they're going to give it to us."

Ben was already thinking ahead. He had a few stronger spells that he had been saving for Vanishing Street, but they would have to be used now. The only problem was, he didn't have enough for all three of them.

Ben was thankful the Old Guard appeared ready to stand there and wait. It gave him time to think, and focus. He pointed his spellshooter at his chest and concentrated. A large blue and white spell started wobbling towards the barrel. Ben grit his teeth, and re-doubled his focus, blanking out the world around him. As soon as the spell reached the cusp of the barrel, he pulled the trigger. The spell that hit him was the size of a tennis ball. A sheen of what looked like metallic armour coated his body, before seeping into his skin.

"What was that?" Charlie asked.

"Steel shield, level four," Ben said, feeling guilty that he had given himself such protection while the other two remained exposed. But he had to get that scabbard out of here.

Charlie gave him an incredulous look. "I didn't know you could cast that."

"First time."

Ben waited for the justified accusations that they could not hope to match Ben's getaway without that sort of spell. Instead, he got two understanding nods.

"Make sure you come and rescue us," Charlie said with a weak smile.

"We're all getting out," Natalie said, giving Charlie a firm poke.

There was no more point in waiting. The Old Guard still hadn't moved, but they weren't going anywhere, and time was ticking by.

Ben moved forwards. Natalie and Charlie went left and right, spreading out, so that they would be more difficult to hit. He didn't run, not while they were out of range. Ben counted twelve of the Old Guard, spread across the room.

Ben placed his finger on the trigger of his spellshooter. The stunning spells had an effective range of approximately thirty paces.

He was still forty paces away.

Ben tried to guess what the Old Guard would fire. Surely

they would shoot to capture or disarm, rather than firing anything fatal. But one look at their stern faces, and Ben wasn't so sure.

Thirty-five paces.

Ben raised his spellshooter. The stunning spells weren't difficult to cast, but shooting several at once made it more difficult.

Thirty paces.

Ben pulled the trigger and unleashed a slew of spells. At that exact moment, the Old Guard raised their spellshooters as one, and fired. Suddenly, Ben was looking at a dozen spells whizzing through the air, coming right at him and his friends.

Ben ducked and swerved, firing again in response. A spell shot passed him; then another. A third clipped him on the shoulder, but it made a metallic sound, and rebounded harmlessly off the armour he'd cast.

Charlie cried out, and Ben flicked a glance over his shoulder. Charlie was down on his knees, but still firing gamely. Three of the Old Guard had detached themselves from the line, and were marching towards Charlie.

Ben had to resist his natural instinct to turn back and help. The line was thinner now with those guards gone. He could see their faces clearly: there was no fear, despite the fact that he was running right at them.

The spells were flying at him, and Ben took several more

hits, without slowing. Two of the guards squared up to him, arms extended, realising the spells weren't doing anything. Ben feinted one way, and then, with a sudden burst of acceleration, aimed for a small gap between the two of them. They tried to grab him, but Ben had been expecting it, and surged past them like a rugby player breaking a tackle.

Suddenly, he was in the clear.

"No!"

Ben barely had time to turn his head to see Natalie being jumped on by another guard. She twisted and fought, but was no match for the strength of the man. Again, Ben resisted the urge to stop, knowing it would be curtains if he did. He whipped round the corner, heading for the stairs. He could hear footsteps behind him, and saw another spell soar over his shoulder. He hit the stairs three at a time, bounding down them at such a pace that he almost lost his balance. He reached the ground floor, and sprinted down the hallway, adrenaline fuelling his muscles.

The exit was just round the corner now. Would the door open easily? If not, he still had his portaler, though that would eat up valuable time. The footsteps behind him told Ben that they were still pursuing him, but he was faster than them. He almost slipped as he leaned into the corner like a motorcyclist at full tilt.

The moment he saw the entrance ahead, he came to a skidding halt.

Guards lined up in front of the door, spellshooters drawn. Ben's heart sunk. There must have been twenty of them, formed in two rows. He looked around desperately for another way out, but saw none. Ben tried to think, while taking in deep breaths. Just like before, the guards weren't moving, but this time that played against him. He needed them to come forwards and spread out, so he could get past them. Could he knock all of them out? Highly unlikely. His armour shield had already taken dozens of hits, and Ben could feel it weakening. Could he plead his innocence? Given that he was trying to make off with one of Elizabeth's possessions, as well as having knocked out countless guards, he was fairly sure that was a non-starter.

Ben was still thinking of a solution when a handful of the guards moved forwards. They quickly moved into range, and fired. Ben ducked and returned fire. He felt one spell graze his shoulder and another hit him full on the leg. The shield sizzled and blinked out. Ben's leg suddenly felt numb, and he cursed.

In that moment, he knew he wasn't going to escape. So he did the next best thing – he charged. With a cry of defiance, Ben half-ran, half-limped, firing like a maniac at anything that moved. Two guards went down. Three. For a moment, he thought he might be able to make it – there were fewer than half a dozen left blocking the door. But Ben took another hit to his shooting arm, and he lost the power to pull the trigger. He dipped his head, and charged like a rhino, bellowing like one too. Something solid hit him on the head and he was vaguely aware that he was falling.

— CHAPTER TWENTY-NINE —

Captain of the Old Guard

Ben woke to the smell of coffee. His nose twitched. That was strong coffee, and may have been the reason he had regained consciousness in the first place. It certainly helped with the grogginess, though his head still hurt a little. He didn't open his eyes, but rather tried to use his senses to get a feeling of his surroundings. He was sitting in an upright chair. To his surprise, he found he wasn't bound. The floor was carpeted beneath his feet, and there was a soft light creeping through his eyelids. He concentrated on sound. He could hear breathing, and the delicate sipping of coffee. Ben resisted the urge to frown, knowing that would give away his consciousness. Where exactly was he? Instinct told him he was still in the museum. But why had they not thrown him into some dark, dank room? It was most puzzling.

Ben opened his eyes, and promptly received his next surprise.

An elderly woman was standing opposite him, drinking a mug of coffee and watching him closely. She wore the uniform of the Old Guard, with the addition of several medals on her chest. Though she was clearly old enough to be his grandmother, she stood with her back perfectly straight.

"Ah, there you are," the woman said in a perfectly spoken English voice that could have come from the queen. "I was wondering when you might venture to open your eyes."

"Where am I?" Ben asked, looking around. The room was small, but cosy, and looked very much like an office, minus the technology.

"Elizabeth's museum, of course," the lady said. "My office, to be precise."

Ben's head was slowly getting back into gear. To his great surprise, the scabbard was leaning against his chair, and hadn't been confiscated or returned to where it came from.

"Where are my friends?"

"Safe," the lady answered. She took another sip of her coffee, and put it down on the desk. "Now, I believe we are getting ahead of ourselves. Shall we do introductions?"

Ben still couldn't understand why he wasn't in deep trouble or why this lady seemed so calm about their attempted robbery, but he didn't complain.

"Ben Greenwood," Ben said.

The lady leant forwards, and extended her hand. "A pleasure to meet you, Ben Greenwood. My name is Anna Farland. I am captain of the Old Guard, and have been for the past fifty years."

Ben took the old woman's hand and was surprised by the firmness of her shake. Questions swirled round his head. He was fairly certain Anna would address them in her own time, but she appeared in no hurry, and he couldn't wait.

"What's going on?" Ben asked. "Why am I here? Why have I not been reported to the authorities?"

Anna smiled, her many wrinkles creasing around her thin lips. "Ah, the impatience of youth. I remember that wonderful feeling – I still get it occasionally, you know. I might be eighty years old, but I don't feel it. Now, where were we? I'm rambling. Ah yes, why are you here, and why have you not been reported? Both those questions have the same, simple answer: we were expecting you."

That was arguably the last thing Ben expected to hear. He leaned forwards on his chair, to get a fraction closer to Anna, fearing he may have misheard her crisp, upper-class accent.

"Yes, you heard correct," Anna confirmed. "For eight years, to be precise."

"I don't understand," Ben said.

"I feel a story coming on," Anna said. "Let's see now –

yes, it happened eight years last summer, in fact. Your father, Greg Greenwood, came in to this very office with Elizabeth's scabbard. You can imagine my surprise and delight at receiving such an item for the museum. But to my astonishment, he said he only wanted to keep it here temporarily for safekeeping, and that one day you would come and claim it."

Ben's mouth opened, but no words came out and, after a pregnant pause, Anna continued.

"I, of course, refuted his claim to the scabbard. It belonged to Queen Elizabeth, and hence its rightful place was in the museum. But he immediately put me straight, showing the most remarkable letter from the queen herself, giving your family, the Greenwoods, the responsibility of safeguarding the sword, and its scabbard, and to do with it what he wished."

Ben couldn't help glancing at the scabbard. "But there is no sword."

"Correct," Anna said. "Your father said he would return later with the sword, but he never did. I was most disappointed. The scabbard is a remarkable item, but if we could have displayed the sword as well, that would have been something to behold."

Ben felt strangely breathless, though he was dimly aware it was also very late, and his body had been through a lot recently. He tried to sift through the multitude of revelations, to make some sort of sense from it. Eventually he found the right questions.

"Why didn't you just give it to me when I came in?" Ben asked.

"Your father was very specific about that. You had to claim it. Additionally, your father said there were powerful spells connected to the scabbard, and if anyone but you tried to leave the room with it, there would be unpleasant consequences."

"But once I claimed it, why did you summon pretty much every single guard in the building to stop us from leaving?"

"Again, your father's instructions. He said you were to be tested upon escape, that it was necessary. He would not give a reason."

Ben was momentarily silent. Did his dad think that by the time he came to claim the scabbard, the sword would also be there? Surely not – he would have mentioned it when he saw him just moments ago in the void. Even so, something didn't sit right. He stood up, and immediately had to grab the chair to stop himself falling. His head was still throbbing from the strike, though he'd barely noticed it while talking to Anna.

"Am I free to go?" Ben asked.

"You always were," Anna said with a smile. "Though I can appreciate that may not have been apparent."

Ben returned the smile and picked up the scabbard. He

walked to the door, but as he was about to exit, he turned back to face Anna.

"Aren't you curious about all this? The scabbard, my dad, me?"

Anna narrowed her eyes and, for the first time, Ben saw a real intelligence there. She gave a thin smile. "Curious? Yes, that, unfortunately, is one of my failings. I wonder the significance of the scabbard, and why you, Ben, should claim it. But the moment I saw the letter from the queen, I've never wavered from my duty to safeguard the scabbard until your arrival."

"Thank you," Ben said.

Anna gave a smart salute. "Good luck, whatever it is you're embarking upon. I have a feeling you may need it."

It was past two o'clock in the morning when Ben, Charlie and Natalie staggered out of Elizabeth's museum, looking rather haggard but jubilant. As they descended the steps, Ben saw a shadow at the bottom.

"Thank god, you made it. I had a bad feeling you weren't going to come out, and I'd have to come looking for you."

"Joshua," Ben said with surprise. "What are you doing here? I thought you had Warden duties."

"I finished them an hour ago, and came straight here."

Joshua's eyes went straight to the scabbard. Even with the lack of light, Ben could tell from the glint in Joshua's eyes that he was impressed.

"Can I hold it?" Joshua asked.

Ben felt strangely reluctant, but he handed the sheath to Joshua, who inspected it closely, drawing it up to his face to run what looked like an expert eye over it.

"It's stunning," Joshua said softly. "The craftsmanship is like nothing I've seen." He handed it back to Ben with something close to an approving nod. "Now we just need the sword to go with it."

"Yeah, I have some news about that, actually," Ben said.

Ben proceeded to tell them all that had happened as they walked to the Dragonway, including his meeting with his parents in the void, which left them all open-mouthed, even Joshua.

"Are you okay?" Natalie asked. Even in the dark, Ben could see her concerned green eyes.

"Yeah, I'm fine. It was a bit of a shock, but it was nice to see them again, even if it was only for a few minutes."

"I can imagine," Joshua said with a sad smile. "I don't understand what your father said about the sword. Why didn't he just tell you where it was?"

"I don't know," Ben replied honestly. "But I think we should trust him. Remember the riddle: *Find me last. I am not hidden.* I have a feeling we will only find the sword after we have found your shield."

Joshua gave a reluctant nod. "You may be right."

"Well, we'll soon find out," Ben said. "How long until we

can get to Vanishing Street?"

"Six days," Joshua replied immediately.

"Are you guys satisfied with all the research you've done?" Natalie asked.

Joshua looked to Charlie, who spoke up. "Outside, yes. Vanishing Street is a highly secretive place, but it's also famous, so I was able to find several references to it. But Lord Samuel's house is another matter. I could find almost nothing on what we might encounter inside."

"The only thing we could find was a few letters from Lord Samuel himself," Joshua said. "And really the only useful thing he would say about the house was that there will be a challenge for everyone. But he doesn't reference who everyone is."

Ben recalled his father's voice. "He means the Guardians. There will be a test for all the Guardians."

"How do you know that?" Joshua asked, frowning.

"My dad. He said all the Guardians would be needed."

"Well, that's good to know," Charlie said. "Though I dread to think what he's come up with for each Guardian."

Ben smiled grimly. "We'll find out in six days' time."

— CHAPTER THIRTY —

Spellsword Apprentices

The Institute was gearing up for war.

Though they had clearly been planning for months, it was now becoming obvious everywhere you looked, as evidenced on their stroll up the hill to the Institute the following morning. There were soldiers everywhere. Humans, elves, dwarves, even giants, ogres and other races Ben couldn't recognise. Institute members were spread among each group. Many of the houses had been temporarily claimed by the Institute to cater for the soldiers. The taverns were busy, but, apart from a few boisterous dwarves and the composed elves, a repressed anxiety filled the air.

An uncomfortable feeling started in the pit of Ben's stomach. Would he be instructed to join one of the units? He had made leaps and bounds in his training, but he didn't feel anywhere near ready to go to war against the dark elves. The very thought of it made him queasy, a feeling that lasted until he reached the Institute.

Ben, Charlie and Natalie had trouble getting through the front door, it was so busy. As soon as they were in, they gave each other a wave, and began heading off to their relative departments.

"Ben Greenwood!"

Ben recognised the friendly voice of Zadaya, one of the weapons instructors. The dark-skinned elf was waving at him.

"Over here, my friend," Zadaya said. He had with him two dozen other apprentices, most of them with four or five colourless diamonds hovering above their shoulder.

"What's that about?" Charlie asked, squinting at the group with curious eyes.

"No idea. I'll see you at lunch and let you know."

Ben was the youngest by some distance, but his reputation with the sword and, more significantly, the spellshooter was well known now, and he got several respectful nods, as if he had passed some silent entry test.

Zadaya took out a scrap of paper he had been referring to. "Good, good! That's everyone. Now, follow me. We go outside."

Ben recognised a few of the apprentices, but it was the muscular, shaven-headed boy near the front who made him feel a little better.

"Do you know what's going on?" Ben asked, after edging his way over to William.

"No clue, Ben," William said, cracking his knuckles idly. "But all of us are Spellsword specialists, so I'm sure you can take a guess."

Ben followed Zadaya and the rest of the apprentices as they bustled their way past members through the over-crowded atrium.

"Excuse me! Coming through," Zadaya commanded in a loud, almost musical voice. He was waving his arms flamboyantly from side to side. "I have here your future Spellsword stars. Such little time, so much to learn!"

Many looked up – some with annoyance, a few with amusement, and one or two in anger. They all moved, eventually, and soon they exited out into the Institute gardens. It was a beautiful winter's day; the air was wonderfully fresh and the blue sky allowed the sun to highlight the vibrant winter flowers and lush green grass. But for once Ben barely noticed the lovely weather; he was too busy wondering where Zadaya was leading them.

Even the gardens, normally a place of retreat and respite, were busy. As they circled the Institute grounds, Ben saw units of soldiers being briefed on the open grass, often by their native captain plus a Spellsword or occasionally a Warden.

Ben started getting a nasty feeling in his stomach. Were they forming some sort of apprentice military unit? Did that mean they were going into battle, after all? He noticed he wasn't the only one who had gone slightly pale. Only William maintained a calm expression, though even he looked a little concerned.

"Aha, here we go. Some space for us," Zadaya said, waving his piece of paper in triumph. He turned to the apprentices. "Line up, five across, by rank."

As the only third-grade apprentice, Ben didn't hesitate going straight to the back.

"Lots of anxious faces," Zadaya said not unkindly. "Do not worry, apprentices. You are not going into battle. You might be good, but you are not ready – not nearly ready."

Despite an effort to maintain a straight face, Ben heard several sighs of relief, including his own.

"However, you are all good Spellswords, useful Spellswords! You will form a combat unit, but your role will be to help defend the Institute. The dark elves may try to take our wonderful building while we are busy dealing with them in the Seen Kingdoms. My job is to turn you from individual apprentices into a group that can fight together." Zadaya's dark, shoulder-length hair whipped in the wind as he thrust a finger skywards for emphasis. "We will train every day, until you know each other's moves like your own. Any questions?"

There were several. Zadaya took one from a grade-four girl near the middle.

"What is our schedule? Are we doing this all day?"

Zadaya nodded enthusiastically. "You are, my friend. We do not have much time, and there is much to learn."

Unlike Dagmar, Zadaya was happy to answer as many questions as the apprentices fielded, before they got into action.

If Ben thought Zadaya's pleasant demeanour was going to make the training any easier, within the first thirty minutes he was thoroughly disabused of that idea.

"You need to be fit, no?" Zadaya said. "I mean elf-fit, not human-fit. Very important. Another twenty. Go!"

Despite the breeze, Ben was already sweating. He wiped his brow, and then rattled off another twenty push-ups, before proceeding to sit-ups and squats. Then there was the running, and the sprinting. Ben considered himself fit, and indeed he always finished within the first half-dozen, but he couldn't remember his lungs being punished quite this much, even in football training with Coach Frank, who Ben strongly suspected was a sadist.

Thankfully, the fitness training was interspersed with combat, leadership and coordination drills. Ben soon learned that a unit of Spellswords fighting together was a very different prospect from fighting alone, and far more effective. Though Ben had the least experience among the apprentices, he more than held his own and, by the end of the third day, he'd been made a squad leader, one of four apprentices in charge of a group of six.

Despite the looming date with Vanishing Street and its significance, Ben was surprised to find that he was so involved with training that he barely had time to think about their mission to find the shield. And it might have stayed that way if not for the news that they received the morning before their invitation to Vanishing Street.

Ben and Charlie stepped off the Dragonway and stopped dead the moment they exited the station, staring with astonishment at the sight before them. The hill up to the Institute, which was normally bustling with soldiers, was half-empty. Several of the taverns were closed and many of the houses that had been appropriated by the Institute were clearly empty.

"What's going on?" Charlie asked.

"Let's find out."

They hurried up to the Institute, which was also far sparser than normal, though on inspection it was the soldiers not the Institute members who were no longer present.

Ben looked around for someone they could get some answers from, and saw Natalie hurrying towards them, a stack of papers in her hand. Her face was creased with worry.

"Dark elf movement," Natalie said, as soon as she approached them. "The Institute thinks they're going to launch an attack on southeast England."

Ben suddenly felt his breakfast rear its ugly head. "When?"

"Literally in the next day or two," Natalie said. "Our spies have reported serious movement in Erellia. They're launching their ships and mobilising an aerial force."

"That's why our soldiers aren't here," Charlie said.

Natalie nodded. "They've gone to Allarr to get ready."

"Allarr?"

"Taecia's military port," Charlie said.

Ben found training difficult that day, and he wasn't the only one. Many of the apprentices were off the mark, and Zadaya had to reprimand them with a sharp clap on more than one occasion.

"Focus, my friends!" Zadaya said. "If the dark elves attack while you are like this, you will not last long."

Ben shook himself, and rallied his group of six. With some effort, he managed to take his attention off the dark elves for the remainder of the training, until six o'clock hit and they broke for dinner.

He met up with Charlie and Natalie at the base of the staircase. But instead of heading to the food hall, Charlie gave a nod to the entrance.

"Want to go see it?" he said. There was a strange look of excitement and curiosity in his eyes.

"See what?"

"Port Allarr," Charlie said. "I've been around Scholars who have been talking about it nonstop all day – logistics; numbers; boats; ships. It only takes half an hour to get there, if we take a taxi."

"Shouldn't we be doing final preparations for Vanishing Street?" Natalie said with a disapproving frown. "We're supposed to be going tomorrow, remember?"

But Ben had caught some of Charlie's curiosity. He too had heard a few things from members passing by throughout the day.

"We've researched Vanishing Street to death," Ben said. "I want to see this port."

Natalie reluctantly agreed, and a jubilant Charlie led them straight to the taxis. Getting there took a little longer than they thought, as many other apprentices had a similar idea of how to utilise their dinner break, so getting a taxi took a little longer than usual.

With some difficulty, they squeezed into a two-man chariot and, in short order, they were flying above the bustling town of Taecia.

"Let me guess – Port Allarr?" the driver said.

"How'd you know?"

The driver gave a gruff laugh. "I've been shipping you apprentices back and forth all day. Can't see why you're all so interested myself, but then I'm not really a ship person."

The taxi buffered against the breeze, and Ben tucked his

jacket a little tighter around his neck to counter the cold, his eyes searching the horizon for the port, and the sea beyond.

Ben had been to several coastal towns at home, and he had seen some large ships moored. But nothing prepared him for the sheer scope of Port Allarr when it finally came into view.

At first, the ships looked like nothing more than little dots, bouncing gently on the sea. As they continued to soar towards the coast, they soon looked like toy ships, yet they were still a good way out.

"Oh my," Natalie gasped.

There were hundreds of them, many of them docked, but the majority were anchored a little way out, and were being gently buffeted against the wind and choppy waters. As the taxi descended, Ben got a bird's eye view of the scene. There were many different types of ships, most likely from different Unseen Kingdoms. Some were incredibly sleek, and looked as though they could cut through water like a motor boat. Then there were steam ships, big and small, pumping a strange kind of smoke into the air. There were barges, dotted with hundreds of troops on board.

Ben's mouth was agape for the entire descent, until a soft bump from the landing shook him from his stupor.

They left the taxi some hundred yards from the sea. As they walked up and down the port, Ben struggled to come to terms with the magnitude of the navy that was being assembled. It was staggering to think the Royal Institute of Magic could summon such a force from all over the Unseen Kingdoms, and he couldn't help but be lifted by the strength of arms. Surely the dark elves couldn't hope to match such numbers?

Ben wasn't sure how long they staggered round for, certainly longer than their allocated break, though they weren't the only apprentices gawking at the sight, and most of the Institute members were far too busy to notice their presence.

"If you break that thing, I'm billing you! That cost me an arm and a leg. And if you can't pay, I'll just hang you instead. Your choice."

Alex's hooded cloak whipped around him in the wind. He was standing next to a ramp where cargo and artillery were being loaded up onto a sleek ship that was primarily manned by sea elves. Ben recognised them by their small gills behind their ears, and their slightly webbed hands.

Alex was so busy issuing orders, his arms gesticulating every which way, that Ben didn't want to disturb him. But Alex caught sight of them in his peripheral vision, and waved them over with a smile.

"How are my favourite apprentices?" Alex said with one of his suave smiles. "Come to see a bit of the action?"

"Kind of," Ben said, returning Alex's smile. "We wanted to see what was happening. I can't believe how many ships there are. Surely the dark elves won't stand a chance?"

Alex's good humour was replaced by rare sincerity. "Actually, they will still outnumber us nearly two to one."

"What?" Ben couldn't believe it. He couldn't even begin to imagine a navy twice as big. "How is that possible?"

"They've been preparing for war for a long time," Alex said. "Suktar has been preparing for hundreds of years, even when he didn't physically have a body. We have superior ships, and the sea elves are the finest seamen in the Unseen Kingdoms, so the battle will be close. We will meet them off the southern coast of England and try to stop them landing."

Ben felt like the air had been sucked out of him. "What happens if we lose?"

"Then things get messy," Alex said. "We haven't been able to convince the government of the dark elf threat. Much of the sea battle will take place without them seeing or believing what's happening. It's only when the dark elves land that the government will realise what they are up against. By then, it may be too late."

The optimism that had been swelling inside Ben eked away, and he shared a daunted look with Charlie and Natalie. The stark truth hit home with considerable force. In a day or two, England could be under siege. The death, horror and destruction were almost too much to think about.

"Chin up," Alex said, giving them a smile. "We haven't lost yet. The Institute has a few tricks up its sleeve, and this war isn't a forgone conclusion."

But for once Ben had a feeling that Alex's light-hearted talk was masking his own fears and beliefs, though Ben wasn't in the mood to challenge them.

They returned to the Institute, a great deal more sombre than when they left, and Ben had trouble staying focused during the final session of training.

Tomorrow was Vanishing Street day. Ben didn't think it possible, but somehow its importance had reached an even higher pitch. So much depended on them gathering Elizabeth's Armour that Ben felt almost overwhelmed.

"See you tomorrow?" Charlie said, as they arrived in Croydon.

Ben nodded. Tomorrow was going to be a hell of a day.

— CHAPTER THIRTY-ONE —

An Unusual Taxi Ride

Ben didn't get much sleep that night, but he still woke up wide awake right at eight o'clock. His heart gave a little flutter just thinking about Vanishing Street, and he hadn't even got out of bed yet.

Ben took extra care packing his bag, having made a list the previous night, before stepping out into a cold but beautiful, blue-skied winter's day. His backpack hung over his shoulder, his scabbard on one side and the spellshooter on the other. Ben took a deep breath, enjoying the feel of the cold air in his lungs, before setting off to the train station. It felt slightly strange, taking an ordinary train, rather than the Dragonway, and he couldn't help thinking the train moved awfully slowly, constantly stopping at regular stations, before it finally pulled into London Victoria station.

291

Ben walked through the busy station and out to the ranks of taxis, where people had lined up.

"Ben!"

He turned, and saw Natalie waving at him, a little distance from the taxis and the underground station, where the commuters swamped.

"Last, as usual," Charlie said. He wore a bright red parka jacket, and yet somehow still managed to strap on his backpack over both shoulders.

"Good morning!" Krobeg said brightly. "This place is wild, isn't it? Makes even the busiest Unseen Kingdoms look like sleepy hollows."

It was strange seeing Krobeg and even stranger seeing Dagmar here, just outside Victoria station. But thankfully they seemed to fit in, or, more likely, the London crowd was so used to slightly unusual people that they simply didn't care. To be fair to Krobeg, he was a big dwarf, at almost five feet, and could pass as a short human without too much difficulty. Ben saw no sign of his breastplate, and so assumed he was wearing it.

Dagmar was wearing her boots, though to the ordinary eye they looked like nothing more than expensive shoes. Only Abigail, with a backpack strapped over her shoulder, chose not to wear her armour.

"I think I'd look a bit silly wearing it, and a bit uncomfortable," she said.

"Are we all ready, then?" Joshua said, after giving Ben a brief, but not unfriendly nod of welcome. "I make it 10:07am and our Vanishing Street appointment is at 10:45am, so we don't have a lot of time."

"Do you know where to go?" Ben asked.

In answer, Joshua pulled out his spellshooter. Ben had become quite used to being able to brandish his weapon without ordinary people observing it, but it felt slightly odd seeing Joshua doing so in the middle of London.

Joshua fired a spell above his head. A glowing white ball shot out from the barrel and hovered a few feet above their heads.

"Taxi-hailing spell," Joshua said. "We need a black cab that's driven by an Unseen. Only they can get us to Vanishing Street."

All the black cabs looked the same to Ben, including the one that pulled over five minutes later.

There were seven of them, and Ben was slightly concerned the taxi wouldn't be large enough, but they stepped inside one by one, without any fuss. When Ben finally followed them in, he found out why. The interior was far bigger than your ordinary taxi, with enough room for a dozen. Ben knew he shouldn't have been surprised – it was an Unseen taxi, after all – but being in London, he had subconsciously slipped back into the scientific way of thinking, rather than magical.

"Where to?" the taxi driver said from the front.

"Vanishing Street, 10:45am," Joshua replied.

The taxi driver turned round in surprise, and Joshua showed him the invitation, which the driver looked at closely, his long nose almost touching the ink.

"Not been there in a while," the taxi driver said with a shrug. "10:45am, eh? Cutting it a bit tight."

The taxi accelerated and then promptly slowed down again, as it joined the morning traffic in the heart of London. They meandered along at less than thirty miles an hour, much to Ben's frustration.

"Any chance you can go any faster?" Joshua asked, leaning forwards.

"I'm a taxi driver, not a miracle worker," the driver said.

"What about, you know, magic?" Ben asked.

The driver laughed. "You think all Unseen taxis are fitted with wings and magical rocket boosters? If I could afford one of them, I wouldn't be driving a taxi."

"How far do we have to go?" Joshua asked.

The taxi driver shrugged. "Twenty minutes, give or take, depending on traffic."

Ben looked anxiously at his watch. That would leave them with less than five minutes to spare. He clenched his teeth. Why hadn't he caught an earlier train? He glanced over at Dagmar, who appeared completely unruffled by their time crunch, and he almost wished she would take over. She would somehow make the taxi driver go faster.

Once the traffic finally cleared, they started to make good progress, and Ben soon saw the River Thames to his left, which they appeared to be running parallel to. He resisted the urge to ask how much longer, until, to a collective groan, they hit more traffic.

"We're in trouble," Charlie said, putting his head against the window to get a better view. There were temporary lights a good distance ahead, and it was gridlock.

Ben couldn't believe it. He felt speechless. Weeks of planning, and they missed the appointment because he got the wrong train?

Joshua, though, had the bit between his teeth. He delved into his pocket, and produced a wad of cash.

"One hundred and fifty quid to get us out of this mess," Joshua said.

Ben frowned. The taxi driver had already made a joke about wings and rocket boosters – what was Joshua playing at?

But to Ben's surprise, further laughter from the taxi man was not forthcoming. Instead, Ben caught a cunning look in the mirror.

"£175."

"Fine. Just get us out of here," Joshua said irritably. He leant forwards and handed over the money. The taxi driver licked his lips as he took it.

"Right you are," the taxi driver said. "Hold on to something."

His hand went to the dashboard and he pressed one of the many buttons.

Ben was thrown back in his seat with great force. The taxi accelerated like a Ferrari. Ben cried out, though only he and Abigail did so in exhilaration, as the taxi sped up to the car in front. Instead of crashing, it went *through* the rear of the car ahead. Within moments, the taxi had sped through dozens more cars and passed the traffic lights responsible for the congestion. The taxi driver reached out and pressed the button again. This time Ben was prepared and he grabbed hold of the armrest, just in time, as the car slowed with violent force. They resumed normal speed, with the traffic safely behind them.

There were a few groans, as they adjusted their necks and rubbed their backs, except for Dagmar, who sat perfectly still and upright, her hands on her lap.

After another set of traffic lights, the driver turned left, and they found themselves on a suspension bridge, crossing the River Thames. Ben's mind shifted subconsciously back to the dark elves – could this famous river be swarming with dark elf ships in the next few days?

Ben shook such thoughts from his mind, and glanced at his watch again with a frown. It was 10:38am; they were supposed to be there in seven minutes, which seemed impossible. He was about to voice his concern, but the taxi driver beat him to it.

"About to turn off onto the E23," the taxi driver said, his hand going to another button on the dashboard.

Ben tensed himself, but his reaction proved unfounded. The taxi's lights switched on, with a strange blue tint. Directly ahead of them a ramp materialised, which led them up to another road that ran parallel to the bridge. It was transparent, made of some sort of plastic or glass. The cars ahead went through the ramp, as if it wasn't there, and continued along the bridge. But the taxi went up the ramp, and onto this new road. Ben grabbed the car handle, and felt Abigail grab his arm, as the road veered to the right. Suddenly, they were driving right over the river. Ben looked down, and could see the choppy Thames below.

He was just starting to relax, and enjoy the feeling of this unprecedented view of the famous river, when he glanced once more at his watch.

The time was 10:40am.

They had just five minutes to get to Vanishing Street. He was about to bring this to the driver's attention, when he saw the road come to an end at a turning circle, just a little way ahead. There was an elf soldier, fully armed, with a long spear, guarding the end of the road, as if someone would be mad enough to jump off it. But it was the stone archway with the all-seeing eye that caught his attention. Unlike the others he had become used to, this one had a black sheen, making it impossible to see through. The taxi came to a stop at the turning circle, just in front of the archway and the elf.

"Entrance to Vanishing Street," he said. "That'll be twenty-four pounds please."

Joshua paid the driver, and they bundled out. Without giving a moment's thought to the return journey, they quickly approached the stern-faced elf blocking the archway.

"Invitation please," the elf said.

Joshua stepped forwards and handed him the invite. To Ben's surprise, and concern, he spent several minutes inspecting it, examining the writing up close, and tracing it with a finger. They watched silently, and Ben thought briefly of what they would do if the elf rejected them. Could they get through the archway without his permission or would they be stuck? He remembered what Krobeg said about the archways swallowing up people who violated security.

Thankfully, such thoughts proved unfounded. The elf gave a nod, and seemed to relax a little. "You have two minutes until you can enter."

Ben wasn't the only one who gave a sigh of relief. He counted the seconds, trying to stare through the blackness of the archway.

"Any idea what we're going to find?" Ben said.

"Yes," Charlie said. But before he could elaborate, the elf waved them through.

Joshua stepped up first. He straightened his shoulders and, with only a moment's hesitation, walked right on through. One by one the others followed, until only Ben remained. *This is it*, he thought to himself. The magnitude and importance of what awaited made him hesitate. He felt the weight of pressure on his shoulders, almost making him physically sag.

This was no good – he couldn't go in feeling like this. He shook himself down, and gave a little smile, throwing the weight of expectation from him, before following the rest through.

— CHAPTER THIRTY-TWO —

Vanishing Street

The words luxury and extravagance didn't really do Vanishing Street justice. Ben almost bumped into a static Charlie; he, as well as the rest, was staring at the street with undisguised awe. Even Dagmar looked a little bemused by it all.

The street itself was wider than your average road, and cobbled with such attention to detail it looked like each stone had been carefully placed. But it was the houses that caught Ben's eye. They were absolutely huge, each one set back a way behind a gated drive. Ben was surprised to see numerous luxury cars parked in the driveways, giving the street an almost contemporary feel. That was offset against the three giant eagles and several griffins he saw flying about, stretching their wings. Many of the houses had chimneys, with coloured smoke that came out in thick, almost velvety swirls.

Predictably, it was Dagmar who recovered first.

"Which house is the baron's, Joshua?" she asked.

Joshua led them along the street, and stopped roughly halfway down, next to one of the larger houses that stood out due to its bright red stone.

"Here it is," Joshua said, confirming the fact with his invitation.

"Now what?" said Natalie. "I guess you need to pay him a visit?"

"Yes," Joshua replied. "We don't want to anger him. It would also not reflect well on the Institute if I didn't turn up."

"How does he even know we're members?" Natalie asked.

"Oh, he knows," Joshua said. "I bet he also knows the names of your parents, your date of birth and your social security number."

"Where do you want us while you visit?" Dagmar said. "I assume it wouldn't do to loiter outside."

"No," said Joshua. "You should continue down the street, so you're out of sight. I'll catch up with you. I shouldn't be more than an hour."

"Good luck," Ben said.

Joshua gave them a slightly anxious smile, then puffed

out his chest, and rang the bell by the gate. Ben and the others didn't hang around. They continued down the street a little way, until Joshua was out of sight.

Ben remembered that Lord Samuel's house was the largest of all, and was located at the end of the road. However, that proved a problem when the road split; they could either continue on or take a right. After a brief debate, they decided to turn right, for it looked like the road that forked off did not last long, and they could easily double-back. Sure enough, after less than a couple of minutes along the offshoot road, they spotted its end in the distance.

"What's that?" Abigail asked.

At the end of the road was a shimmering window – a portal, Ben realised, after a moment. Through the portal he could just make out cars whizzing by. So that was how the cars on Vanishing Street came in and out. The portal took the cars right into the heart of London.

"We need to turn back," Dagmar said, who showed far less interest in the discovery of the road than the rest of them.

They did so, and were soon continuing on the main road. The further they progressed, the larger the houses became, until it was clearly some sort of ludicrous competition between neighbours. Some were so tall they looked more like mini-towers; others floated several feet above the ground, enabling their gardens to run beneath them. Then there were those that slowly rotated, following the path of the sun. Replica houses were also a common sight, Ben's favourite being the floating *Star Trek* battleship. Ben was half-tempted to stop by and see what happened when he got to the entrance, to see if he was beamed up.

As incredible as these houses were, Ben forgot about them the moment he sighted Lord Samuel's house at the end of the road. House wasn't really an apt description – mansion, or even palace, was a better fit. It was a monster, dwarfing the other houses even from a distance. There was a set of golden gates some distance from the house itself, giving enough space for gardens to warrant the attention of the National Trust. A sign was placed near the centre of the gate. Ben could see the gold lettering sparkling in the sunlight, but it wasn't until they were closer that he could read the sign. It consisted only of two words, but those two words were significant.

GUARDIANS ONLY.

"Well, that's not very nice," Natalie said, attempting to make light of the sign. She turned, and specifically avoided Dagmar's stern expression, and Krobeg's concerned one. "A silly sign isn't going to stop us, is it, Charlie?"

Charlie gave an awkward shrug. "It depends what they have in mind." Then, seeing Natalie's green-eyed frown, he added, "Though whatever it is, I'm sure we can deal with it."

Ben was aware Dagmar was looking at him, and he

realised then that she was letting him, as Head Guardian, make the calls. He ran a hand through his ruffled hair.

"I don't want to be responsible if anything happens to you in there," he said softly.

"You won't be, Ben," Natalie said firmly. "We are responsible for our own actions. If anything happens to us, it will be our own fault."

"That's not true," Ben said with a firm shake of the head. "If anything happens to you, it will be my responsibility, because I'm in charge, and I chose to ignore the sign that specifically says Guardians only."

Natalie's face went slightly red, her green eyes narrowing dangerously. Ben was slightly taken aback – he'd never seen her really angry at him before. "You can't dictate the choices we make, Ben. We are not your puppets or your soldiers. We're your friends, and we are going to stick with you, no matter what you say."

Ben hesitated. He knew, instinctively, the decision he should make, but it would cost him a very valuable friendship.

"You can't stop us, Ben," Natalie said, putting her hands on her hips. "Not unless you tie us up to a tree or knock us out."

Ben couldn't help noticing how the argument came from Natalie, not Charlie. But he knew it would be cruel to put his friend on the spot, when it was obvious to Ben where Charlie stood on the matter.

Ben ran a hand through his hair, and sighed. This was the last time, he told himself. This was the absolute last time he was going to risk his friends, no matter what.

"Okay," Ben said, raising a hand. "I have no intention of tying you to a tree or knocking you out, so I guess you're coming with." Natalie's satisfied smile was cut off by Ben's pointing finger. "But," he added, "once we're inside, if I see a situation that I think is too dangerous, then I want you to leave – no questions asked."

Natalie seemed ready to protest, but Ben stared her down and eventually she gave a reluctant nod.

There was an awkward silence, but it was broken by the sound of footsteps, and the arrival of Joshua. Ben was glad for the distraction, and turned to him with a relieved smile.

"How'd it go?" Natalie asked.

"Fine. The baron is an unusual man, with some interesting ideas. But I think he was happy to have company, especially from someone with a prestigious family history."

"So, that's it, then?" Charlie asked. "We're free to do what we like here?"

"Yes. He said when we want to leave, I should just pop by his house and he will arrange it."

It was then that Joshua noticed the sign on the gate.

"Guardians only?"

Ben raised a hand, cutting him off. "We've just had this

discussion – they're coming with."

Joshua frowned. "That's ridiculous. What if they jeopardise the mission? What if—?"

"Joshua."

Dagmar's voice cut him short. She was looking at him with her usual impassiveness, but there was a hint of impatience in her voice.

"Ben has made his decision. That is the end of it."

Joshua clearly wasn't happy, but he wasn't prepared to argue the point with Dagmar, as his voice trickled to a disgruntled mumble, before fading off. Not for the first time, Ben was glad Dagmar was with them.

With the matter resolved, Ben turned his attention back to Lord Samuel's house. It was hard not to get slightly intimidated by its scope and size.

"Will we face many obstacles to get inside?" Krobeg asked. "Or are the challenges all within the house?"

Ben noticed Krobeg slowly twirling his axe, and licking his lips. He couldn't be looking forward to meeting the enemy, could he?

"We couldn't find much information on the outside," Joshua said. "But see all the statues? They might be an issue."

Some of the statues were clearly of famous people, most likely family members or possibly Samuel himself. But there were also creatures, perched on tall columns. Ben spotted several gargoyles, as well as other creatures he couldn't recognise. There must have been at least thirty of them, spread over the large grounds.

"You think they'll come to life or something?"

"It's possible," Charlie said.

Ben felt his spellshooter by his waist, and eyed the front door in the distance. "Should we make a run for it, then?"

"No," Joshua said. "Not unless we have to. We don't know what else is out there. If we're careless, we might trigger other traps."

Ben turned to the others. "Once we pass these gates, we have no idea how long it will be before we will eat or drink again." He put down his backpack and then, to everyone's surprise, sat down. "We should take advantage of eating while we can."

As it was almost lunchtime, few disagreed. Even Joshua, who was eager to get inside, sat himself down promptly. Only Krobeg, who normally leapt at the chance of food, lingered for a moment, eyeing up the house and the statues in the garden, before the smell of food finally drew him down.

Ben handed out sandwiches, crisps, and bottles of water.

"Not bad," Krobeg said, eyeing the middle. "What ham did you use?"

"It's from a butcher's my parents used to go to," Ben said. "It's expensive, but once you try it, there's no going back."

When they each had full stomachs, Ben took all the rubbish and stuffed it into a side compartment, before strapping the backpack over both shoulders, Charlie-style. He didn't want the thing falling off if they had to suddenly run or fight, where vigorous movement was required.

Abigail took out Elizabeth's Helm from her own backpack, and gently placed it over her head. She looked at her backpack in question.

"I don't really need this anymore," she said. "I kind of like it, though, so I don't want to just blast it to smithereens."

Ben took the backpack. He folded it up as best he could, and placed it within his own. Then he looked around, inspecting each of them. To his surprise, he found they were all looking at him. Could they actually be waiting for orders?

"Arm yourselves. We're going in. If something unexpected happens, follow my lead," Ben said.

Joshua didn't appear overly pleased with the command, but he didn't complain. They drew and checked their spellshooters. Ben touched his orb and ran a mental check – it was loaded with some serious spells, which gave him comfort. Finally, he checked his scabbard, to make sure it was still well fastened onto his trousers.

"Everyone ready?" he asked, summoning an encouraging smile, despite his beating heart, which was rapidly starting to accelerate.

One by one, they nodded. Charlie looked the most

anxious, and kept fiddling with his jacket. Abigail appeared surprisingly serene, and Ben wondered if Dagmar had been giving her lessons on staying calm; as usual Dagmar herself appeared unflustered, though there was a determined glint in her eye. Krobeg had his axe out, and seemed almost to be relishing the challenge; but then with Elizabeth's Breastplate on, he was practically a one-man army.

Joshua stepped forwards to the gate, and produced a key. It was the same key that Ben had seen him collect from the antique store what seemed like an age ago. With a soft click, the gate opened and Joshua pushed it open. Ben went in first, the rest just behind. He walked quietly, as if the lack of noise might reduce the chance of setting off some trap. His eyes darted left and right, constantly on the lookout for movement. If it wasn't for the obvious threat, the garden itself would have been a pleasure to walk in. There were neat paths, the grass was well tended, and even a few winter flowers imported from the Unseen Kingdoms gave the flowerbeds some unusual colour for this time of year. But it was the statues that Ben focused most on as he inched his way towards the front door. He counted at least two dozen gargoyles, with their bat-like wings and menacing faces.

Step by step, they got closer, and Ben started to wonder if the trials began inside, not outside. What if this was just a garden, after all?

The creaking noise quickly changed his mind.

Ben stopped dead, his head whipping round to his left. He spotted the statue immediately. How had he not noticed *that*? It looked like a gargoyle, except that it was three times the size of the others. A red pigment suddenly filled its eyes, and it turned its mighty head left and right. Small fragments of stone crumbled down, as it loosened its joints. It let out a puff of what looked like green smoke, and then extended bat-like wings, which must have spanned at least twenty feet.

"A queen gargoyle," Joshua whispered.

Charlie was shuffling his feet anxiously. "Should we run?"

But there was no time. With a mighty leap, the gargoyle took to the air. Ben was stunned how quick it moved, shooting skywards, and then diving towards them with such speed that Ben took an instinctive step back. Those red eyes focused right on him. The gargoyle landed with such impact that Ben almost lost his footing.

The queen gargoyle looked down upon them. Ben could sense an intelligence in those red, calculating eyes.

"This way is barred," she said in a strange, almost metallic voice. "Go back now, and I will spare your lives."

Ben had dealt with enough of these types of creatures to know that debating the matter was normally pointless. He was about to inch his spellshooter upwards, to get an angle on a shot, when Joshua stepped forwards. He raised his chin and wore that slightly pompous expression that Ben found so irritating.

"I am here to inherit the Shield of Elizabeth, which we know to be in Lord Samuel's household. It is mine by right, so step aside and this can remain civil."

Ben knew it was a mistake the moment Joshua spoke, though he had admired his bravery, if not his conceit.

The queen gargoyle turned her attention to Joshua, and opened her mouth, revealing a set of razor-sharp teeth carved of stone.

"Back!" Ben cried, grabbing Joshua and pulling him away, just as the gargoyle fired her green smoke towards them. Ben could smell the acid as it shot past.

"Foolish human," the gargoyle said. "Nobody enters the house while I live. Those were Lord Samuel's orders."

And with that, Ben heard the cracking of the other gargoyle statues, as they came to life, shaking off years, possibly centuries, of being statuesque, bits of stone crumbling from their joints.

"Enough of this," Krobeg said from behind. "Coming through!"

With one mighty step, Krobeg stepped forwards and heaved his battle axe into the gargoyle's midriff. The strength of the dwarf, combined with the magic from Elizabeth's Breastplate, cut a huge chunk of stone from the queen gargoyle's body. The gargoyle stumbled back, even as its children took flight and soared towards them.

"Run!" Ben cried.

He darted past the stricken queen, and sprinted towards the front door of the house, heedless of any traps or spells he might trigger. Behind him, he could hear the path being pounded and heavy breathing as the others followed. He glanced back, and cursed. The sky was full of gargoyles, flying right at them. The noise of their flapping wings, combined with their screeching, was deafening.

Ben focused on the door, which was now less than fifty paces away, and closing fast. It was up a series of steps, set on a porch, between two Greek columns.

A ball of acid sailed past his head and seared the pathway. Ben glanced over his shoulder in shock. The gargoyles were now almost above them, raining acid. Ben raised his spellshooter skywards and fired, without giving much attention to direction. He heard several screams, and the satisfactory sound of gargoyles hitting the floor.

"Get the key ready!" Ben shouted.

Joshua nodded, and whipped it out. The two of them leapt up the stairs and reached the door in a couple of mighty leaps. Joshua fumbled with the key trying to insert it into lock. Ben spun, and saw the others sprinting up the stairs, the gargoyles hot on their heels, coming from every angle. Thankfully, the porch was covered, so the gargoyles couldn't fly over them; instead they dived right at them.

Ben unloaded powerful fireballs like a maniac, firing at

anything that moved. The gargoyles went down like flies, but others took their place. A few dived under the porch and grabbed Abigail just as she was running up the steps.

"Oh no! Get off me," Abigail said, turning and giving one of the gargoyles a hard, but largely ineffective slap.

"Get that door open," Ben shouted, rushing down the steps to Abigail's aid.

"Working on it," Joshua grunted. "It's stiff."

Ben fired a couple of spells from point-blank range right into the gargoyles surrounding Abigail. He grabbed her arm and hauled her up the stairs. Something grabbed his leg, but even as he turned to tackle the offending gargoyle, a fireball from another ended its life.

"It's open! I just need—" Joshua cried, pushing the door ajar.

The rest of Joshua's words were lost as something huge hit the porch roof and it exploded. The queen gargoyle's claws could be seen ripping the remainder of the porch roof to shreds, its red eyes peeking through the gap.

"Get in!" Ben shouted.

They flew inside, almost crashing into one another. Ben aimed one last fireball at the queen. At the same time, the queen gargoyle launched its own ball of acid, the size of a basketball. Ben turned and dived through the front door, the acid crashing just outside.

Something seared the back of his shoes, but he barely

noticed as he hit the welcome mat, and Joshua slammed the door shut behind them.

They had made it inside Lord Samuel's house.

— CHAPTER THIRTY-THREE —

Lord Samuel's House

Stay on the welcome rug," Joshua said.

Thankfully, the welcome rug was big enough to accommodate them all, even those who had dived in. It looked like the fur from some stripy Unseen animal Ben couldn't recognise. They were all breathing hard, even Dagmar. Ben noticed that a few of them had their clothes scorched by acid, and Natalie was tending to Joshua's shoulder, which had a nasty welt on it.

Ben was happy to wait there until the first aid was complete, and his heart rate approached something close to normal. While the others were being tended to, he took the opportunity to take the place in.

The inside of Lord Samuel's house was every bit as magnificent as the exterior. They were standing in a grand entrance hall, lit by a sparkling chandelier. At the end of the hall was a staircase that split left and right to an open gallery. Looking up, Ben counted at least eight floors; the place couldn't have been much smaller than the Institute. Then there were the antiques on display, treasures and peculiar objects Ben could only assume came from the Unseen Kingdoms. The hallway led to a large living room to the left, which Ben could see only part of from their current angle.

Ben wasn't the only one admiring the house. Six sets of eyes stared at the surroundings with something approaching awe; even Dagmar looked impressed, most likely due to its similar scope to the Institute.

"Well, we haven't left the welcome rug," Krobeg said. He had a cloth out and was wiping his axe. "Now what?"

"We might trigger something if we leave the mat," Charlie said.

"What would we trigger?"

Charlie rubbed his chin. "Honestly, it could be anything. I couldn't find any specific references to what lay where."

"Is there any way of knowing if stepping off the mat will trigger a spell, without actually doing it?" Abigail asked.

"No," Joshua said. "Which is why we need to be prepared. Are you all ready?"

"No," Charlie said immediately, drawing his spellshooter.

Nobody moved except Ben, who inched forwards to the

end of the mat, blood thumping in his ears. He cringed a little as he extended his foot, and placed it on the ground, just beyond the mat.

For a second, he thought they were in the clear. Then the place lit up. Dozens of spotlights materialised and expanded, all around the entrance hall, quickly becoming bigger and brighter.

"Stay where you are!" Ben ordered.

The spells exploded like fireworks of all shapes and colours, of every element, each honing in on the group. Ben had only seconds, but he knew he couldn't rush the spell he was about to cast – it was too powerful. He had time to take just one breath, and then with a huge force of will that involved somehow staying calm and composed, he aimed the spellshooter in the middle of the mat, and fired.

The dome formed seconds before the first spell hit, making a sizzling noise as it smashed against the shield and was neutralised. Ben flinched – the impact rocked the balance of the spell, and he had to re-focus before he lost it. Within seconds there were sizzling noises everywhere, as the spells smashed into the dome, including a fireball the size of a football, which made them duck instinctively. Ben didn't see any of it; his eyes were closed. He focused on maintaining the spell and nothing else. It took several minutes, but eventually the spells became more sporadic and, after a final flurry, came to a halt. Ben knew he should wait another minute, just to make sure they were finished, but he couldn't hold the spell a moment longer. He released the spell, and his legs almost gave way.

"That was incredible," Abigail said, staring at Ben in open-mouthed awe.

"Good job," Joshua said with a nod.

Even Dagmar was looking at him slightly oddly. "That was a level-five shield."

"Yeah," Ben said. "It's one of the easiest level-five spells to cast, though, and in one of my strongest elements."

"Regardless, I've never seen a third-grader cast a level-five spell before," Dagmar said. Ben was pretty sure she was impressed, but, as usual, it was hard to tell.

"Okay, so *now* can we leave the mat?" Abigail said.

Ben turned back to the mat's edge, and once more tested the waters, putting a foot on the marble floor beyond the mat.

Nothing happened. He took another step, so both feet were off the mat.

"Seems okay," Ben said.

They made their way ever so slowly from the entrance hall into the grand living hall adjacent to it. Ben was constantly looking at where he was stepping, tense and ready for something to shoot at him from any angle.

"This doesn't look too bad," Krobeg said. "This Lord Samuel has good taste at least. I like that sofa. We could use something like that in my tavern."

The living room certainly didn't scream danger. It was a typical wealthy living space, with an assortment of expensive furniture, carefully arranged about the place. Ben wondered how the place remained so spotless – where was the dust, after centuries of being empty? Ben almost felt silly holding his spellshooter at the ready.

"Now what?" Ben said, looking to Joshua.

"We have to search the place," Joshua said. "The mansion is huge, and it could be anywhere."

"We should stay together," Charlie said immediately.

Joshua gave him a doubtful look. "It will be faster if we split up."

"If we split up, some of us won't make it back," Charlie said with a straight face. "This isn't a holiday home, Joshua. This place was designed specifically to stop anyone reaching the shield."

"Charlie is right," Dagmar said. "Splitting up here would be foolish."

Dagmar's intervention signalled the end of the debate.

"Fine," Joshua said. "But I lead. This is my piece of armour, after all."

"I'm not complaining," Ben said with a shrug. "Lead on."

They followed Joshua, still tight and tense, expecting to be fired or shot at any moment. Charlie flinched at the slightest sound, and jumped when Ben sneezed.

After a thorough search of the living room to establish there was indeed no shield hidden, Joshua glanced to the doors. There were half a dozen in this room alone. Joshua inspected each one, clearly unsure which one to take.

"Just take any," Ben said. "They're all the same to me."

"They're not the same," Joshua said reproachfully. His hand was trailing the lines of wood. "But I can't identify a factor that would lead me to pick one over the other, so we will take this one."

Joshua had chosen the one that looked the cleanest, with the least stains on the wood. He opened the door and everyone followed him through.

To Ben's surprise, they entered a bedroom, complete with a huge, curtained four-poster bed and a small suite of furniture tastefully arranged near the window. He stared at the sunlight coming through the window, and could see only blue sky from where he stood. That was strange; Ben would have expected to see some of the gardens outside. Remembering to walk cautiously, he eased his way over to the window to get a better look.

"What the—?"

Ben found himself staring at the gardens below.

They were three floors up.

He waved the others over, and they crowded around the window.

"How interesting," Charlie said, rubbing his cheeks. "I

wonder..."

He walked back to the door and opened it. Ben saw Charlie nod, as if he was expecting something. Ben quickly hurried over, and peered out the door Charlie had opened. It led into an unfamiliar hallway.

"The doors act as mini portals to other parts of the house," Charlie said, shutting the door again.

"How are we supposed to search the house if we keep getting portaled all over the place?" Krobeg asked.

"With difficulty," Charlie admitted. "It's a good thing we stuck together, or else we'd be sprawled all over the house by now."

"It's not in here," Joshua said.

Ben turned, and saw Joshua bending down, searching underneath the bed.

"Let's keep searching," Ben said. "But since this place is now officially a maze, try to remember each room, so we know where we've been and which rooms we've searched already."

Joshua insisted on leading again. They left the bedroom and entered the hallway. Ben groaned inwardly when he saw all the doors on both sides. Thankfully, Joshua appeared to be tackling the problem in a logical manner. He went all the way to the end of the hallway, and took the last door on the left.

So eager was Joshua to keep searching that he had

opened the door and marched several paces inside the room before the others had a chance to follow.

Ben heard the spell trigger before he saw it. Joshua cried out and dived to his right, just about avoiding the spell. The ball of energy tried to follow Joshua's path, but had too much momentum, and crashed into the wall.

"Patience!" Dagmar said with unusual severity as she and the others followed Joshua in. "Charging in like a bull will not do anyone any good."

Joshua nodded, his eyes shocked and his hair frazzled. To his credit, he shook it off and immediately started searching the place. They found themselves in another bedroom, this one smaller than the last. After making sure there were no other booby traps, the seven of them searched the room thoroughly, before concluding the shield was not there.

Joshua gave a little groan when they exited back out the same door into another space entirely. They were in a large kitchen, replete with all the modern conveniences. There were large French windows looking out to the garden. Again, they searched the room. Charlie received a nasty shock when he opened the oven and a group of pixies attacked him, but they dealt with them in short order.

"This is going to get tiresome, if we can't systematically search the house," Joshua said after the kitchen revealed nothing.

"I think that's the point," Abigail said. "Lord Samuel wanted to make the shield hard to get. It's not always just about using brute force; sometimes other talents are required."

Joshua looked at her, slightly irritated. "What talent can we use to search this house properly?"

"Easy, Joshua," Krobeg said, his eyes narrowing. "It's not the girl's fault that we're stuck."

"Let's keep going. We just need to get lucky," Natalie said.

And so they continued their search. Bedrooms, lounges, kitchens, dining rooms, offices, music rooms, recreational rooms, more kitchens and bathrooms. They entered them all, cautiously at first, but soon with something approaching reckless haste. Half an hour passed; an hour; then two. When hunger set in, they stopped at a smaller dining room and stopped for a quick break. This time it was Charlie who dished out the food.

They ate in silence, and felt a little better for it, but nobody except Joshua felt in a hurry to resume the search.

"We must be doing something wrong," Charlie said, licking his fingers.

"What could we possibly be doing wrong?" Joshua asked. "It's pretty straightforward – we search each room and then move on if we don't find anything."

"Think of it from Lord Samuel's perspective. He wouldn't

want the Guardians to stumble upon the shield by luck, would he? Abigail was right – there must be some sort of skill or something involved that we aren't using, which would help us find the shield."

Charlie's logic made sense, and even Joshua acknowledged it with a reluctant nod. It made Ben think of his parents, and their advice. *You will need all the Guardians to find the shield.*

Why, though? Ben wondered. That hadn't been the case so far. None of them had done anything special, except fumble their way into the house and promptly get thoroughly lost. He thought through each of the Guardians, and what they offered. Krobeg was the easiest: he gave them brute force, and would come in handy if they ran into any serious physical obstacles. Abigail, with Elizabeth's Helm, could possibly prove useful if they had some mental or even spiritual task. And Dagmar, what did she offer as a Guardian? The boots were apparently the key to finding their way to Suktar. So she was a guide or a navigator. Ben's eyes widened as realisation hit him.

Of course. Why hadn't he thought of it before?

"Dagmar, I think you should lead," Ben said.

Dagmar looked at Ben with a mild frown. "I can do that if you want. But why?"

"Elizabeth's Boots," he said. "They act as a kind of navigational tool, right? To eventually get us to Suktar. What if you could harness that power to help us find the shield?"

A silence fell upon the group, and Ben could feel a sense of hope and expectation from them, except for Dagmar, who gave Ben one of her measured looks.

"I don't know if that's possible," she said slowly. "But I can try. We certainly need to change something, or else we'll be stuck here indefinitely."

She gave a pointed look at Joshua, who had the good grace to blush.

"I need silence while I see what I can harness from the boots," Dagmar said.

Ben wanted to ask for how long, but Dagmar had already zoned out. She sat down, cross-legged, and closed her eyes.

Ten minutes passed, with not a peep from Dagmar. Twenty. Thirty. Ben's mind drifted to the sword, and how much time he would have to learn how to use it before he was forced to confront Suktar. Much depended on when the dark elves attacked. He couldn't imagine having more than a few days, and he just hoped the sword wouldn't be too difficult to master. But that seemed unlikely, given that he would be wielding the only weapon capable of killing the dark elf king.

An hour passed, with the only sound coming from Charlie and Krobeg, trying to eat some crisps without making a crunching noise.

Finally, Dagmar opened her eyes and stood up. Ben

expected a yawn, a stretch or some sign that she had just kept her body perfectly still for the past hour, but it was as if she had been on the floor for only a few minutes.

"I am ready," she announced.

Ben wanted to ask what exactly she did to become ready, but now wasn't the time.

Dagmar walked up to the door and put a hand on the handle. But instead of opening it immediately, she paused, for a good minute, concentrating on what looked like a spot on the door. Ben recalled the hallway they had entered from, with its large portraits and polished wooden floorboards.

Dagmar opened the door. They found themselves staring at an airy conservatory, one that Ben seemed to recognise from before.

There was a soft groan, which Dagmar silenced with one quick look. Instead of walking through, she closed the door, and they all remained in the dining room. She focused again, her hand on the handle. Another five minutes passed, and she re-opened it. Another bedroom. More groans of disappointment, again silenced by Dagmar, who shut the door and tried once more. The next five attempts resulted in three bathrooms, yet another unexplored kitchen, and a master bedroom.

Ben's frustration was building, but he knew how difficult Dagmar's task was, and he kept it bottled up. The others did the same, with contrasting levels of success. Abigail seemed as serene as always, but Joshua looked as if he was mentally pulling his hair out.

The next attempt resulted in a hallway. Not the same hallway as the original one they came through, but a hallway nevertheless. Dagmar gave a satisfied nod, and shut the door again. She opened the door again relatively quickly, and another hallway was revealed. Ben felt a flutter of excitement in his belly, and exchanged a look with Natalie. More hallways revealed themselves, until, on the tenth attempt, Dagmar opened the door to the original hallway from which they had entered.

"Good job," Krobeg said.

Dagmar led them into the hallway, and immediately put her hand on another door. She took her time over this one, before opening it to reveal another hallway. To Ben's surprise, she shut the door and, a moment later, opened it again. The same hallway remained.

Dagmar gave a satisfied nod, and one of her rare smiles. "I have countered the portal spells on each door, so we can search the house without getting lost. I believe I can also harness the boots' magic to hone in on the shield."

"That would be incredible," Ben said. "Do you need anything from us?"

"Just silence," Dagmar said. "And protection. I will be entering doors more quickly now, and all my attention will be on following the trail of the shield. You will need to block any traps or spells that are aimed at me."

Ben pulled out his spellshooter. "That won't be a problem. You just do your thing; we'll make sure nothing blows your head off."

They lined up very specifically, with Ben and Joshua directly behind Krobeg; then came Abigail, and last, Charlie and Natalie.

Dagmar started slowly, feeling her way through each door, but soon sped up, moving through the rooms at such a pace that Ben, Krobeg and Joshua had their work cut out, deflecting spells, casting shields and taking out occasional enemies. Ben even had to sweep Dagmar up and stop her from walking directly into quicksand disguised as floorboards. He expected a reaction from Dagmar, but she gave him only a thankful nod, and continued onwards.

Dagmar stopped her furious pace only when they arrived in a small cloakroom. Her hand went to the handle, but the moment she touched it, she recoiled, as if burnt.

"Are you okay?" Ben asked.

Dagmar took a measured breath. "Yes. The room next door is the large living room we first entered when we came in to Lord Samuel's house." She stopped, and appeared to be listening or calculating something. Her eyes narrowed, before she nodded. "This is the room we need to be in."

Joshua frowned. "But we searched there already – we found no shield."

"No, the shield isn't there," Dagmar agreed. "But something else is – something we need to overcome to find the shield."

"What is it?"

"I'm not sure," Dagmar said. "But it is powerful." She turned to Ben. "You said each of the Guardians would be tested. I have received my test. I think in the next room, the next Guardian will receive theirs."

Ben felt his blood freeze. Surely it wouldn't be him or Joshua, as they hadn't claimed their armour yet, which left Krobeg or Abigail. If it was Krobeg, then it would undoubtedly involve some sort of combat. But what of Abigail?

Ben turned to the others. "Are you guys ready?"

He got six sets of determined nods, even from Charlie, though the anxiety was palpable.

Dagmar nodded, and put her small hand on the door.

She turned and, with unusual caution, entered the living room.

— CHAPTER THIRTY-FOUR —

A Test of Resolve

The room looked the same, with its luxuriously spacious layout, but there was one key difference: the girl in the middle. Deep down Ben knew she must be dangerous, but it was hard to believe, when he first set eyes on her.

She was a child, surely no more than ten years old, sitting cross-legged on a red cushion. She had a mass of wavy, blonde hair, the sort you see on Barbie dolls. The Barbie analogy suited her well, with her cream, almost pale skin, sparkling blue eyes and perfect teeth. For a young child, she seemed perfect in every way, Ben thought.

"You arrived!" the girl said in a suitably young, enthusiastic voice. She clapped her hands in excitement. "Good! For a while, I thought you might not make it. The doors here can be really horrible."

Despite the lack of danger the child appeared to pose, Ben and the others approached her cautiously, stopping a good twenty feet away. If she was part of the test, then she would have something up her sleeve. But, once again, Joshua intervened before Ben could begin to properly formulate a plan.

"My name is Joshua Wistletop. I am the Guardian of the Shield, which I have come to claim," Joshua said. He tried to sound authoritative, but Ben could see he was having trouble talking sternly to the child. It was as if her cute demeanour was acting as a kind of shield, softening all those around.

"Joshua," the girl said, nodding. "Very nice to meet you. My name is Alaya, and I am the second gatekeeper for the shield." She turned to the others and, for a moment, Ben felt a most peculiar tickle in his mind, but it disappeared as soon as it had come.

"Let me see," she said, pointing a dainty finger at each of them. "Ben, Charlie, Natalie, Abigail, Krobeg, and Dagmar. Am I right?"

"You got it," Ben said.

"I thought so," Alaya said with another clap of the hands. She gave them a cute pout. "Now, why are you all standing while I'm sitting? Please, sit down. I don't have any more cushions, but the carpet is nice and fluffy, just like Iggy, my poodle."

Ben sat down, but he was one of the few who did.

Krobeg, Dagmar and Joshua remained standing.

"We're in a bit of a rush, actually," Joshua said, sounding a little impatient. "We're looking for Elizabeth's Shield. Are you able to help us or not?"

Alaya gave a small frown, a subtle crinkling of her smooth brow.

"I asked you to sit down," she said, pointing a reproachful finger at him. "How can we talk if we can't see eye to eye?"

Joshua gave a startled cry, and his legs were taken from under him, his backside landing on the carpet. Krobeg and Dagmar went down at exactly the same time.

"That's better!" Alaya said with another delighted clap. "Now we can talk properly, can't we?"

Joshua immediately attempted to get back up, but a horrified look crossed his rapidly paling face. "What have you done? I can't move my legs."

Alaya clucked her tongue. "You were being naughty, so I had to take over. You'll get them back once I see you're being good again."

Ben exchanged a quick, alarmed look at Charlie, who was seated next to him. He very gently tried to move his leg. Nothing happened. He tried again, harder this time. Panic threatened to set in, but he forced it back. What was going on? Somehow he had lost access to the muscular function in his legs. He was sending the order to his brain, but it wasn't being carried out. Ben tried his arms, but they too would not respond.

"Are we all settled now? Everyone comfortable?" Alaya asked, giving them a sparkling smile.

"Where is the shield?" Joshua snarled.

Ben was impressed by his display of anger rather than fear. Ben himself had to hold back a spark of anxiety that threatened to unleash itself every time he tried to move his limbs. The idea that he couldn't move his body made his hairs stand on end.

"Oh, the shield is close by," Alaya said, waving a hand vaguely. "However, it is my job, as a gatekeeper, to stop you from getting the shield."

"What are you going to do to us?" Ben asked.

"Oh, nothing nasty," Alaya said, putting her hand to her chest, and sounding genuinely shocked. "You will stay here. Indefinitely. With me. I think you'll enjoy it. In fact, I know you will."

"Indefinitely?" Krobeg asked. Ben could see he was still trying to struggle to move, shifting his torso, while his arms hung limply by his sides.

"Why, yes," Alaya said. "I could never actually kill someone." She gave a little shiver. "However, after a few days, you may find yourself getting weak and hungry. And if you do pass away, that would be your own doing, you see."

"You're mad," Joshua said.

"Oh no, I'm not," Alaya said, shaking her head, so that her thick, wavy hair danced and bobbed. "I'm quite the opposite!"

Alaya turned and ran a critical eye over them all, stopping at Natalie and Charlie. "Now, before we begin, I see a couple of people who aren't Guardians." She clucked her tongue again. "You two shouldn't be here. You must have seen the sign in front of Lord Samuel's house."

"We saw the sign," Natalie said grimly. "We just chose to ignore it."

"Oh no, you shouldn't have done that," Alaya said, shaking her head and sounding grave. "We will have to correct that mistake now, won't we?"

"Try your worst," Natalie said, giving Alaya a murderous look.

Alaya gave a light shrug. "Oh, I don't need to do that. However, we can't have you here, so it's time to say goodbye to your friends."

It took Ben a moment to realise what Alaya was suggesting. He cried out in desperation and tried to move, but his body simply wouldn't respond.

Alaya gave a little smile and pointed her finger towards Charlie and Natalie. They suddenly rose several feet into the air. They still had no control over their limbs, but they could use their vocal cords, and they did, extensively, especially Charlie.

"Stop!" he shouted. "There's got to be a solution to this. Can't we discuss this properly?"

Alaya ignored their protests, and gave them a little finger-wave. "Bye bye!"

Charlie and Natalie accelerated at an alarming pace and, with a mighty crash, smashed through the window. Ben cringed as they landed with a thump, somewhere outside the house. Immediately Ben heard groans and curses from Charlie, and even more vocally, Natalie.

Ben cried out in anguish, and then anger, but no matter how furious he became, his body wouldn't respond to his orders. After a minute of cursing violently at Alaya, he realised he should be aiming it at himself, not her. He was the one who had made the call for them to come in, despite the "Guardians Only" sign. How could he have been so irresponsible? Natalie had been very convincing, but there could be no excuse for jeopardising his friends. None. He thought of the final journey to Suktar, which only solidified his resolve. At least now he knew what course of action to take. Should they make it out of here alive, Charlie and Natalie would most certainly not be coming.

"I'm glad we got that unpleasantness out the way," Alaya said. "I am a gentle soul and I do so hate using force, even when it's needed."

Ben was watching her very closely now. Even though she looked like a child, it was clear she wasn't one. What did she have planned for them? Whatever it was, they appeared powerless to stop it. They couldn't even move, let alone act.

Alaya gave them a little dainty wave, and a slight shrug of her shoulders. "Well, this is it. It's time to go to sleep. Good night, sleep tight!"

Ben had a second to wonder what she was going on about, when he collapsed onto the floor, and the world around went black. It was an odd feeling; he was awake, but his body was clearly sleeping. He could hear the rhythmic beating of his heart, and his breathing, which had slowed as his metabolism function began to slow. He wanted to do something, but he was stuck inside his body, unable to wake it up. Ben tried again and again, but to no avail. He felt strange, wrong almost. He wanted to scream, but, of course, his vocal cords didn't work while he was asleep. There was nothing he could do – he was completely trapped inside his body.

"Don't try to fight it."

Alaya's voice seemed to come from afar, but he heard it clear enough.

"It will be more relaxing if you descend into unconsciousness. Trust me, you'll find it easier."

Alaya's voice was soft, almost hypnotic, and for a moment Ben almost let himself go. The idea of just relaxing and not having to think or be conscious of the tiny space inside his body was extremely tempting. But he caught himself just before he entered the black hold of unconsciousness. *Don't be an idiot! Stay focused.* But it was a lot easier said than done. He concentrated on just being aware, and not dropping off into oblivion.

"*Don't fight it, Ben,*" Alaya crooned again. " *The others aren't.*"

But fight it Ben did. Every minute, every second, he made sure he was aware and didn't drift off into the blackness that loomed before him. Time lost all sense of meaning – minutes could have passed or it could have been days. Slowly, very slowly, Ben started winning the battle, and the blackness became less menacing, and further away.

Alaya started singing just as Ben was starting to think he was getting on top. It was a soft, crooning noise, almost like a bird humming, and Ben immediately found himself relapsing. The song was hypnotic, the perfect piece to fall asleep to. Ben fought like crazy, but he was tired now – mentally tired – and he didn't have the energy. He needed a break. Just a small break, then he would try again. Surely that made sense, to re-gain his energy?

"*Ben!*"

Abigail's voice came to him loud and clear inside his head, temporarily breaking the hold Alaya's soft singing had on him.

"*Abigail, you reached me just in time. I was almost gone.*"

"I can't reach the others," Abigail said in a worried voice. *"Not even Dagmar."*

"That's okay. We'll wake them together, once we've dealt with the girl."

Ben could feel Abigail's anxiety, even without hearing or seeing her.

"She's strong, Ben. Really strong. I'm not sure I can overcome her."

Of course. This was Abigail's trial. It was obvious, when you thought about it, but Ben had been too pre-occupied to give it any thought.

"You can do it," Ben said. *"You've done so many incredible things already. You're so strong."*

There was a slight pause, which Ben hoped was due to his words sinking in. When Abigail's thoughts came through again, they did feel a little stronger.

"I know what I have to do. I have to break free of this trance, and then knock her out." She paused for a moment, and then continued with remarkable calm. *"If I fail, I will be stuck in here, forever."*

"You won't fail," Ben said sternly. *"Is there anything I can do to help?"*

"You might be able to," Abigail said after a moment.

From out of the darkness, a glowing ball of light appeared, bathing Ben in warmth and contentment that made him want to groan, had he a body to do so.

"That is my 'soul' or essence, I guess you'd call it," Abigail said. *"When I attack her, she will attack back, and try to destroy me. I need you to focus on my essence, and try to keep it strong. You cannot restore it or make it grow, but just putting your attention on me will act as a kind of shield. Does that make sense?"*

"Yes. You can rely on me," Ben said. *"I'll make sure the crazy girl doesn't take you down."*

Ben felt, rather than saw, Abigail smile, and some of her inherent courage seemed to return.

"Okay, here I go. I will project my thoughts, and hers, to you, so you know what's going on."

The glowing essence that was Abigail didn't move, but Ben could tell she was no longer focused on him, but somewhere else. He placed his attention on the essence, and immediately saw a thin white halo surround it. He concentrated, and the halo became thicker.

"Oh goodie, you made it. For a while I thought you might leave little old me by myself. I was starting to get despondent."

Alaya's thoughts came to him, via Abigail, right down to her babyish tone. A black ball of energy appeared, just feet from Abigail's white one. They were of comparable size, though Ben thought Abigail's might be a fraction bigger.

"I am going to give you one chance to let us go," Abigail said.

Alaya gave a titter. "Don't be silly. I can't do that, nor would I want to. You are all now my play things, and are very precious to me."

"I was hoping you would say that," Abigail said.

Ben felt surprise emanating from the black thing that was Alaya, but she didn't have time to reply, because Abigail attacked. A streak of white energy lanced out and latched on to the black mass, like a bolt of electricity, forming a permanent connection that flickered and pulsed.

"Oh, you tricky thing!" Alaya said. Her voice was still soft, babyish, but Ben detected just a hint of anger behind it. She fired back, and suddenly half the energy flow turned black, so it looked as if they met halfway, crackling with power.

Immediately, both the white and black balls of energy started shrinking. Ben, who had been distracted by the spectacle, re-doubled his efforts to focus. Immediately the shrinking of Abigail's ball of energy slowed a fraction.

"Cheater! You have help," Alaya said. *" He won't save you. I am too strong. See?"*

Indeed, the black mass, having shrunk a little, seemed to be maintaining its size, whereas Abigail's continued to shrink. It had started off approximately two feet wide, and was now half that, and shrinking. Ben knew instinctively that if it disappeared, Abigail would too.

"Do you know what it's like not to exist?" Alaya said,

almost conversationally. *"Some say it's impossible, but they've never had their life force wiped out. It's a peculiar feeling. I've heard it's like you never were. Can you imagine that?"*

Ben was pleased when Abigail didn't reply. He could feel Alaya's annoyance, and her black mass started to shrink just a fraction quicker.

"I might consider saving a fraction of you and adding you to my collection, if you plead towards the end," Alaya said. *"I can do that, you know – keep a bit of your soul in a glass container. Glass is a wonderful thing – so pretty, but it also has useful properties for holding energies. Then, if you're a good girl, I'll let you out every so often."*

Again, Abigail didn't respond. The black mass had now almost shrunk as much as Abigail's white ball of energy; both were now less than eight inches in diameter. For what seemed like forever, the bolts continued to push against each other, black and white sparks flying like fireworks into the darkness.

They were both shrinking slowly now and at the same pace. Ben calculated that at the current rate of deterioration, one of them would be extinguished. Alaya must have recognised this, because he felt a sudden shift in her presence.

"You can't win this, you stupid girl," she said.

Ben was almost caught off-guard and nearly let his shield

down. Gone was her sickly sweet tone, replaced with a snarl.

"I can, and I will," Abigail said, the very model of calm.

"I will not be destroyed! I am immortal. You cannot defeat me."

Though Alaya appeared to be panicking, Ben was concerned. There was now just six inches left from both of them. What would happen if they both extinguished at the same time? Ben had a feeling the one that was microscopically bigger would survive. He threw the last of his reserves into the shield. Had he a voice, he would have been screaming with effort.

Five inches.

Three.

Two.

Abigail's was now fractionally bigger. Or was his mind playing tricks on him?

One inch. Both were now just specks of intense light, white and black and, for a moment, neither refused to vanish, both throwing forth one last effort to stay alive.

And then came the explosion. Even outside his body, Ben felt the lounge shake, and heard bits of furniture break, and god knew what crash onto the floor.

The black speck was gone. The white one had returned to its former glory.

— CHAPTER THIRTY-FIVE —

Krobeg's Call

Ben sat up, just as the others did the same, though their expressions of bemusement suggested they had been oblivious to Abigail's heroics.

Alaya was gone. In her place was a frail old lady, clothed in black, lying lifeless on the floor.

"What just happened?" Joshua asked.

Ben got to his feet and moved cautiously over to the old lady, spellshooter in hand. Her skin was horribly pocked, and she had a peculiar double-boned chin. There was a horrible rotting smell emanating from her. At the risk of contaminating his shoe, Ben poked the lady, softly at first; then he gave her a kick, which he rather enjoyed. She didn't move.

"She's not there," Abigail said softly, looking down at the

343

lady. To Ben's surprise, she looked upset; her lips were even quivering a little. "I've never killed anyone before. I didn't really like it, to be honest."

Ben immediately stepped in and gave her a hug, and spoke softly into her ear. "It was you or her, remember? You didn't have a choice."

Abigail's face was buried in Ben's chest and Ben could feel a little dampness. She gave a nod, then pulled away and wiped her eyes.

"What happened?" Dagmar asked.

Abigail was clearly in no state to re-tell the incident, so Ben did, resisting the urge to highlight Abigail's incredible strength and bravery, knowing it would only embarrass her. Nevertheless, the bare facts of the story had them all staring at Abigail with a mixture of astonishment and awe; Dagmar was smiling with satisfaction. Before Abigail knew what was happening, they were hugging and thanking her. Even Joshua came in and gave her a hug, full of gratitude.

"You saved us," he said simply.

Dagmar was looking at Abigail like a proud teacher. "Your learning is complete."

"Really?" Abigail said. "You think I'm ready?"

"Ready or not, when the student surpasses the teacher, it is time to move on."

Ben's elation was suddenly and dramatically cut short the moment he remembered what had happened to Charlie and Natalie. He ran over and looked out of the broken window into the garden. They were nowhere to be seen. Part of him wanted to jump out the window and find them, but he knew that could jeopardise their entire mission.

"They're fine," Krobeg said, appearing by his side. The others quickly followed, their eyes scouring the gardens.

"How do you know?" Ben asked.

"I don't. But being thrown out the window isn't going to kill anyone. I've done it myself on numerous occasions to troublemakers at my tavern."

Ben turned away with a heavy heart, determined to find them the moment they were outside. He guessed they would have tried to get back into the house. The most obvious route was through the broken window, but Ben had a feeling that, as they weren't Guardians, their way in would be barred. Knowing Natalie, she wouldn't give up easily, and had probably tried to find an alternate way in.

They would be fine, he told himself. With some effort, Ben put the matter from his mind, and turned away from the window, to see Joshua standing over the old woman in black.

"Who or what was she?"

"She was a high priestess from the kingdom of Praal," Dagmar said. "They are a tribal people and happen to be extremely gifted with spirit spells."

"How did Lord Samuel get her? And has she been in this house for the past five hundred years?"

"Yes, which would explain why she had gone mad. I have no idea how Lord Samuel found and caught her."

Nobody felt like hanging around near the priestess, least of all Joshua, who already appeared eager to continue their search. Dagmar led them to one of the many doors that lined the walls, but she didn't open it.

"Assuming Joshua and Ben won't get tested as they don't have their pieces of armour yet, you are the only one left, Krobeg," Dagmar said.

Krobeg nodded, spinning his axe slowly in his hands. "I figured that."

"Which means the next challenge is going to be a physical one. And given that you're almost invulnerable while wearing Elizabeth's Breastplate, any enemy we face is going to be formidable."

Krobeg nodded, his face suddenly sombre. "I have been thinking about that. I think it might be better if I go alone."

"What? No," Ben said immediately. "That's crazy. We can help you."

"Can you?" Krobeg asked. "Whatever we face is going to be almost as indestructible as I am. It will be quick, it will certainly be strong, and none of you have the armour's protection."

"Krobeg has a point," Dagmar said. "We might just get in the way."

Ben stared at her. She wasn't scared, was she? No, of

course not. That wasn't Dagmar. He turned to Joshua, who clearly didn't like the idea either, but didn't seem as put out about it as Ben did.

"Even if we can't hurt it, we could distract it," Ben said. He wasn't giving up easily. "Maybe we could give you an opening."

"Possibly," Krobeg conceded. "But I don't think I could focus properly if you were in there. I would be too worried about you all. Remember, we all need to survive this if we're going to get Elizabeth's Armour. The Seen and Unseen Kingdoms are doomed if we lack even one piece."

In that moment, Ben knew he had lost the argument. He ran a hand through his ruffled and now sweaty hair. "Okay, but at least connect me to a beacon spell that you will fire if you run into trouble, okay?"

Krobeg nodded. He drew his spellshooter, and touched orbs with Ben's, linking them up.

Ben didn't like it; in fact, he detested it, but he could see Krobeg's argument. It was like they were jumping out of the plane and he was the only one with a parachute.

Dagmar sensed the argument was done. She put her hand on the door and focused, before turning and looking up at Krobeg.

"This is the one," she said. "Ben is right – call us if you are in trouble. We might be vulnerable, but we can still fight."

"I will," Krobeg promised.

He took several deep breaths, his big chest heaving, axe in both hands. There was a fiery light in his eyes, and Ben got that strange feeling that, despite the danger and importance of the mission, Krobeg might actually be relishing the challenge. Indeed, he gave a flicker of a smile as he turned back to Dagmar.

"Alright, I'm ready. Let's see what Lord Samuel has for me."

— CHAPTER THIRTY-SIX —

The Waiting Game

You won't hear him," Dagmar said.

As soon as Krobeg left, Ben had plastered his ear against the door.

"The portal magic on the doors will stop any vibrations passing through."

"You could disable that, though, couldn't you?" Ben asked, still trying to listen, despite Dagmar's warning.

"If I was touching the door and concentrating, I could create a link, yes. But I'm not going to."

Ben thought about protesting, but then remembered who he was talking to. Instead, he started pacing the room, checking his orb every minute to see whether it was flashing, signalling a call from Krobeg. On more than one occasion he thought he heard something, and turned towards the door, almost putting his neck out.

"I suggest you calm down," Dagmar said. "Think of something else to take your mind off it."

"Like what?"

"Your apprenticeship," Dagmar said immediately. "You can go over what you've learnt, and what you have left on your checklist in preparation for your third-grade exam, which will be coming up shortly."

Ben looked at her as if she were mad. Was she joking? No, of course not. Dagmar never joked.

"That's not really in the forefront of my mind, to be honest," Ben said.

"What about you?" Joshua asked. "Surely you must be concerned about Krobeg. How do you remain so calm?"

"Knitting," Dagmar said with that perfectly straight face of hers. "It's a hobby of mine. I have several pieces I'm in the middle of, and I amuse myself by pondering which colours I should use."

Ben turned to Joshua, and they exchanged incredulous looks. But Abigail smiled. "I enjoy knitting, but I'm not very good at it. Maybe you could teach me, Dagmar?"

"I would be happy to," Dagmar replied with an indulgent smile.

"Moving back on topic, what do you think Krobeg could be up against?" Joshua asked. "Surely there aren't many things in the Unseen Kingdoms that could beat him while he's wearing Elizabeth's Breastplate?"

"There are some very powerful people and creatures in the Unseen Kingdoms," Dagmar said. "There are many formidable creatures from the dragon family, and some of the rare golems are almost indestructible. Then there are some extraordinarily powerful magic users, though I'm more inclined to think Samuel will want someone of a physical nature to face Krobeg."

"Dragons?" Ben said. "How on earth would Samuel get a dragon into the house? And how would it stay there?"

"Oh, that's not difficult, if you have the resources," Dagmar said with an indifferent wave of the hand. "The dragon-taming industry is a lucrative one, even five hundred years ago, and he would have hired the best in the business. With some powerful sleeping spells, they could have knocked the dragon out and shipped it here."

"How would he stay here, though?" Abigail asked. "Surely once it woke up, it would break free?"

"Not in this house," Dagmar said. "There is magic everywhere, and they would use it to contain him. Though I'll admit the spells required to keep a dragon in the house for five hundred years would be extensive and they would have to be renewed every so often."

Ben rubbed his chin thoughtfully. "Someone would have to be here to do it, right?"

"Yes, they would."

"And what about food and drink?" Joshua asked.

"That would also be required," Dagmar admitted. "Which leads me to believe that the creature is more likely to be something like a golem, which requires no nourishment, rather than a carnivorous animal."

"Well, that's good, I guess," Ben said. "Golems can't be as bad as dragons, surely?"

Joshua piped up. "Have you ever heard of the Egyptian golem?"

"No, but if I was to take a stab in the dark, I would say they are golems that come from Egypt?"

"They are extinct now, but five hundred years ago there were still a handful left. They were rumoured to be almost twenty feet tall and immune to magic. They were made of a metal that looks like golden sand, which is both soft and yet reforms under pressure."

Ben frowned. "If they are so strong, why are they extinct?"

"They liked to fight," Joshua said with a shrug. "And since there was nobody around worthy except other golems, they basically fought each other to death. That's what I heard, anyway."

"You are right." Dagmar nodded. "The last one was killed in the eighteenth century, by order of the Institute."

"Unless Samuel managed to capture one before then."

"That would surprise me," Dagmar said, looking

decidedly unsurprised.

Ben checked his watch. Fifteen minutes had now passed since Krobeg had left. The anxiety that he had managed to push aside through conversation came flooding back. Fights, by their very nature, didn't normally last long. He noticed Joshua biting his nails and staring at the floor; Abigail sat, with her legs crossed, looking anxious, but with that steely determination Ben had come to expect from her; only Dagmar remained unflustered, though she did occasionally glance at the door.

Twenty minutes passed, and Ben took to checking his orb with increasing frequency.

"Have patience," Dagmar said upon seeing their expressions. "Remember, Krobeg and whatever he is fighting will be very tough to kill. They might be at each other for some time before a victor is confirmed."

The thought calmed Ben but alarmed him at the same time. Krobeg might have the powers of regeneration through Elizabeth's Breastplate, but fighting for such a length of time would still be absolutely exhausting, and a test of perseverance, courage and endurance beyond anything Ben had experienced.

And so it proved.

Half an hour passed, which soon became a full hour.

Ben was now collapsed on one of the sofas. He felt exhausted, and he wasn't the only one. Joshua had joined him, and even Dagmar was now sitting down, with a faint crease of concern running across her brow. What if Krobeg had lost the fight? The thought had crept upon him some time ago. Initially he had swept it aside, but as time went on, it slowly moved to the front of his mind. If he had lost, they would never know, and they could end up sitting here indefinitely.

"This is ridiculous," Joshua said, breaking a silence that had enveloped them for the last half an hour. "We can't sit here forever."

"Joshua's right," Ben said, turning to Dagmar, glad that he wasn't the one who had capitulated over the wait. "We need to do something."

To Ben's surprise, Dagmar did not immediately disagree. She pursed her lips, and looked once more to the door. But after a considered moment, she shook her head.

"If the fight is with an Egyptian golem, which I fear it might be, none of us will stand a chance."

"I don't care," Ben said, his voice etched with frustration. "I'm sick of doing nothing."

"Why don't we give it fifteen more minutes?" Joshua suggested. "If we don't hear anything, we go in. If it is an Egyptian golem, we go out again."

"Unless something has happened to Krobeg," Ben said.

"That sounds like a good idea," Abigail said, looking to Dagmar.

Dagmar had her hands on her lap. She sat there thoughtfully, before nodding. "I agree to this. Ben?"

Ben had almost forgotten that as Head Guardian, Dagmar deferred all decisions to him. He almost regretted not going in earlier.

"Fine, fifteen minutes. Then we go."

Time seemed to have a habit of slowing just when he wanted it to pass quickly. Ben started pacing round the room with a new vigour, energised by the prospect that, very soon, they'd be doing something pro-active. He hoped they weren't too late, though quite what they'd do if it was an Egyptian golem fighting Krobeg, he wasn't sure. He dismissed it from his mind – they didn't know what Krobeg was facing, so it was pointless to worry about it.

With ten minutes to go, Ben started checking his watch more regularly. On the five-minute mark, even Dagmar started running a cursory check over her spellshooter.

Four minutes. Ben's heart started picking up, fuelling his body with the adrenaline he would be needing very soon.

Three minutes. Ben did a few jumps, and then shook his limbs out, loosening his muscles.

"Good luck," Ben said to Dagmar, Joshua, and Abigail.

"I don't believe in luck, but thank you," Dagmar said.

"I do," Joshua replied with feeling. "And I hope we get plenty of it."

Two minutes.

Ben's orb suddenly blasted, making him jump and cry out in shock.

"Krobeg's signal!"

The orb was flashing brightly like a siren. He touched it, to turn it off and let Krobeg know they had received the call, then quickly moved to the door. Dagmar had beaten him to it, her hand flying to the door handle. With one quick look to make sure Ben, Joshua and Abigail were right behind, she focused, and opened the door.

— CHAPTER THIRTY-SEVEN —

The Impossible Duel

Ben's heart was pounding and his hands were sweaty, as he followed Dagmar in, knowing they could well be walking right into death. But the thought that Krobeg needed their help fuelled his courage, knocking his fear aside.

The first thing he saw was broken chairs scattered across the floor in a room that looked more like a meeting hall than anything else. His eyes quickly scanned the large, empty space, expecting to find one huge golem and a dwarf in desperate trouble, though hopefully still alive.

He saw no golems. He saw no dragons. What he saw were two dwarves.

Two Krobegs, to be precise.

Ben looked on in astonishment, as they faced up to each other, hacking and cutting with their axes in the middle of the room. Even from a distance, he could hear their ragged breathing and see the sweat pouring down their faces – hardly surprising, given the length of time they'd been fighting. How were they still standing? More importantly, which one was the actual Krobeg?

Ben didn't want to shout his name, for fear that he might distract the real Krobeg. With the others following, Ben walked round until he was adjacent to the two dwarves so he could get a good look at both of them, with enough of a gap to stay out of harm's way.

Both the dwarves were too involved in combat to even glance their way.

"Which is ours?" Joshua asked.

"I cannot tell," Dagmar admitted, scrutinising both closely.

Ben bit his lip in frustration. They couldn't help if they didn't know who was who.

"Ben!" the Krobeg on the left grunted, glancing his way for a split second. "I can't best him! We're too evenly matched."

Ben immediately aimed his spellshooter and launched a rocket at the enemy Krobeg. It hit his chest full on, and seemed to be absorbed, with almost no effect.

Ben frowned. That wasn't possible.

"He has the armour too," Krobeg said, as he launched a vicious cut, which evil Krobeg deflected. The two dwarves looked at each other and gave a tired nod. Both stepped back momentarily, to catch their breath.

"Only got a minute," Krobeg panted, leaning wearily on his axe. Despite the armour, he was cut in several places and looked a mess. More than that, he looked exhausted. Ben couldn't see how he could keep fighting.

"Why have you stopped?" Abigail asked. "I've never seen that before. Have you agreed to take regular breaks?"

"I honestly don't know," Krobeg said. "He started it, and I wasn't about to complain, as I was ready to collapse. Now we fight for several minutes, and then take mini breaks. It draws out the fight, but it's the only reason I'm still alive."

"That is most peculiar," Dagmar said. "Don't you think it might be significant?"

"Possibly," Krobeg said with a shrug. "I haven't had much time to think on it, though, to tell the truth. I'm either fighting or taking a couple of minutes to recover."

"Are you hurt?" Abigail asked. "I've learnt some good healing spells if you need some."

"Oh, these?" Krobeg said, glancing at his wounds dismissively. "These are nothing compared to the gaping wounds we've both had, only to be regenerated by Elizabeth's Breastplate. No, I'm fine, but thank you for asking."

"How is it possible that your opponent also wears the armour?" Joshua said. "There is only one breastplate."

Krobeg barely managed to lift his shoulders with a shrug.

"Some ridiculously powerful mirror spell, I guess. I've spent a long time thinking about it. I'm sure it would expire at some point, and I bet it only works in certain areas. But we've been fighting forever and I can't lure him out of this hall. The point is, how am I supposed to beat myself? We're exactly equal."

"Isn't it obvious?" Ben said. "We help you. That will throw the odds in your direction. If we can't use magic, we can still fight him."

To Ben's surprise, Krobeg didn't like the idea, and he gave a grim look back towards his doppelgänger. "I have a feeling that might make it worse."

"How?" Ben said with surprise.

But before he could reply, evil Krobeg made a noise, and started forwards. Krobeg heaved his axe up, and charged. Ben couldn't believe how quickly Krobeg had recovered; he seemed to be fighting like a renewed dwarf. But his momentary optimism was dealt a blow when he saw that evil Krobeg was also fighting with new vigour. After a few minutes, it became blindly obvious there would be no winner until someone dropped dead from exhaustion – but could that even happen while wearing the breastplate?

There seemed to be only one solution, and it seemed a rather obvious one to Ben, despite Krobeg's misgivings. He drew his spellshooter, focused on the evil Krobeg, and put his finger on the trigger. He had blocked one spell, but could he block a dozen in quick succession? Surely evil Krobeg would at worst get distracted, allowing good Krobeg a way in. But before he could unleash hell, evil Krobeg raised an arm. A ball of white energy formed in his palm, which he pointed towards Ben. Without even looking, evil Krobeg shot the ball of energy, and it landed in front of Ben, less than half a dozen paces away.

At first, Ben thought that evil Krobeg had missed, for he hadn't even looked where he was shooting. But a form began to materialise just a few paces away. A very familiar-looking form.

Ben gaped in astonishment as evil Ben formed, right in front of his eyes.

"You've got to be kidding," he whispered.

"I knew that was a bad idea," Abigail said, looking wide-eyed at mirror Ben. "What should we do?"

"Nothing," Ben said firmly. "I don't want you fighting yourself. You won't win."

Evil Ben gave real Ben a wink and a smile that he had seen in the mirror countless times.

"You ready?" evil Ben asked.

Without waiting for an answer, evil Ben drew his spellshooter, and fired a spell into his hand, forming a sword. Then he attacked.

Ben summoned his own sword just in time to block the first slice, a vicious cut to the neck. Evil Ben was fast, but Ben grit his teeth and matched his enemy step for step, blow for blow. He knew all evil Ben's moves, and was able to predict each attack. But on the flip side, Ben found it impossible to land his own blows. He launched a sizzling, fast-paced attack, but somehow evil Ben got to each thrust just in time, as if he knew where it was going. Which he probably did.

Ben was beginning to tire, but so was evil Ben. To Ben's surprise, evil Ben took a step back and gave a little nod. A break? Ben frowned. A break from trying to kill each other? Ben didn't know what was going on, but he had seen evil Krobeg do it, and didn't object. He stepped back to catch his breath and wipe the sweat from his face. Dagmar and Abigail had joined him, while Joshua remained with Krobeg.

"If you've got any bright ideas, I'd love to hear them," Ben said, trying for a smile.

"I'm thinking," Dagmar said. "It is difficult. We can't attack without creating versions of ourselves who we cannot overcome. What does that mean?"

"It means we're in trouble," Ben said. "Especially me."

"No, Dagmar's right: it does mean something," Abigail said, pursing her lips thoughtfully.

But whatever Abigail was about to say was lost, as evil Ben came forwards, more cautiously this time. They circled each other, making occasional stabs. Ben tried to apportion a section of his mind to think about what Dagmar and Abigail had just said. He had to remind himself that this was a test,

362

intended primarily for Krobeg, and that all tests can be passed. So how could you pass this test? Even if he threw everything into his attack, he knew that somehow evil Ben would just about repel it, and then launch a quick counter attack, as Ben had done so often in the past, which he would in turn fend off. And so it would go on.

Even as he had the thought, evil Ben came forwards like a whirlwind, and Ben went on the defensive, back-pedalling like mad. But as close as evil Ben came to taking Ben's head off, he never felt in any real danger, because he knew where each attack would come from, and he met it with a solid clash of blades, before finally launching a counter attack, and pushing evil Ben away.

Evil Ben gave another nod, and Ben was more than glad to step away for another break.

Ben had time to cast a quick glance over at Krobeg and saw that little had changed – they were still caught in a deadlock, much like he and his doppelgänger.

"Are you okay, Ben?" Abigail asked. She moved forwards and dabbed his shoulder. He hadn't even realised he was bleeding. One glance at evil Ben and he saw a similar wound in the opposite shoulder.

"An unusual convention, these breaks," Dagmar mused.

"Do you think I should ignore them?" Ben asked. "I could keep on attacking, maybe that's the secret."

"I don't think so. You are still evenly matched; it would

just result in you both deteriorating quicker. Yet I do believe these breaks somehow provide a clue to passing this test."

Ben glanced back at evil Ben, and found to his surprise that evil Ben was looking at him intently. Was he waiting for something? Ben got the distinct feeling that evil Ben was waiting for him to do something that might not be combat related. But whatever it was, Ben had clearly taken too long to do it, as evil Ben came forwards again and once more they clashed swords.

Unlike Krobeg, who with the armour could recover almost fully with each rest and so go on indefinitely, Ben was starting to tire despite the breaks, which meant their fight would be over all the sooner. Ducking under a sweeping strike, Ben tried desperately to think while maintaining focus on the fight. He now had several pieces of the puzzle: the breaks; the fact that evil Ben seemed to expect something from him during those breaks; and finally, the knowledge that he couldn't possibly win through brute force.

Ben froze as the realisation hit him.

Evil Ben's sword bit into his arm, and he cried out loud, quickly bringing his guard back up. Thankfully, the searing pain was momentarily diminished by his sudden brainwave. What if he wasn't supposed to win the fight? What if combat wasn't the point at all, but quite the opposite? The more he thought about it, the more sense it made. The breastplate turned one into an almost invulnerable killing machine.

There could be no real test in combat while wearing it. The real test would be to have the strength to take it off and perhaps even seek a peaceful resolution, despite the lure of the breastplate. Ben remembered quite vividly how eager Krobeg had been to get into combat whilst wearing the armour.

First, though, he would need to try it out on his doppelgänger. He might not have the armour, but the same principles should still apply. Just the thought of refusing to fight, especially when charged upon, made him baulk, and he received another nick from evil Ben, as his concentration wavered. Ben made sure he defended resolutely until, once more, evil Ben signalled a retreat.

This was it. Ben took a deep breath. Could he do this? If he was wrong, he was in big trouble – big, dead trouble. But the alternative was to keep fighting until one of them dropped, and that someone would most likely be him, as his mind kept on drifting, messing with his concentration.

He had to give it a go, and he had to do it soon, before evil Ben decided to attack again.

Ben extinguished his sword and, while staring right into the eyes of his doppelgänger, removed his spellshooter and placed it carefully on the floor.

"Ben! What are you doing?" Abigail asked. He didn't need to look at her to feel the shock in her voice.

"I think he might be on to something," Dagmar said.

Evil Ben continued to watch Ben, clearly intrigued. Ben felt tense, his hands itching to grab his spellshooter. This wasn't going to work, unless he calmed down, he realised. With a deep breath, and supreme force of will, he made himself forget about his spellshooter, his one form of attack, and stood straight, staring evil Ben right in the eye.

Evil Ben smiled, then nodded, and gave a deep bow. With a flash of white light, evil Ben vanished.

Ben almost collapsed with relief.

"You did it!" Abigail said with a delighted clap.

Dagmar gave one of her rare approving nods. "Very good, Ben. The test is about peace in spite of all, not combat. How very clever to give such a test to the Guardian of the Breastplate."

Ben would have liked to bathe in the compliment, but a shout from Krobeg made him turn. Incredibly, he was still fighting, though perhaps a little slower now. Ben waited until evil Krobeg backed away, and Krobeg stepped back to them, breathing heavily. He now had a nasty wound on his forehead and he was limping a bit.

"How'd you do it?" Krobeg asked, as soon as he joined them.

"You need to stop fighting," Ben said immediately. "The test isn't about combat, but the ability to refuse its temptation, despite all impulse, desire and even apparent necessity."

"Stop fighting?" Krobeg said doubtfully. "I can't believe that's the solution. He'll just tear me to pieces."

"No. It worked for me."

Krobeg didn't look convinced.

"Oh, and you'll need to take Elizabeth's Breastplate off."

"What?" Krobeg's hand went to his chest, and he shook his head. "No, I can't do that. I need the breastplate. I won't survive without it."

"You won't need it," Ben said. "Once you determine without a doubt that you will not fight, and remove the breastplate, your doppelgänger will disappear."

Krobeg was shaking his head even before Ben had finished speaking. "No. I need the breastplate. It gives me strength. I need it."

There was a wild look in Krobeg's eyes that Ben didn't like.

"Remove the breastplate, Krobeg," Dagmar said in an authoritative voice Ben had heard so many times before. "It is clouding your mind."

"I cannot. I will not," Krobeg said. He turned away from them to face his doppelgänger, who had been watching the scene closely – no doubt wondering if Krobeg was going to relinquish the armour and end the fight, Ben thought bitterly.

Instead, the two of them clashed again, and Ben looked on helplessly as Krobeg gave and received several nasty blows, before returning to them looking ready to collapse.

"Krobeg, you need to trust me," Ben said.

But Krobeg raised a hand and shook his head, claiming no interest.

"Foolish dwarf," Dagmar said with a flash of anger. "You're killing yourself, and you're going to jeopardise our whole mission. Remember our mission? We are the only ones who can stop the dark elves by removing their king. The fate of the kingdoms rests on our shoulders, and you're blowing it."

Krobeg turned to Dagmar, a torn look on his face. "The mission – that's right. But the armour—"

"Take it off!" Abigail shouted with such force and conviction that Krobeg jumped.

His eyes widened, and his face cleared. "Take it off." He took a deep, heaving breath. "Take it off. Yes, I can do that – I think."

But time had run out. His doppelgänger was advancing, and Krobeg was forced to endure another round. Ben watched, tense, knowing that they both looked ready to collapse. Krobeg was clearly no longer focused on battle, and he took a nasty blow to the shoulder so that he could hardly use his axe. It was only time that saved him, with evil Krobeg retreating just as he looked certain to win, further reinforcing Ben's belief that he was on the right track. This was not about winning or losing in combat.

Krobeg stumbled back, dragging his axe.

"Off," Dagmar snapped. "Get rid of your weapons, and remove the breastplate. Do it now, before it's too late."

Krobeg dropped the axe and, with some difficulty, removed his jacket, revealing the breastplate beneath. His hands went to remove the straps, and he hesitated.

"Krobeg," Ben said. "Don't stop now. You're almost there."

Ben sensed a brief conflict and, for one horrible moment, Ben thought Krobeg was going to change his mind. But he shook his head, as if trying to rid himself of some evil thoughts, and undid each of the straps. With tender care, he then removed the breastplate, and placed it softly on the floor. He gave it one last longing look, before turning back to Ben.

"Okay, now what?"

"Now you have to decide that whatever happens, you're not going to fight. You have to show that you are willing to resolve conflict through peaceful means, not just bloodshed."

"What if he attacks me?" Krobeg asked.

"You stand your ground, but do not attack back. If you do, or if you even think about doing so, you will fail," Ben said.

"So basically be a sitting duck – got it," Krobeg said.

"You'll be fine," Ben assured him.

Evil Krobeg was watching the scene with interest, but

made no move to relinquish his own weapons. Ben frowned – his own doppelgänger had bowed and disappeared upon seeing Ben's submission. Why wasn't evil Krobeg doing the same?

"You don't have any thoughts of combat lingering in your head, do you?" Ben asked.

"No, they're all gone," Krobeg said. Despite his weariness and injuries, he even managed a small smile. "It's quite refreshing actually. With the breastplate on, I couldn't stop thinking about fighting."

Evil Krobeg took a single step forwards.

"Shouldn't he be disappearing, like your one did?" Abigail asked.

"I'm not sure. This one is obviously different."

Krobeg maintained his smile, but it was starting to become strained. "Ben? He's coming forwards, and he's still armed."

So he was. Evil Krobeg was now walking back into combat, preparing for the next round of attack, grim-faced, battle axe in hand.

"Stay where you are," Ben ordered, holding a hand out. "It's a test."

"Are you sure?" Krobeg said, his voice breaking slightly. "My life is on the line here."

Ben watched in horror as evil Krobeg broke into a run and charged forwards, with a sudden terrifying cry.

"Hold your position!" Ben screamed.

Krobeg's eyes were like saucers, watching his doppelgänger charge at him, but he didn't move; he didn't even raise his arms when evil Krobeg raised his axe.

In the fleeting moment before evil Krobeg struck, Ben had the horrible feeling that he'd got it all wrong. He raised his arms over his head, as if he were the one who needed protecting, and tried shouting for Krobeg to duck, to move, to do anything to avoid being sliced open. But his voice wouldn't function.

Evil Krobeg jumped, swung his axe, and exploded in a flash of light.

Ben stood there for a moment, gasping for breath. Joshua and Abigail did likewise, and even Dagmar looked put out, her face slightly pale.

Only Krobeg remained calm. His eyes were shut, and he was taking deep breaths.

"That was incredible," Krobeg said.

He opened his eyes, and Ben immediately saw a new Krobeg emerge. He looked calmer, more relaxed and at peace with himself. He glanced at the breastplate with a purse of the lips.

"I guess I need to put that back on," he said reluctantly.

"Just while we're in this house," Ben said. "As soon as we get outside, you can take it off."

Krobeg nodded. "I knew it was affecting me, but I never

realised how much."

"You beat it, though," Joshua said.

"For now," Krobeg agreed, lifting the breastplate up and slowly strapping it back on.

Ben felt exhausted. The few chairs in the hall had long since been shattered, most likely in the fight between the Krobegs. So Ben sat himself down on the floor.

Dagmar immediately approached him and raised her spellshooter. "Brace yourself."

Ben gasped as she fired a series of healing spells. They coursed through his body like ice, making him go rigid, as they worked on the cuts and bruises. After a painful few minutes, he felt a little better.

"I've got a bit of food left," Ben said. "Abigail, can you dish it out?"

The five of them sat in a circle, and tucked into a rather meagre feast. Even though Ben received only half a ham sandwich and a few gulps of water, he felt a lot better for it.

"I could use another ten of those sandwiches," Krobeg admitted, patting his stomach.

"I could use a bed," Ben said, stretching his legs out.

For the next ten minutes, they sat there resting. It was a wonderful feeling being able to relax, without the constant threat of danger lurking over your shoulder. Unsurprisingly, it was Joshua who started looking towards the two end doors of the hall first.

"We should get going," Joshua said. "Time is still against us, with the dark elves."

"What will we face next?" Abigail asked.

"The shield, hopefully," Ben said, reluctantly getting to his feet. "And whatever is guarding it."

Feeling a little refreshed from the food, drink and rest, they walked to the end of the hall, where Dagmar eyed up both doors, before choosing the one on the left.

She put her hand on the door handle, and immediately recoiled with a gasp.

"What is it?" Ben asked, the others chorusing in with variations of the same question.

"There is a great deal of magic and power in the next room," Dagmar said. "I can feel it the moment I connect the door to the room."

"The shield?" Joshua asked eagerly.

Dagmar nodded. "Most likely." She pursed her lips thoughtfully, her eyes flicking to Ben. "And something else – something I can't quite place, but it has significant power."

"Could that be whatever is guarding the shield?" Abigail asked.

"Possibly," Dagmar said, though she didn't seem convinced.

Ben smiled grimly. "Well, let's go find out, shall we?"

Dagmar re-placed her hands on the door handle, and gently pushed it open.

— CHAPTER THIRTY-EIGHT —

Elizabeth's Shield

Ben followed Dagmar in, spellshooter drawn, the others right behind. After everything they had been through, Ben felt like he was prepared for anything, but the fear of the unknown was always unnerving, and yet he was too weary to get too worked up about it.

The moment he entered this new, rectangular room, Ben knew they had come to the end of their journey. Weapons and pieces of armour covered nearly every space on the walls, bar a pair of large double doors across from them.

Joshua surged past him, all thought of caution forgotten.

"This is it!" he said, scouring the walls. "It must be here."

And it was.

The shield wasn't hard to spot. It was the only piece of armour housed in a glass cabinet, occupying one of the smaller walls. The cabinet itself was a wonderful piece of craftsmanship: gold trimmed with jewels embedded along its frame. But it was the shield within that Ben and the others stared at. Just like the other pieces of Elizabeth's Armour, it was relatively simple, but stunningly crafted. It was a somewhat small, circular shield, with blue precious stones running round its rim.

"It's beautiful," Abigail said.

Ben wasn't sure how long the five of them stood there, admiring the shield, but eventually he tore his eyes away and inspected the rest of the room, looking for signs of trouble. So far, so good. Nevertheless, he kept his spellshooter primed and ready as he turned back to the cabinet.

"How do we get the thing out?" he asked.

There appeared to be no handle or any method of opening the glass.

"Look below," Krobeg said, pointing.

Ben had been so fixated on the shield, he had missed the lock combination just below the cabinet. It was a series of small blocks that could be rotated to produce any given number. There were eight of them.

Joshua frowned the moment he spotted the numbers, and the delight on his face was immediately replaced with something approaching concern.

"Give me some space, please. I need to concentrate," he said.

They backed up, and let Joshua focus. The first four digits he seemed sure about, for he keyed in three-two-six-one immediately. But the last four had him biting his lower lip and muttering to himself. They watched him anxiously as he tried combination after combination, but nothing happened.

Finally, he took a step back, his face etched in frustration. "My grandfather only gave me four digits, not eight. How am I supposed to unlock the thing?"

"Have you tried entering the same digits twice?" Abigail asked.

"Of course," Joshua said. "It was the first thing I did. Then I tried it backwards, and in all sorts of different orders. I've also tried other numbers significant to our family. Nothing works."

Krobeg walked up to the glass and put a hand on it. "It doesn't seem that strong. We could try to smash it."

"You can try," Dagmar said dryly. "I would be very surprised if it did you any good."

Krobeg shrugged. "Worth a shot."

He hefted his axe, gave it a mighty swing and crashed the blade directly into the thin-looking glass. The axe rebounded with such force it flew out of Krobeg's hands, and Ben ducked as it sailed over his head and across the room.

"What a surprise," Dagmar said, crossing her arms. "We need to come up with those final four digits. Does anyone else have any suggestions?"

"Let me try again," Joshua insisted. "It's got to have something to do with Lord Samuel."

"His birth date?" Ben suggested.

"Tried it."

"The date he joined the Institute? The date he became director?"

"Tried both of them," Joshua said, shaking his head. "No, it's something else. Something I must know, but haven't thought of."

As Joshua continued to rattle off guesses, Ben started to become a little concerned that too many wrong combinations might somehow lock them out, or worse, trigger some sort of reaction. But Joshua was so intent on guessing the code, Ben thought it best not to distract him. Instead, he thought upon Dagmar's words. *Does anyone else have any suggestions?* He knew of several four-digit combinations, but nothing that had anything to do with Lord Samuel's family or the shield. Indeed, the only combination that had anything to do with Elizabeth's Armour was his own four digits he had obtained from his dad, which turned out to be the address, in reverse order, of Elizabeth's museum. But those were surely the last numbers that might fit. After all, Michael Greenwood and Lord Samuel were practically enemies – the thought that they would share numbers for the code for the shield was almost laughable.

Except, the more Ben thought about it, the less he felt like laughing. Was it too crazy to think that they might have shared the eight numbers, and that only the Guardian of the Shield working with the Guardian of the Sword could unlock the cabinet? Certainly, all the other Guardians had already been used. The more Ben thought about it, the more excited he became.

"Try two-three-seven-one," Ben said.

Joshua turned, his face flushed with pure frustration. "What's that? I don't recognise that combination."

"A number," Ben said. He certainly didn't want to say where he got it from. "Just try it."

For a moment, Ben thought Joshua was going to refuse. But then he saw him arrange the numbers accordingly.

"Nothing," Joshua said. "Hardly surprising. Please don't interrupt me again; I've thought of some other possibilities."

His hand was just about to re-arrange them when there was a loud click. Joshua jumped, and almost fell over, his head jerking up with wide-eyed astonishment at the glass protecting the shield.

The glass faded away, revealing the shield in all its glory.

Joshua turned back to Ben in astonishment. "What were those numbers?"

When Ben told him, he expected disbelief or at least denial from Joshua. Instead, he received a distant look that even contained a hint of a smile.

"They must have resolved their difficulties," Joshua said, almost to himself. "It's the only way. Incredible."

Joshua reached forwards with the sort of reverence that Ben could fully understand, and gently eased the shield from the wall. Ben and the others surrounded Joshua as he turned the shield over, examining every inch of the magnificent piece of armour.

"It's stunning," Joshua said softly.

He slipped his arm under the straps, and put the shield on. He gave an involuntary gasp, and his mouth stayed open for a good few seconds, before he got it under control.

"The magic," he said. "I can feel it. It is incredible."

"Yeah, they all have that," Krobeg said with a rueful look.

"We did it," Abigail said with a delighted smile. "Can we go now? I would really like to see the sky again. It feels like we've been in this house forever."

"In a moment," Dagmar said. She turned to Ben. "The sword?"

Ben felt his empty scabbard. "I don't understand it. The riddle said, 'Find me last. I am not hidden' But if we can't find the thing, then it's obviously hidden."

"We must be missing something," Joshua said. His eyes had finally returned to something approaching normal size, though he kept the shield strapped to his arm. "We have all the pieces now, so we are certainly trying to find the sword last. What are we not doing?"

Ben rubbed a hand through his hair, forcing back a growing desperation. He had thought – hoped – that maybe the sword would somehow materialise within the scabbard the moment the shield was found, but that hadn't happened. What else could he do? He had no other clues. Now he cursed himself for not getting more exact information from his dad while he had the chance. But the way his dad had addressed the issue led him to believe that finding the sword would simply be a matter of course, once they had the other pieces.

Having the four Guardians staring at him expectantly was both off-putting and compounded his desperation and feeling of failure. He clenched his fist. There had to be a solution. He must be missing something.

Ben scanned the room and the double doors that he had spotted when he first entered caught his eye. A small flicker of hope welled up inside him, and he walked over to them. They were made of stone and, just like the glass, had no obvious handle or way to open them.

Ben stepped back, hands on hips. "This could be something."

"I didn't even see these," Joshua said with sudden optimism. "I was so focused on the shield. How do we open them?"

"There must be a handle or a knob somewhere," Krobeg said. "These look dwarf-made, so we might be searching for a while."

Even searching methodically, with five sets of eyes, it took them a good twenty minutes before Abigail gave a delighted shout.

"I've found something!" she said, waving her hand and bouncing up and down.

Ben had to get on his knees to see the small button that Abigail had found at the bottom right edge of the door. It was difficult to see even when staring right at it, but Ben could just about make out the button's outline, no more than an inch in diameter.

"Good job, Abigail." He looked up at the others, trying and failing to hold back a mounting excitement. "Let's see what this does, shall we?"

Ben pressed the button.

There was no click or any indication that a mechanism had been set in motion. Ben tried again, and a third time. Nothing. He frowned. Was there more than one button to press, perhaps?

Ben was searching so diligently for a second button that it took him a moment before he saw the white mist that was beginning to accumulate to his right, just within his peripheral vision.

"Oh my," Abigail said, her face going pale as she stared towards the mist, tapping Ben on the shoulder with increasing urgency.

Ben turned and quickly stood up. The mist started to solidify, and a female, ethereal figure began to form. She had auburn hair and a strong nose. Her posture and dress oozed regality. Her long-fingered hands rested on the hilt of a magnificent sword.

Ben stared into the dark brown eyes of Queen Elizabeth and saw an intelligence and determination that took his breath away.

"Directors," she said. Her voice was soft, but spoke with an intention even Dagmar would struggle to match. "The time has come. The power of Suktar draws close, and must be stopped." She paused, and once more inspected them. "You have united my armour, bar the sword, which I myself watch over. Are you ready, Michael Greenwood, to claim the sword?"

Ben managed a nod. He wasn't sure if the queen was seeing them or the original directors, and he certainly wasn't going to argue the point.

"I'm ready, Your Majesty," he said.

"Very well," Queen Elizabeth said.

To Ben's surprise, she turned to Joshua. "Lord Samuel, are you ready to assume your role as protector to the sword-bearer?"

Joshua responded with admirable dignity. "I am, Your Majesty."

Queen Elizabeth nodded. "Good. Your commitment to

the cause will be sorely tested during your struggle, especially as I know the regard in which you hold Michael Greenwood. However, it is because of this, not in spite of it, that I chose you to bear the shield and take this responsibility. Now, let us see if you can pass the first test."

Elizabeth raised a hand and the double doors slowly opened, sliding away from each other. Ben watched as a narrow corridor was revealed beyond. At the end of the corridor was a small room with a single pedestal. Upon that pedestal, floating upright, seemingly held in place by thin air, was Elizabeth's Sword.

Ben forgot to breathe. His heart threatened to explode from his chest and he was vaguely aware that there was pooling in his mouth. It must have been over fifty paces away, but even from a distance the sword shone and seemed to light up the small room by itself.

"The sword is protected by spells that were given to me by the High Council. They cannot be stopped, except by my shield. Your test, Lord Samuel, is to put your own life at risk to protect Michael's, so he can retrieve the sword. Are you prepared to do this?"

Ben turned to Joshua, who had gone a slightly sickly colour, but, to his utmost credit, he nodded immediately.

"So be it," Queen Elizabeth said. She turned to Ben, who once again felt the full force of her gaze. Ben had time to wonder just how she must have been in real life.

"Michael Greenwood, I give you my permission to retrieve my sword."

— CHAPTER THIRTY-NINE —

The Final Test

The urge to rush over and grab the sword was extremely tempting, but Ben knew that would be suicide. He turned to Joshua, who was looking down the passage, as if trying to guess what lay in store.

"How do you want to do this?" Ben asked.

"I'll lead," Joshua said. "You follow right behind me."

Joshua extended his shield in front of him. Ben noted his hands were shaking a little, and he didn't blame him. Ben recalled Queen Elizabeth's words. *The sword is protected by spells that were given to me by the High Council.* Who or what was the High Council? They sounded impressive – Ben made a mental note to ask Charlie once they were out.

The moment they stepped into the corridor, the double doors slid shut behind them. Joshua started shuffling forwards slowly, eyes darting this way and that, looking for the spells they knew they were going to trigger. Ben followed right behind, eyes on the sword ahead, using Joshua as his human shield.

Ben estimated fifty feet until they reached the cubicle containing the sword. Joshua continued to inch forwards. Forty feet. Ben glanced at the walls – could the attacks come from there? Would Joshua have the necessary reflexes to block them if they did?

The first spell materialised from the cubicle. It was barely a speck of light, but its brightness was such that it stung Ben's eyes. The speck grew to the size of a pea, and Ben had to squint. The spell radiated a power that almost knocked Ben from his feet.

"Here it comes!" Ben said.

Joshua raised his shield, just as the spell struck. It moved like a bullet, leaving a trail of silver dust as it rocketed towards Joshua. The spell hit the centre of the shield and exploded. Joshua fell backwards and knocked Ben over, landing on top of him.

Joshua scrambled to his feet, his face scrunched with pain. His whole body was shaking. Ben was about to ask Joshua if he was okay, when another speck of light formed.

This time they braced themselves, and Joshua took the impact of the spell without falling. But his groan was more pronounced than before. Nevertheless, he took the impact, and moved forwards – or tried to. Joshua was already struggling to put one foot in front of the other.

The shield might take the majority of the impact, but clearly it was having some other effect on Joshua. He managed just two stumbling pigeon steps before the next spell smashed into the shield, throwing him back into Ben, who caught and held on to him.

"Can't move," Joshua said between gritted teeth. "Body shaking too much."

But despite that, he continued to shuffle forwards, each step ripping a cry of pain from his lips. Ben wanted desperately to help – he hadn't been hit, and felt perfectly fresh. There had to be something he could do, even if it wasn't taking the brunt of the spells. An idea came to him.

"I've got you," Ben said. He wrapped his arms underneath Joshua's and helped prop him up. Joshua was shaking so violently it was as if he had hypothermia.

Together they inched forwards.

Twenty feet.

"Almost there, Josh!" Ben said. Ben wasn't sure how Joshua was still holding the shield, but it remained propped out in front of him, remarkably still compared to the rest of his body.

Ten feet.

To Ben's horror, another white speck started to materialise when they were just a few paces from the cubicle.

Ben cried out with frustration. He barely had time to prepare himself before the white flash of light crashed into Joshua. The impact sent both of them sprawling, and Joshua lost his grip on the shield.

Ben blinked rapidly, trying to regain his eyesight after the blinding flash. It took him a moment to realise he was lying face down. He groaned, and scrambled to his feet.

Joshua was still lying down, shaking violently.

Ben knew he had just seconds to act. If another spell went off, they were curtains. He grabbed the shield, placed it in Joshua's outstretched arm, and then physically dragged him towards the cubicle, praying another spell wouldn't materialise.

They made it, and Ben collapsed alongside Joshua, breathing raggedly. In the back of his mind, he wondered if the spells might still ignite; if so, they were done for. Joshua wasn't fit to block an ant, let alone another one of those monstrously powerful spells.

"Did we make it?" Joshua asked. He was still lying on his back, but his shaking was starting to recede just a fraction.

"We did," Ben said. "You were great. Magnificent even."

Joshua managed to ease himself up into a sitting position, leaning against the wall. "I'll tell you what's magnificent –*that*."

Joshua nodded, and Ben turned towards the pedestal in the middle of the room.

Ben stood up slowly, his eyes locked on Elizabeth's Sword, which hovered just above a red cushion. Like the other pieces of Elizabeth's Armour, it was a work of beauty, but to Ben this one seemed even more so. The blade was perfect, and in the centre of the hilt was a blue gemstone that seemed to glow. It was only a short sword, but Ben could feel the magic emanating from it.

This was it, he realised. Ben licked his lips and slowly reached both hands towards the hilt. Slowly, almost delicately, he attempted to lift the sword away from its position.

Ben gasped with shock the moment his hands made contact, and he very almost dropped the sword on the floor. Raw energy flowed through his body, his perceptions heightened to a fever pitch – not just the regular perceptions, but other ones he was not normally aware of, such as time, orientation, balance, instinct, and dozens of others.

There was too much power; Ben couldn't control it. His heart started accelerating to dangerous levels, and the world began to blink, as he became light-headed. He stumbled backwards, his head spinning. He needed to let go of the sword before it did lasting damage, and he needed to do it *now*.

The scabbard.

The thought came to him as he glanced down, looking for a place to put the sword. With trembling movements, Ben managed to sheathe the sword in the scabbard. The moment he let go, the magic ceased to channel through him and, incredibly, the scabbard housed the sword and contained the magic within. Ben let out an audible sigh of relief.

"Are you okay?" Joshua asked.

Ben hadn't realised, but Joshua had got to his feet, and was looking at him with concern.

"Yeah," Ben said, wiping his brow. "You?"

Joshua nodded. "I am now."

The two of them looked at each other, and there was an awkward silence. Ben was a mixture of emotions. He seemed to recall that he strongly disliked Joshua, but he was having trouble remembering why.

"We did it," Ben said with a sudden smile.

To Ben's surprise, Joshua smiled back and extended his hand, which Ben shook.

"We did it," Joshua agreed. "Now the hard work begins. We need to take out Suktar."

— CHAPTER FORTY —

Guardians Unite

Ben sat cross-legged on the vast expanse of lawn that spread across Lord Samuel's front garden, its perfection ruined only by the broken gargoyles that had returned to their stone form. They lay in crumbled heaps everywhere, though the queen gargoyle was nowhere to be seen. Ben was looking at the sky, revelling in the winter sun, the crisp air, and just being outside. There was nothing more wonderful than a sense of freedom after being trapped.

He wasn't the only one enjoying the freedom. The other Guardians had adopted similar positions. Dagmar sat cross-legged, contentedly tucking into a packet of crisps. Krobeg had devoured several sandwiches, and was busy searching the bag for more.

They had found Charlie and Natalie anxiously waiting for

them in the front garden as soon as they left Lord Samuel's house. As Ben had suspected, they had tried and failed to get back inside.

Thinking about Charlie and Natalie momentarily clouded his thoughts. He still had to face talking to them about the final journey to defeat Suktar. Ben cast the thought from his mind – he'd worry about that later.

"I can't believe we did it," Natalie said. "All the Guardians, all the pieces of Elizabeth's Armour."

Ben popped a cherry into his mouth, and glanced round at each of the Guardians. They were a mixed bunch, but each one suited their piece of armour perfectly and, on reflection, he wouldn't have picked anyone else.

"It's crazy," Ben said. "I feel like I deserve a holiday or something."

"Why don't we go back to my tavern? I'll cook us a celebratory meal," Krobeg said.

"We just ate."

"What? This?" Krobeg picked up a half-eaten sandwich. "This hardly counts. I need a proper meal."

"I need to get back to the Institute," Dagmar said. "I've already been gone too long."

Eventually they eased themselves up and started down Vanishing Street. Ben couldn't help smiling with satisfaction every time he thought about what they had achieved.

"I guess we need to ask the baron how to get home?"

Natalie said.

"Yes. He will phone a taxi for us," Joshua said.

Ben cast only a cursory glance when they passed the left turning on the street, but he came to a standstill the moment he spotted the portal.

Even from this distance, Ben had a good view through the shimmering portal into the heart of London, and it was immediately obvious that something was wrong.

The cars on the street weren't moving.

Even stranger, the portal was supposed to block out all the noise, but Ben could swear he could hear something, even from this distance.

He heard screams.

With a concerned look at his colleagues, Ben turned, and started down the road, his eyes focused on the shimmering portal. The closer he got, the worse it looked, and his walk quickly turned into a run. He could hear the others pounding the cobbled stone right behind him.

Ben could now see several people stepping out of their cars, right in the middle of the busy London road.

A horrible feeling started to form in the pit of Ben's stomach. Ben dashed through the portal. The moment he entered the streets of London, his blood froze.

There were screams of fear and horror, coupled with gasps of astonishment and disbelief, as people looked to the skies.

Dragons ridden by dark elves filled the air – huge, purple, flying animals, ridden by strange purple-cloaked beings with long spears and glowing purple hands. Buildings were rapidly catching fire as the riders swept down and lit them up with dragon fire and elf magic. Others scorched the roads, sending people running and screaming for safety.

Ben stood there, unable to take it all in. A part of him couldn't believe it was really happening. Even as he tried to come to terms with the attack, the sound of sirens began to fill the air, as the emergency services responded. Ben saw police cars attempt to weave their way through the chaos, with little success.

"Ben!"

He turned and saw Dagmar looking at him, her face urgent.

"We need to get back to the Institute, *now*. The shit has just hit the fan."

Ben wasn't sure if it was Dagmar's voice or her choice of words that snapped him out of his shock.

"How far are we from London Victoria?" Krobeg asked.

"Not far," Charlie said. "I know it took us a while to get to Vanishing Street from Victoria, but this portal has thrown us out just ten minutes from the station. Three if we could drive."

"Nobody's driving," Ben said, eyeing the roads. "We go by foot."

Ben checked his scabbard and spellshooter, scanning the ground for any dark elf movement, recalling the pods that had sprung up all over Croydon. No doubt they had done the same here. It didn't take him long to spot a small group of dark elves coming round the street. Most people were running away, but the braver ones, and several police officers, tried stopping them. They were all mercilessly cut down.

"Is it that way to the station?" Ben asked, pointing towards the dark elves.

"No, but we can take a little detour," Charlie said, eyeing up the dark elves with intent.

"Good." Ben drew his spellshooter. "Let's get going."

The seven of them walked against the tide, as people fled past them in horror.

Even from a distance, Ben could tell the dark elves were enjoying themselves, shooting balls of purple fire almost casually, not caring if they hit person or building – either was a hit in their eyes. They took turns aiming at a small group of Chinese tourists, who appeared more agile than most, and even managed to dodge a few purple balls, before one of them went down. The elves laughed – a horrible, evil sound. The elf in the centre began lining up his next spell.

It was a long shot, and Ben didn't have a clear line of sight, but he had learnt how to get round that. Ben raised his spellshooter and, in one smooth motion, aimed and fired.

A spinning, spiked disc shot out from his barrel, and whirled its way through the crowd, swaying and pitching to avoid the terrified citizens. The moment it had a clear run at the elf, it seemed to accelerate, and hit the elf right in the forehead. The elf's eyes widened, first in shock, then in disbelief, and he collapsed to the floor, unmoving.

Charlie raised an arm, palm extended upwards. Ben slapped it, but they barely even exchanged glances, both still focused on the elves.

They had the dark elves' attention now. Their good humour and joviality disappeared, replaced with a mixture of surprise and anger.

The dark elves formed a line, and started forwards.

"Don't fire until you have a line of sight," Ben said. "You guys ready?"

"Oh yes," Krobeg said. "Just let me get within range."

"We will," Ben said. "Form a line. Krobeg, next to me. Charge when I give you the go-ahead."

Krobeg moved alongside him, twirling his axe.

Ben sidestepped an oncoming lady, who barely noticed him in her hurry to get away from the oncoming elves.

"Almost there," Ben said. "Three, two, one, now!"

Charlie, Dagmar, Natalie and Joshua raised their spellshooters, and fired in unison. Four coloured spells shot towards the dark elves.

Ben waited until the elves were clearly distracted by the

spells, before ordering Krobeg to join the fight. He couldn't help smiling as the spells made contact, and Krobeg crashed into the remaining dark elves like a sledgehammer. The fight was over in minutes.

"Now what?" Joshua said, turning straight to Ben the moment Krobeg downed the last dark elf. "Do we search about for more dark elves? I bet they are everywhere."

All eyes, even Dagmar's, were on him, awaiting orders. He desperately wanted to hunt for more dark elves, but he knew instinctively what the right call was.

"No, we go back to the Institute. They will want to brief all members and apprentices urgently. Plus, there are some very important issues we need to discuss. The dark elves have forced our hand. We have all the pieces of Elizabeth's Armour. So that begs just one very important question: when do we begin the final journey?"

"You are right: there is much to discuss, and it must be done in the sanctuary of the Institute," Dagmar said.

Ben nodded. "Let's get out of here and make some serious decisions."

With some difficulty, the seven of them ignored the mayhem around them, and moved in a bubble of calm towards London Victoria and the Dragonway.

The war had begun.

THE END

FROM THE AUTHOR

Thank you for reading Royal Institute of Magic: The Last Guardian - I hope you enjoyed it. I am busy working on book 6!

If you would like to stay in touch, please visit my website at **www.royalinstituteofmagic.com** where you can also sign up to the newsletter in order to receive information on upcoming releases, exclusive content, and free giveaways!

If you feel so inclined, I would also greatly appreciate it if you could write a little review on **Amazon.** It only takes a few minutes and gives other potential readers a better idea of what the book is like.

Writing can be a pretty lonely business, so it's always nice to hear from readers. Please feel free to get in touch at **victor@royalinstituteofmagic.com** and I'll reply within 24 hours - promise!

I look forward to hearing from you.

Regards,
- Victor

ABOUT THE AUTHOR

Victor Kloss was born in 1980 and lived his first five years in London, before moving to a small town in West Sussex. By day he builds websites, by night he writes (or tries to).

His love for Children's Fantasy stems from Enid Blyton, Tolkien, and recently, JK Rowling. His hobbies include football, golf, reading and taking walks with his wife and daughter.

Visit Victor's website at www.royalinstituteofmagic.com or contact him at victor@royalinstituteofmagic.com.

Also By

59606919R00243

Made in the USA
Lexington, KY
10 January 2017